綠野仙蹤

原著雙語彩圖本

The Wizard of Oz

作者──李曼・法蘭克・鮑姆
（Lyman Frank Baum）

譯者──朱文宜

Contents — The Wizard of Oz

Chapter 1	The Cyclone	6
Chapter 2	The Council with the Munchkins	12
Chapter 3	How Dorothy Saved the Scarecrow	22
Chapter 4	The Road Through the Forest	32
Chapter 5	The Rescue of the Tin Woodman	39
Chapter 6	The Cowardly Lion	48
Chapter 7	The Journey to the Great Oz	56
Chapter 8	The Deadly Poppy Field	65
Chapter 9	The Queen of the Field Mice	75
Chapter 10	The Guardian of the Gate	83
Chapter 11	The Wonderful City of Oz	93
Chapter 12	The Search for the Wicked Witch	110
Chapter 13	The Rescue	128
Chapter 14	The Winged Monkeys	135
Chapter 15	The Discovery of Oz, the Terrible	144
Chapter 16	The Magic Art of the Great Humbug	157
Chapter 17	How the Balloon Was Launched	163
Chapter 18	Away to the South	168
Chapter 19	Attacked by the Fighting Trees	175
Chapter 20	The Dainty China Country	181
Chapter 21	The Lion Becomes the King of Beasts	189
Chapter 22	The Country of the Quadlings	194
Chapter 23	Glinda The Good Witch Grants Dorothy's Wish	200
Chapter 24	Home Again	207

目錄 — 綠野仙蹤

Chapter 1	龍捲風	210
Chapter 2	遇見芒奇金的居民	216
Chapter 3	救出稻草人	226
Chapter 4	穿越森林的路	236
Chapter 5	拯救鐵錫樵夫	243
Chapter 6	膽小的獅子	252
Chapter 7	驚險的旅程	259
Chapter 8	致命的罌粟花田	267
Chapter 9	田鼠皇后	276
Chapter 10	大門守衛	283
Chapter 11	奧茲的翡翠城	292
Chapter 12	尋找邪惡女巫	307
Chapter 13	救援	323
Chapter 14	飛猴	329
Chapter 15	露出馬腳	337
Chapter 16	大騙子的魔法	349
Chapter 17	熱氣球怎麼起飛的	355
Chapter 18	前往南方	360
Chapter 19	樹林警察	366
Chapter 20	精緻的瓷器國	371
Chapter 21	獅子成為萬獸之王	379
Chapter 22	垮德林人的國度	384
Chapter 23	善良女巫葛琳達實現女孩的願望	389
Chapter 24	重返家園	396

The Wizard of Oz

Introduction

Folklore, legends, myths and fairy tales have followed childhood through the ages, for every healthy youngster has a wholesome and instinctive love for stories fantastic, marvelous and manifestly unreal. The winged fairies of Grimm and Andersen have brought more happiness to childish hearts than all other human creations.

Yet the old-time fairy tale, having served for generations, may now be classed as "historical" in the children's library; for the time has come for a series of newer "wonder tales" in which the stereotyped genie, dwarf and fairy are eliminated, together with all the horrible and blood-curdling incidents devised by their authors to point a fearsome moral to each tale. Modern education includes morality; therefore the modern child seeks only entertainment in its wonder tales and gladly dispenses with all disagreeable incident.

Having this thought in mind, the story of "The Wonderful Wizard of Oz" was written solely to please children of today. It aspires to being a modernized fairy tale, in which the wonderment and joy are retained and the heartaches and nightmares are left out.

L. Frank Baum
Chicago, April, 1900.

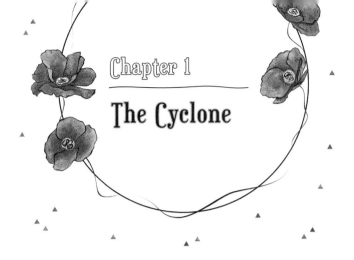

Chapter 1

The Cyclone

Dorothy lived in the midst of the great Kansas prairies, with Uncle Henry, who was a farmer, and Aunt Em, who was the farmer's wife. Their house was small, for the lumber to build it had to be carried by wagon many miles. There were four walls, a floor and a roof, which made one room; and this room contained a rusty looking cooking stove, a cupboard for the dishes, a table, three or four chairs, and the beds. Uncle Henry and Aunt Em had a big bed in one corner, and Dorothy a little bed in another corner. There was no garret at all, and no cellar—except a small hole dug in the ground, called a cyclone cellar, where the family could go in case one of those great whirlwinds arose, mighty enough to crush any building in its path. It was reached by a trap door in the middle of the floor, from which a ladder led down into the small, dark hole.

When Dorothy stood in the doorway and looked around, she could see nothing but the great gray prairie on every side. Not a tree nor a house broke the broad sweep of flat country that reached to the edge of the sky in all directions. The sun had baked the plowed land into a gray mass, with little cracks running through it. Even the grass was not green, for the sun had burned the tops of the long blades until they were the same gray color to be seen everywhere. Once the house had been painted, but the sun blistered the paint and the rains washed it away, and now the house was as dull and gray as everything else.

When Aunt Em came there to live she was a young, pretty wife. The sun and wind had changed her, too. They had taken the sparkle from her eyes and left them a sober gray; they had taken the red from her cheeks and lips, and they were gray also. She was thin and gaunt, and never smiled now. When Dorothy, who was an orphan, first came to her, Aunt Em had been so startled by the child's laughter that she would scream and press her hand upon her heart whenever Dorothy's merry voice reached her ears; and she still looked at the little girl with wonder that she could find anything to laugh at.

Uncle Henry never laughed. He worked hard from morning till night and did not know what joy was. He was gray also,

from his long beard to his rough boots, and he looked stern and solemn, and rarely spoke.

It was Toto that made Dorothy laugh, and saved her from growing as gray as her other surroundings. Toto was not gray; he was a little black dog, with long silky hair and small black eyes that twinkled merrily on either side of his funny, wee nose. Toto played all day long, and Dorothy played with him, and loved him dearly.

Today, however, they were not playing. Uncle Henry sat upon the doorstep and looked anxiously at the sky, which was even grayer than usual. Dorothy stood in the door with Toto in her arms, and looked at the sky too. Aunt Em was washing the dishes.

From the far north they heard a low wail of the wind, and Uncle Henry and Dorothy could see where the long grass bowed in waves before the coming storm. There now came a sharp whistling in the air from the south, and as they turned their eyes that way they saw ripples in the grass coming from that direction also.

Suddenly Uncle Henry stood up.

"There's a cyclone coming, Em," he called to his wife. "I'll go look after the stock." Then he ran toward the sheds where the cows and horses were kept.

Aunt Em dropped her work and came to the door. One glance told her of the danger close at hand.

"Quick, Dorothy!" she screamed. "Run for the cellar!"

Toto jumped out of Dorothy's arms and hid under the

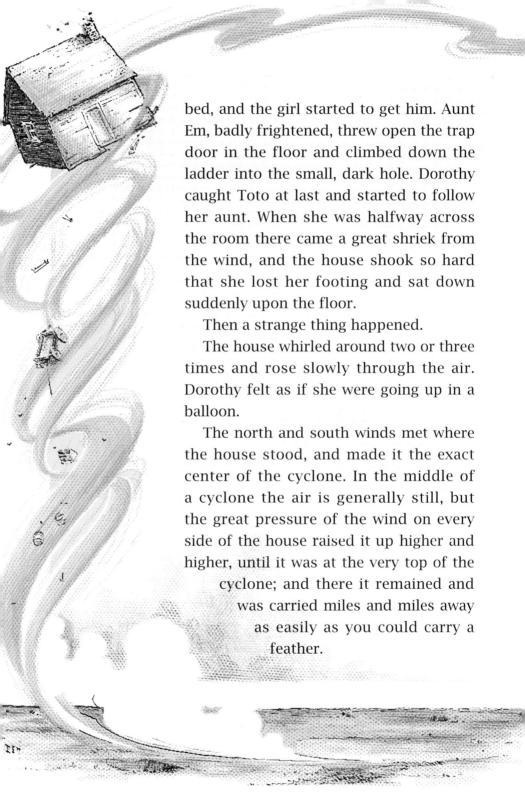

bed, and the girl started to get him. Aunt Em, badly frightened, threw open the trap door in the floor and climbed down the ladder into the small, dark hole. Dorothy caught Toto at last and started to follow her aunt. When she was halfway across the room there came a great shriek from the wind, and the house shook so hard that she lost her footing and sat down suddenly upon the floor.

Then a strange thing happened.

The house whirled around two or three times and rose slowly through the air. Dorothy felt as if she were going up in a balloon.

The north and south winds met where the house stood, and made it the exact center of the cyclone. In the middle of a cyclone the air is generally still, but the great pressure of the wind on every side of the house raised it up higher and higher, until it was at the very top of the cyclone; and there it remained and was carried miles and miles away as easily as you could carry a feather.

She caught Toto
by the ear.

It was very dark, and the wind howled horribly around her, but Dorothy found she was riding quite easily. After the first few whirls around, and one other time when the house tipped badly, she felt as if she were being rocked gently, like a baby in a cradle.

Toto did not like it. He ran about the room, now here, now there, barking loudly; but Dorothy sat quite still on the floor and waited to see what would happen.

Once Toto got too near the open trap door, and fell in; and at first the little girl thought she had lost him. But soon she saw one of his ears sticking up through the hole, for the strong pressure of the air was keeping him up so that he could not fall. She crept to the hole, caught Toto by the ear, and dragged him into the room again, afterward closing the trap door so that no more accidents could happen.

Hour after hour passed away, and slowly Dorothy got over her fright; but she felt quite lonely, and the wind shrieked so loudly all about her that she nearly became deaf. At first she had wondered if she would be dashed to pieces when the house fell again; but as the hours passed and nothing terrible happened, she stopped worrying and resolved to wait calmly and see what the future would bring. At last she crawled over the swaying floor to her bed, and lay down upon it; and Toto followed and lay down beside her.

In spite of the swaying of the house and the wailing of the wind, Dorothy soon closed her eyes and fell fast asleep.

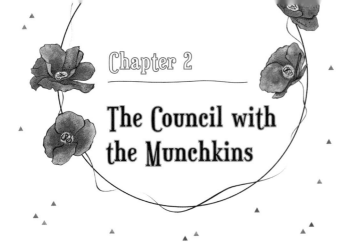

Chapter 2

The Council with the Munchkins

She was awakened by a shock, so sudden and severe that if Dorothy had not been lying on the soft bed she might have been hurt. As it was, the jar made her catch her breath and wonder what had happened; and Toto put his cold little nose into her face and whined dismally. Dorothy sat up and noticed that the house was not moving; nor was it dark, for the bright sunshine came in at the window, flooding the little room. She sprang from her bed and with Toto at her heels ran and opened the door.

The little girl gave a cry of amazement and looked about her, her eyes growing bigger and bigger at the wonderful sights she saw.

The cyclone had set the house down very gently—for a cyclone—in the midst of a country of marvelous beauty. There were lovely patches of greensward all about, with stately trees bearing rich and luscious fruits. Banks of gorgeous flowers were on every hand, and birds with rare and brilliant plumage sang and fluttered in the trees and bushes. A little way off was a small brook, rushing and sparkling along between green banks, and murmuring in a voice very grateful to a little girl who had lived so long on the dry, gray prairies.

While she stood looking eagerly at the strange and beautiful sights, she noticed coming toward her a group of the queerest people she had ever seen. They were not as big as the grown folk she had always been used to; but neither were they very small. In fact, they seemed about as tall as Dorothy, who was a well-grown child for her age, although they were, so far as looks go, many years older.

Three were men and one a woman, and all were oddly dressed. They wore round hats that rose to a small point a foot above their heads, with little bells around the brims that tinkled sweetly as they moved. The hats of the men were blue; the little woman's hat was white, and she wore a white gown that hung in pleats from her shoulders. Over it were sprinkled little stars that glistened in the sun like diamonds. The men were dressed in blue, of the same shade as their hats, and wore well-polished boots with a deep roll of blue at the tops. The men, Dorothy thought, were about as old as Uncle Henry, for two of them had beards. But the little woman was doubtless much older. Her face was covered with wrinkles, her hair was nearly white, and she walked rather stiffly.

When these people drew near the house where Dorothy was standing in the doorway, they paused and whispered among themselves, as if afraid to come farther. But the little old woman walked up to Dorothy, made a low bow and said, in a sweet voice:

"You are welcome, most noble Sorceress, to the land of the Munchkins. We are so grateful to you for having killed the Wicked Witch of the East, and for setting our people free from bondage."

Dorothy listened to this speech with wonder. What could the little woman possibly mean by calling her a sorceress, and saying she had killed the Wicked Witch of the East? Dorothy was an innocent, harmless little girl, who had been carried by a cyclone many miles from home; and she had never killed anything in all her life.

But the little woman evidently expected her to answer; so Dorothy said, with hesitation, "You are very kind, but there must be some mistake. I have not killed anything."

"Your house did, anyway," replied the little old woman, with a laugh, "and that is the same thing. See!" she continued, pointing to the corner of the house. "There are her two feet, still sticking out from under a block of wood."

Dorothy looked, and gave a little cry of fright. There, indeed, just under the corner of the great beam the house rested on, two feet were sticking out, shod in silver shoes with pointed toes.

"Oh, dear! Oh, dear!" cried Dorothy, clasping her

hands together in dismay. "The house must have fallen on her. Whatever shall we do?"

"There is nothing to be done," said the little woman calmly.

"But who was she?" asked Dorothy.

"She was the Wicked Witch of the East, as I said," answered the little woman. "She has held all the Munchkins in bondage for many years, making them slave for her night and day. Now they are all set free, and are grateful to you for the favor."

"Who are the Munchkins?" inquired Dorothy.

"They are the people who live in this land of the East where the Wicked Witch ruled."

"Are you a Munchkin?" asked Dorothy.

"No, but I am their friend, although I live in the land

I am the Witch of the North.

of the North. When they saw the Witch of the East was dead the Munchkins sent a swift messenger to me, and I came at once. I am the Witch of the North."

"Oh, gracious!" cried Dorothy. "Are you a real witch?"

"Yes, indeed," answered the little woman. "But I am a good witch, and the people love me. I am not as powerful as the Wicked Witch was who ruled here, or I should have set the people free myself."

"But I thought all witches were wicked," said the girl, who was half frightened at facing a real witch.

"Oh, no, that is a great mistake. There were only four witches in all the Land of Oz, and two of them, those who live in the North and the South, are good witches. I know this is true, for I am one of them myself, and cannot be mistaken. Those who dwelt in the East and the West were, indeed, wicked witches; but now that you have killed one of them, there is but one Wicked Witch in all the Land of Oz—the one who lives in the West."

"But," said Dorothy, after a moment's thought, "Aunt Em has told me that the witches were all dead—years and years ago."

"Who is Aunt Em?" inquired the little old woman.

"She is my aunt who lives in Kansas, where I came from."

The Witch of the North seemed to think for a time, with her head bowed and her eyes upon the ground. Then she looked up and said, "I do not know where Kansas is, for I have never heard that country mentioned before. But tell me, is it a civilized country?"

"Oh, yes," replied Dorothy.

"Then that accounts for it. In the civilized countries I believe there are no witches left, nor wizards, nor sorceresses, nor magicians. But, you see, the Land of Oz has never been civilized, for we are cut off from all the rest of the world. Therefore we still have witches and wizards amongst us."

"Who are the Wizards?" asked Dorothy.

"Oz himself is the Great Wizard," answered the Witch, sinking her voice to a whisper. "He is more powerful than all the rest of us together. He lives in the City of Emeralds."

Dorothy was going to ask another question, but just then the Munchkins, who had been standing silently by, gave a loud shout and pointed to the corner of the house where the Wicked Witch had been lying.

"What is it?" asked the little old woman, and looked, and began to laugh. The feet of the dead Witch had disappeared entirely and nothing was left but the silver shoes.

"She was so old," explained the Witch of the North, "that she dried up quickly in the sun. That is the end of her. But the silver shoes are yours, and you shall have them to wear." She reached down and picked up the shoes, and after shaking the dust out of them handed them to Dorothy.

"The Witch of the East was proud of those silver shoes," said one of the Munchkins, "and there is some charm connected with them; but what it is we never knew."

Dorothy carried the shoes into the house and placed them on the table. Then she came out again to the Munchkins and said:

"I am anxious to get back to my aunt and uncle, for I am sure they will worry about me. Can you help me find my way?"

The Munchkins and the Witch first looked at one another, and then at Dorothy, and then shook their heads.

"At the East, not far from here," said one, "there is a great desert, and none could live to cross it."

"It is the same at the South," said another, "for I have been there and seen it. The South is the country of the Quadlings."

"I am told," said the third man, "that it is the same at the West. And that country, where the Winkies live, is ruled by the Wicked Witch of the West, who would make you her slave if you passed her way."

"The North is my home," said the old lady, "and at its edge is the same great desert that surrounds this Land of Oz. I'm afraid, my dear, you will have to live with us."

Dorothy began to sob at this, for she felt lonely among all these strange people. Her tears seemed to grieve the kind-hearted Munchkins, for they immediately took out their handkerchiefs and began to weep also. As for the little old woman, she took off her cap and balanced the point on the end of her nose, while she counted "One, two, three" in a solemn voice. At once the cap changed to a slate, on which was written in big, white chalk marks:

"LET DOROTHY GO TO THE CITY OF EMERALDS."

The little old woman took the slate from her nose, and having read the words on it, asked, "Is your name Dorothy, my dear?"

"Yes," answered the child, looking up and drying her tears.

"Then you must go to the City of Emeralds. Perhaps Oz will help you."

"Where is this city?" asked Dorothy.

"It is exactly in the center of the country, and is ruled by Oz, the Great Wizard I told you of."

"Is he a good man?" inquired the girl anxiously.

"He is a good Wizard. Whether he is a man or not I cannot tell, for I have never seen him."

"How can I get there?" asked Dorothy.

"You must walk. It is a long journey, through a country that is sometimes pleasant and sometimes dark and terrible. However, I will use all the magic arts I know of to keep you from harm."

"Won't you go with me?" pleaded the girl, who had begun to look upon the little old woman as her only friend.

"No, I cannot do that,"
she replied, "but I will
give you my kiss, and no
one will dare injure a person who
has been kissed by the Witch of the
North."

She came close to Dorothy and
kissed her gently on the forehead.
Where her lips touched the girl they
left a round, shining mark, as Dorothy
found out soon after.

"The road to the City of Emeralds is
paved with yellow brick," said the Witch, "so
you cannot miss it. When you get to Oz do not
be afraid of him, but tell your story and ask him
to help you. Good-bye, my dear."

The three Munchkins bowed low to her and
wished her a pleasant journey, after which they
walked away through the trees. The Witch gave Dorothy
a friendly little nod, whirled around on her left heel
three times, and straightway disappeared, much to
the surprise of little Toto, who barked after her loudly
enough when she had gone, because he had been afraid
even to growl while she stood by.

But Dorothy, knowing her to be a witch, had expected
her to disappear in just that way, and was not surprised
in the least.

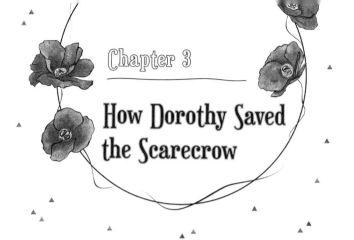

Chapter 3

How Dorothy Saved the Scarecrow

When Dorothy was left alone she began to feel hungry. So she went to the cupboard and cut herself some bread, which she spread with butter. She gave some to Toto, and taking a pail from the shelf she carried it down to the little brook and filled it with clear, sparkling water. Toto ran over to the trees and began to bark at the birds sitting there. Dorothy went to get him, and saw such delicious fruit hanging from the branches that she gathered some of it, finding it just what she wanted to help out her breakfast.

Then she went back to the house, and having helped herself and Toto to a good drink of the cool, clear water, she set about making ready for the journey to the City of Emeralds.

Dorothy had only one other dress, but that happened to be clean and was hanging on a peg beside her bed. It was gingham, with checks of white and blue; and although the blue was somewhat faded with many washings, it was still a pretty frock. The girl washed herself carefully, dressed herself in the clean gingham, and tied her pink sunbonnet on her head. She took a little basket and filled it with bread from the cupboard, laying a white cloth over the top. Then she looked down at her feet and noticed how old and worn her shoes were.

"They surely will never do for a long journey, Toto," she said. And Toto looked up into her face with his little black eyes and wagged his tail to show he knew what she meant.

At that moment Dorothy saw lying on the table the silver shoes that had belonged to the Witch of the East.

"I wonder if they will fit me," she said to Toto. "They would be just the thing to take a long walk in, for they could not wear out."

She took off her old leather shoes and tried on the silver ones, which fitted her as well as if they had been made for her.

Finally she picked up her basket.

"Come along, Toto," she said. "We will go to the Emerald City and ask the Great Oz how to get back to Kansas again."

She closed the door, locked it, and put the key carefully in the pocket of her dress. And so, with Toto trotting along soberly behind her, she started on her journey.

There were several roads nearby, but it did not take her long to find the one paved with yellow bricks. Within a short time she was walking briskly toward the Emerald City, her silver shoes tinkling merrily on the hard, yellow roadbed. The sun shone bright and the birds sang sweetly, and Dorothy did not feel nearly so bad as you might think a little girl would who had been suddenly whisked away from her own country and set down in the midst of a strange land.

She was surprised, as she walked along, to see how pretty the country was about her. There were neat fences at the sides of the road, painted a dainty blue color, and beyond them were fields of grain and vegetables in abundance. Evidently the Munchkins were good farmers and able to raise large crops. Once in a while she would pass a house, and the people came out to look at her and bow low as she went by; for everyone knew she had been the means of destroying the Wicked Witch and setting them free from bondage. The houses of the Munchkins were odd-looking dwellings, for each was round, with a big dome for a roof. All were painted blue, for in this country of the East blue was the favorite color.

Toward evening, when Dorothy was tired with her long walk and began to wonder where she should pass the night, she came to a house rather larger than the rest.

On the green lawn before it many men and women were dancing. Five little fiddlers played as loudly as possible, and the people were laughing and singing, while a big table nearby was loaded with delicious fruits and nuts, pies and cakes, and many other good things to eat.

The people greeted Dorothy kindly, and invited her to supper and to pass the night with them; for this was the home of one of the richest Munchkins in the land, and his friends were gathered with him to celebrate their freedom from the bondage of the Wicked Witch.

Dorothy ate a hearty supper and was waited upon by the rich Munchkin himself, whose name was Boq. Then she sat upon a settee and watched the people dance.

When Boq saw her silver shoes he said, "You must be a great sorceress."

"Why?" asked the girl.

"Because you wear silver shoes and have killed the Wicked Witch. Besides, you have white in your frock, and only witches and sorceresses wear white."

"My dress is blue and white checked," said Dorothy, smoothing out the wrinkles in it.

"It is kind of you to wear that," said Boq. "Blue is the color of the Munchkins, and white is the witch color. So we know you are a friendly witch."

Dorothy did not know what to say to this, for all the people seemed to think her a witch, and she knew very well she was only an ordinary little girl who had come by the chance of a cyclone into a strange land.

When she had tired watching the dancing, Boq led

You must be a great sorceress.

her into the house, where he gave her a room with a pretty bed in it. The sheets were made of blue cloth, and Dorothy slept soundly in them till morning, with Toto curled up on the blue rug beside her.

She ate a hearty breakfast, and watched a wee Munchkin baby, who played with Toto and pulled his tail and crowed and laughed in a way that greatly amused Dorothy. Toto was a fine curiosity to all the people, for they had never seen a dog before.

"How far is it to the Emerald City?" the girl asked.

"I do not know," answered Boq gravely, "for I have never been there. It is better for people to keep away from Oz, unless they have business with him. But it is a long way to the Emerald City, and it will take you many days. The country here is rich and pleasant, but you must pass through rough and dangerous places before you reach the end of your journey."

This worried Dorothy a little, but she knew that only the Great Oz could help her get to Kansas again, so she bravely resolved not to turn back.

She bade her friends good-bye, and again started along the road of yellow brick. When she had gone several miles she thought she would stop to rest, and so climbed to the top of the fence beside the road and sat down. There was a great cornfield beyond the fence, and not far away she saw a Scarecrow, placed high on a pole to keep the birds from the ripe corn.

Dorothy leaned her chin upon her hand and gazed thoughtfully at the Scarecrow. Its head was a small sack

Dorothy gazed thoughtfully at the Scarecrow.

stuffed with straw, with eyes, nose, and mouth painted on it to represent a face. An old, pointed blue hat, that had belonged to some Munchkin, was perched on his head, and the rest of the figure was a blue suit of clothes, worn and faded, which had also been stuffed with straw. On the feet were some old boots with blue tops, such as every man wore in this country, and the figure was raised above the stalks of corn by means of the pole stuck up its back.

While Dorothy was looking earnestly into the queer, painted face of the Scarecrow, she was surprised to see one of the eyes slowly wink at her. She thought she must have been mistaken at first, for none of the scarecrows in Kansas ever wink; but presently the figure nodded its head to her in a friendly way. Then she climbed down from the fence and walked up to it, while Toto ran around the pole and barked.

"Good day," said the Scarecrow, in a rather husky voice.

"Did you speak?" asked the girl, in wonder.

"Certainly," answered the Scarecrow. "How do you do?"

"I'm pretty well, thank you," replied Dorothy politely. "How do you do?"

"I'm not feeling well," said the Scarecrow, with a smile, "for it is very tedious being perched up here night and day to scare away crows."

"Can't you get down?" asked Dorothy.

"No, for this pole is stuck up my back. If you will please take away the pole I shall be greatly obliged to you."

Dorothy reached up both arms and lifted the figure off the pole, for, being stuffed with straw, it was quite light.

"Thank you very much," said the Scarecrow, when he had been set down on the ground. "I feel like a new man."

Dorothy was puzzled at this, for it sounded queer to hear a stuffed man speak, and to see him bow and walk along beside her.

"Who are you?" asked the Scarecrow when he had stretched himself and yawned. "And where are you going?"

"My name is Dorothy," said the girl, "and I am going to the Emerald City, to ask the Great Oz to send me back to Kansas."

"Where is the Emerald City?" he inquired. "And who is Oz?"

"Why, don't you know?" she returned, in surprise.

"No, indeed. I don't know anything. You see, I am stuffed, so I have no brains at all," he answered sadly.

"Oh," said Dorothy, "I'm awfully sorry for you."

"Do you think," he asked, "if I go to the Emerald City with you, that the great Oz would give me some brains?"

"I cannot tell," she returned, "but you may come with me, if you like. If Oz will not give you any brains you will be no worse off than you are now."

"That is true," said the Scarecrow. "You see," he continued confidentially, "I don't mind my legs and arms and body being stuffed, because I cannot get hurt. If anyone treads on my toes or sticks a pin into me, it doesn't matter, for I can't feel it. But I do not want people to call me a fool, and if my head stays stuffed with straw instead of with brains, as yours is, how am I ever to know anything?"

"I understand how you feel," said the little girl, who was truly sorry for him. "If you will come with me I'll ask Oz to do all he can for you."

"Thank you," he answered gratefully.

They walked back to the road. Dorothy helped him over the fence, and they started along the path of yellow brick for the Emerald City.

Toto did not like this addition to the party at first. He smelled around the stuffed man as if he suspected there might be a nest of rats in the straw, and he often growled in an unfriendly way at the Scarecrow.

"Don't mind Toto," said Dorothy to her new friend. "He never bites."

"Oh, I'm not afraid," replied the Scarecrow. "He can't hurt the straw. Do let me carry that basket for you. I shall not mind it, for I can't get tired. I'll tell you a secret," he continued, as he walked along. "There is only one thing in the world I am afraid of."

"What is that?" asked Dorothy; "the Munchkin farmer who made you?"

"No," answered the Scarecrow; "it's a lighted match."

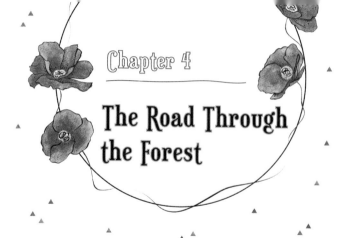

Chapter 4

The Road Through the Forest

After a few hours the road began to be rough, and the walking grew so difficult that the Scarecrow often stumbled over the yellow bricks, which were here very uneven. Sometimes, indeed, they were broken or missing altogether, leaving holes that Toto jumped across and Dorothy walked around. As for the Scarecrow, having no brains, he walked straight ahead, and so stepped into the holes and fell at full length on the hard bricks. It never hurt him, however, and Dorothy would pick him up and set him upon his feet again, while he joined her in laughing merrily at his own mishap.

The farms were not nearly so well cared for here as they were farther back. There were fewer houses and fewer fruit trees, and the farther they went the more dismal and lonesome the country became.

At noon they sat down by the roadside, near a little brook, and Dorothy opened her basket and got out some bread. She offered a piece to the Scarecrow, but he refused.

"I am never hungry," he said, "and it is a lucky thing I am not, for my mouth is only painted, and if I should cut a hole in it so I could eat, the straw I am stuffed with would come out, and that would spoil the shape of my head."

Dorothy saw at once that this was true, so she only nodded and went on eating her bread.

"Tell me something about yourself and the country you came from," said the Scarecrow, when she had finished her dinner. So she told him all about Kansas, and how gray everything was there, and how the cyclone had carried her to this queer Land of Oz. The Scarecrow listened carefully, and said, "I cannot understand why you should wish to leave this beautiful country and go back to the dry, gray place you call Kansas."

"That is because you have no brains," answered the girl. "No matter how dreary and gray our homes are, we people of flesh and blood would rather live there than in any other country, be it ever so beautiful. There is no place like home."

The Scarecrow sighed.

"Of course I cannot understand it," he said. "If your heads were stuffed with straw, like mine, you would probably all live in the beautiful places, and then Kansas would have no people at all. It is fortunate for Kansas that you have brains."

"Won't you tell me a story, while

we are resting?" asked the child.

The Scarecrow looked at her reproachfully, and answered,

"My life has been so short that I really know nothing whatever. I was only made day before yesterday. What happened in the world before that time is all unknown to me. Luckily, when the farmer made my head, one of the first things he did was to paint my ears, so that I heard what was going on. There was another Munchkin with him, and the first thing I heard was the farmer saying, 'How do you like those ears?'

"'They aren't straight,'" answered the other.

"'Never mind,'" said the farmer. "'They are ears just the same,'" which was true enough.

"'Now I'll make the eyes,' said the farmer. So he painted my right eye, and as soon as it was finished I found myself looking at him and at everything around me with a great deal of curiosity, for this was my first glimpse of the world.

"'That's a rather pretty eye,' remarked the Munchkin who was watching the farmer. 'Blue paint is just the color for eyes.'

"'I think I'll make the other a little bigger,' said the farmer. And when the second eye was done I could see much better than before. Then he made my nose and my mouth. But I did not speak, because at that time I didn't know what a mouth was for. I had the fun of watching them make my body and my arms and legs; and when they fastened on my head, at last, I felt very proud, for I

"I was only made day before yesterday," said the Scarecrow.

thought I was just as good a man as anyone.

"'This fellow will scare the crows fast enough,' said the farmer. 'He looks just like a man.'

"'Why, he is a man,' said the other, and I quite agreed with him. The farmer carried me under his arm to the cornfield, and set me up on a tall stick, where you found me. He and his friend soon after walked away and left me alone.

"I did not like to be deserted this way. So I tried to walk after them. But my feet would not touch the ground, and I was forced to stay on that pole. It was a lonely life to lead, for I had nothing to think of, having been made such a little while before. Many crows and other birds flew into the cornfield, but as soon as they saw me they flew away again, thinking I was a Munchkin; and this pleased me and made me feel that I was quite an important person. By and by an old crow flew near me, and after looking at me carefully he perched upon my shoulder and said:

"'I wonder if that farmer thought to fool me in this clumsy manner. Any crow of sense could see that you arc only stuffed with straw.' Then he hopped down at my feet and ate all the corn he wanted. The other birds, seeing he was not harmed by me, came to eat the corn too, so in a short time there was a great flock of them about me.

"I felt sad at this, for it showed I was not such a good Scarecrow after all; but the old crow comforted me, saying, 'If you only had brains in your head you would be as good a man as any of them, and a better man than some of them. Brains are the only things worth having in this world, no matter whether one is a crow or a man.'

"After the crows had gone I thought this over, and decided I would try hard to get some brains. By good luck you came along and pulled me off the stake, and from what you say I am sure the Great Oz will give me brains as soon as we get to the Emerald City."

"I hope so," said Dorothy earnestly, "since you seem anxious to have them."

"Oh, yes; I am anxious," returned the Scarecrow. "It is such an uncomfortable feeling to know one is a fool."

"Well," said the girl, "let us go." And she handed the basket to the Scarecrow.

There were no fences at all by the roadside now, and the land was rough and untilled. Toward evening they came to a great forest, where the trees grew so big and close together that their branches met over the road of yellow brick. It was almost dark under the trees, for the branches shut out the daylight; but the travelers did not stop, and went on into the forest.

"If this road goes in, it must come out," said the Scarecrow, "and as the Emerald City is at the other end of the road, we must go wherever it leads us."

"Anyone would know that," said Dorothy.

"Certainly; that is why I know it," returned the Scarecrow. "If it required brains to figure it out, I never should have said it."

After an hour or so the light faded away, and they found themselves stumbling along in the darkness. Dorothy could not see at all, but Toto could, for some dogs see very well in the dark; and the Scarecrow declared he could see as well as by day. So she took hold of his arm and managed to get along fairly well.

"If you see any house, or any place where we can pass the night," she said, "you must tell me; for it is very uncomfortable walking in the dark."

Soon after the Scarecrow stopped.

"I see a little cottage at the right of us," he said, "built of logs and branches. Shall we go there?"

"Yes, indeed," answered the child. "I am all tired out."

So the Scarecrow led her through the trees until they reached the cottage, and Dorothy entered and found a bed of dried leaves in one corner. She lay down at once, and with Toto beside her soon fell into a sound sleep. The Scarecrow, who was never tired, stood up in another corner and waited patiently until morning came.

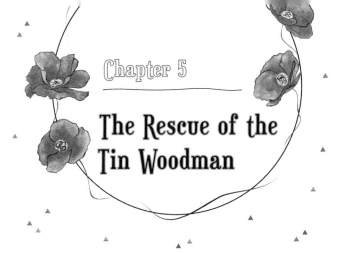

Chapter 5

The Rescue of the Tin Woodman

When Dorothy awoke the sun was shining through the trees and Toto had long been out chasing birds and squirrels. She sat up and looked around her. There was the Scarecrow, still standing patiently in his corner, waiting for her.

"We must go and search for water," she said to him.

"Why do you want water?" he asked.

"To wash my face clean after the dust of the road, and to drink, so the dry bread will not stick in my throat."

"It must be inconvenient to be made of flesh," said the Scarecrow thoughtfully, "for you must sleep, and eat and drink. However, you have brains, and it is worth a lot of bother to be able to think properly."

They left the cottage and walked through the trees until they found a little spring of clear water, where Dorothy drank and bathed and ate her breakfast. She saw there was not much bread left in the basket, and the girl was thankful the Scarecrow did not have to eat anything, for there was scarcely enough for herself and Toto for the day.

When she had finished her meal, and was about to go back to the road of yellow brick, she was startled to hear a deep groan nearby.

"What was that?" she asked timidly.

"I cannot imagine," replied the Scarecrow; "but we can go and see."

Just then another groan reached their ears, and the sound seemed to come from behind them. They turned and walked through the forest a few steps, when Dorothy discovered something shining in a ray of sunshine that fell between the trees. She ran to the place and then stopped short, with a little cry of surprise.

One of the big trees had been partly chopped through, and standing beside it, with an uplifted axe in his hands, was a man made entirely of tin. His head and arms and legs were jointed upon his body, but he stood perfectly motionless, as if he could not stir at all.

Dorothy looked at him in amazement, and so did the Scarecrow, while Toto barked sharply and made a snap at the tin legs, which hurt his teeth.

"Did you groan?" asked Dorothy.

"Yes," answered the tin man, "I did. I've been groaning for more than a year, and no one has ever heard me before or come to help me."

"What can I do for you?" she inquired softly, for she

was moved by the sad voice in which the man spoke.

"Get an oil-can and oil my joints," he answered. "They are rusted so badly that I cannot move them at all; if I am well oiled I shall soon be all right again. You will find an oil-can on a shelf in my cottage."

Dorothy at once ran back to the cottage and found the oil-can, and then she returned and asked anxiously, "Where are your joints?"

"Oil my neck, first," replied the Tin Woodman. So she oiled it, and as it was quite badly rusted the Scarecrow took hold of the tin head and moved it gently from side to side until it worked freely, and then the man could turn it himself.

"Now oil the joints in my arms," he said. And Dorothy oiled them and the Scarecrow bent them carefully until they were quite free from rust and as good as new.

The Tin Woodman gave a sigh of satisfaction and lowered his axe, which he leaned against the tree.

"This is a great comfort," he said. "I have been holding that axe in the air ever since I rusted, and I'm glad to be able to put it down at last. Now, if you will oil the joints of my legs, I shall be all right once more."

So they oiled his legs until he could move them freely; and he thanked them again and again for his release, for he seemed a very polite creature, and very grateful.

"I might have stood there always if you had not come along," he said; "so you have certainly saved my life. How did you happen to be here?"

"We are on our way to the Emerald City to see the

"This is a great comfort," said the Tin Woodman.

Great Oz," she answered, "and we stopped at your cottage to pass the night."

"Why do you wish to see Oz?" he asked.

"I want him to send me back to Kansas, and the Scarecrow wants him to put a few brains into his head," she replied.

The Tin Woodman appeared to think deeply for a moment. Then he said:

"Do you suppose Oz could give me a heart?"

"Why, I guess so," Dorothy answered. "It would be as easy as to give the Scarecrow brains."

"True," the Tin Woodman returned. "So, if you will allow me to join your party, I will also go to the Emerald City and ask Oz to help me."

"Come along," said the Scarecrow heartily, and Dorothy added that she would be pleased to have his company. So the Tin Woodman shouldered his axe and they all passed through the forest until they came to the road that was paved with yellow brick.

The Tin Woodman had asked Dorothy to put the oil-can in her basket. "For," he said, "if I should get caught in the rain, and rust again, I would need the oil-can badly."

It was a bit of good luck to have their new comrade join the party, for soon after they had begun their journey again they came to a place where the trees and branches grew so thick over the road that the travelers could not pass. But the Tin Woodman set to work with his axe and chopped so well that soon he cleared a passage for the entire party.

Dorothy was thinking so earnestly as they walked along that she did not notice when the Scarecrow stumbled into a hole and rolled over to the side of the road. Indeed he was obliged to call to her to help him up again.

"Why didn't you walk around the hole?" asked the Tin Woodman.

"I don't know enough," replied the Scarecrow cheerfully. "My head is stuffed with straw, you know, and that is why I am going to Oz to ask him for some brains."

"Oh, I see," said the Tin Woodman. "But, after all, brains are not the best things in the world."

"Have you any?" inquired the Scarecrow.

"No, my head is quite empty," answered the Woodman. "But once I had brains, and a heart also; so, having tried them both, I should much rather have a heart."

"And why is that?" asked the Scarecrow.

"I will tell you my story, and then you will know."

So, while they were walking through the forest, the Tin Woodman told the following story:

"I was born the son of a woodman who chopped down trees in the forest and sold the wood for a living. When I grew up, I too became a woodchopper, and after my father died I took care of my old mother as long as she lived. Then I made up my mind that instead of living alone I would marry, so that I might not become lonely.

"There was one of the Munchkin girls who was so beautiful that I soon grew to love her with all my heart. She, on her part, promised to marry me as soon as I could earn enough money to build a better house for her; so I set to work harder than ever. But the girl lived with an old woman who did not want her to marry anyone, for she was so lazy she wished the girl to remain with her and do the cooking and the housework. So the old woman went to the Wicked Witch of the East, and promised her two sheep and a cow if she would prevent the marriage. Thereupon the Wicked Witch enchanted my axe, and when I was chopping away at my best one day, for I was anxious to get the new house and my wife as soon as possible, the axe slipped all at once and cut off my left leg.

"This at first seemed a great misfortune, for I knew a one-legged man could not do very well as a wood-chopper. So I went to a tinsmith and had him make me a new leg out of tin. The leg worked very well, once I was used to it. But my action angered the Wicked Witch of the East, for she had promised the old woman I should not marry the pretty Munchkin girl. When I began chopping again, my axe slipped and cut off my right leg. Again I went to the tinner, and again he made me a leg out of tin. After this the enchanted axe cut off my arms, one after the other; but, nothing daunted, I had them replaced with tin ones. The Wicked Witch then made the axe slip and cut off my head, and at first I thought that was the end of me. But the tinner happened to come along, and he made me a new head out of tin.

"I thought I had beaten the Wicked Witch then, and I worked harder than ever; but I little knew how cruel my enemy could be. She thought of a new way to kill my love for the beautiful Munchkin maiden, and made my axe slip again, so that it cut right through my body, splitting me into two halves. Once more the tinsmith came to my help and made me a body of tin, fastening my tin arms and legs and head to it, by means of joints, so that I could move around as well as ever. But, alas! I had now no heart, so that I lost all my love for the Munchkin girl, and did not care whether I married her or not. I suppose she is still living with the old woman, waiting for me to come after her.

"My body shone so brightly in the sun that I felt very proud of it and it did not matter now if my axe slipped, for it could not cut me. There was only one danger— that my joints would rust; but I kept an oil-can in my cottage and took care to oil myself whenever I needed it. However, there came a day when I forgot to do this, and, being caught in a rainstorm, before I thought of the danger my joints had rusted, and I was left to stand in the woods until you came to help me. It was a terrible thing to undergo, but during the year I stood there I had time to think that the greatest loss I had known was the loss of my heart. While I was in love I was the happiest man on earth; but no one can love who has not a heart, and so I am resolved to ask Oz to give me one. If he does, I will go back to the Munchkin maiden and marry her."

Both Dorothy and the Scarecrow had been greatly interested in the story of the Tin Woodman, and now they knew why he was so anxious to get a new heart.

"All the same," said the Scarecrow, "I shall ask for brains instead of a heart; for a fool would not know what to do with a heart if he had one."

"I shall take the heart," returned the Tin Woodman; "for brains do not make one happy, and happiness is the best thing in the world."

Dorothy did not say anything, for she was puzzled to know which of her two friends was right, and she decided if she could only get back to Kansas and Aunt Em, it did not matter so much whether the Woodman had no brains and the Scarecrow no heart, or each got what he wanted.

What worried her most was that the bread was nearly gone, and another meal for herself and Toto would empty the basket. To be sure neither the Woodman nor the Scarecrow ever ate anything, but she was not made of tin nor straw, and could not live unless she was fed.

Chapter 6

The Cowardly Lion

All this time Dorothy and her companions had been walking through the thick woods. The road was still paved with yellow brick, but these were much covered by dried branches and dead leaves from the trees, and the walking was not at all good.

There were few birds in this part of the forest, for birds love the open country where there is plenty of sunshine. But now and then there came a deep growl from some wild animal hidden among the trees. These sounds made the little girl's heart beat fast, for she did not know what made them; but Toto knew, and he walked close to Dorothy's side, and did not even bark in return.

"How long will it be," the child asked of the Tin Woodman, "before we are out of the forest?"

"I cannot tell," was the answer, "for I have never been to the Emerald City. But my father went there once, when I was a boy, and he said it was a long journey through a dangerous country, although nearer to the city where Oz dwells the country is beautiful. But I am not afraid so long as I have my oil-can, and nothing can hurt the Scarecrow, while you bear upon your forehead the mark of the Good Witch's kiss, and that will protect you from harm."

"But Toto!" said the girl anxiously. "What will protect him?"

"We must protect him ourselves if he is in danger," replied the Tin Woodman.

Just as he spoke there came from the forest a terrible roar, and the next moment a great Lion bounded into the road. With one blow of his paw he sent the Scarecrow spinning over and over to the edge of the road, and then he struck at the Tin Woodman with his sharp claws. But, to the Lion's surprise, he could make no impression on the tin, although the Woodman fell over in the road and lay still.

Little Toto, now that he had an enemy to face, ran barking toward the Lion, and the great beast had opened his mouth to bite the dog, when Dorothy, fearing Toto would be killed, and heedless of danger, rushed forward and slapped the Lion upon his nose as hard as she could, while she cried out:

"Don't you dare to bite Toto! You ought to be ashamed of yourself, a big beast like you, to bite a poor little dog!"

You ought to be ashamed of yourself!

"I didn't bite him," said the Lion, as he rubbed his nose with his paw where Dorothy had hit it.

"No, but you tried to," she retorted. "You are nothing but a big coward."

"I know it," said the Lion, hanging his head in shame. "I've always known it. But how can I help it?"

"I don't know, I'm sure. To think of your striking a stuffed man, like the poor Scarecrow!"

"Is he stuffed?" asked the Lion in surprise, as he watched her pick up the Scarecrow and set him upon his feet, while she patted him into shape again.

"Of course he's stuffed," replied Dorothy, who was still angry.

"That's why he went over so easily," remarked the Lion. "It astonished me to see him whirl around so. Is the other one stuffed also?"

"No," said Dorothy, "he's made of tin." And she helped the Woodman up again.

"That's why he nearly blunted my claws," said the Lion. "When they scratched against the tin it made a cold shiver run down my back. What is that little animal you are so tender of?"

"He is my dog, Toto," answered Dorothy.

"Is he made of tin, or stuffed?" asked the Lion.

"Neither. He's a—a—a meat dog," said the girl.

"Oh! He's a curious animal and seems remarkably small, now that I look at him. No one would think of biting such a little thing, except a coward like me," continued the Lion sadly.

"What makes you a coward?" asked Dorothy, looking at the great beast in wonder, for he was as big as a small horse.

"It's a mystery," replied the Lion. "I suppose I was born that way. All the other animals in the forest naturally expect me to be brave, for the Lion is everywhere thought to be the King of Beasts. I learned that if I roared very loudly every living thing was frightened and got out of my way. Whenever I've met a man I've been awfully scared; but I just roared at him, and he has always run away as fast as he could go. If the elephants and the tigers and the bears had ever tried to fight me, I should have run myself—I'm such a coward; but just as soon as they hear me roar they all try to get away from me, and of course I let them go."

"But that isn't right. The King of Beasts shouldn't be a coward," said the Scarecrow.

"I know it," returned the Lion, wiping a tear from his eye with the tip of his tail. "It is my great sorrow, and makes my life very unhappy. But whenever there is danger, my heart begins to beat fast."

"Perhaps you have heart disease," said the Tin Woodman.

"It may be," said the Lion.

"If you have," continued the Tin Woodman, "you ought to be glad, for it proves you have a heart. For my part, I have no heart; so I cannot have heart disease."

"Perhaps," said the Lion thoughtfully, "if I had no heart I should not be a coward."

"Have you brains?" asked the Scarecrow.

"I suppose so. I've never looked to see," replied the Lion.

"I am going to the Great Oz to ask him to give me some," remarked the Scarecrow, "for my head is stuffed with straw."

"And I am going to ask him to give me a heart," said the Woodman.

"And I am going to ask him to send Toto and me back to Kansas," added Dorothy.

"Do you think Oz could give me courage?" asked the Cowardly Lion.

"Just as easily as he could give me brains," said the Scarecrow.

"Or give me a heart," said the Tin Woodman.

"Or send me back to Kansas," said Dorothy.

"Then, if you don't mind, I'll go with you," said the Lion, "for my life is simply unbearable without a bit of courage."

"You will be very welcome," answered Dorothy, "for you will help to keep away the other wild beasts. It seems to me they must be more cowardly than you are if they allow you to scare them so easily."

"They really are," said the Lion, "but that doesn't make me any braver, and as long as I know myself to be a coward I shall be unhappy."

So once more the little company set off upon the journey, the Lion walking with stately strides at Dorothy's side. Toto did not approve this new comrade at first, for he could not forget how nearly he had been crushed between the Lion's great jaws. But after a time he became more at ease, and presently Toto and the Cowardly Lion had grown to be good friends.

During the rest of that day there was no other adventure to mar the peace of their journey. Once, indeed, the Tin Woodman stepped upon a beetle that was crawling along the road, and killed the poor little thing. This made the Tin Woodman very unhappy, for he was always careful not to hurt any living creature; and as he walked along he wept several tears of sorrow and regret. These tears ran slowly down his face and over the hinges of his jaw, and there they rusted. When Dorothy presently asked him a question the Tin Woodman could not open his mouth, for his jaws were tightly rusted together. He became greatly frightened at this and made many motions to Dorothy to relieve him, but she could not understand. The Lion was also puzzled to know what was wrong. But the Scarecrow seized the oil-can from Dorothy's basket and oiled the Woodman's jaws, so that after a few moments he could talk as well as before.

"This will serve me a lesson," said he, "to look where I step. For if I should kill another bug or beetle I should surely cry again, and crying rusts my jaws so that I cannot speak."

Thereafter he walked very carefully, with his eyes on the road, and when he saw a tiny ant toiling by he would step over it, so as not to harm it. The Tin Woodman knew very well he had no heart, and therefore he took great care never to be cruel or unkind to anything.

"You people with hearts," he said, "have something to guide you, and need never do wrong; but I have no heart, and so I must be very careful. When Oz gives me a heart of course I needn't mind so much."

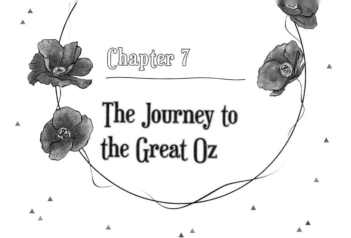

Chapter 7

The Journey to the Great Oz

They were obliged to camp out that night under a large tree in the forest, for there were no houses near. The tree made a good, thick covering to protect them from the dew, and the Tin Woodman chopped a great pile of wood with his axe and Dorothy built a splendid fire that warmed her and made her feel less lonely. She and Toto ate the last of their bread, and now she did not know what they would do for breakfast.

"If you wish," said the Lion, "I will go into the forest and kill a deer for you. You can roast it by the fire, since your tastes are so peculiar that you prefer cooked food, and then you will have a very good breakfast."

"Don't! Please don't," begged the Tin Woodman. "I should certainly weep if you killed a poor deer, and then my jaws would rust again."

But the Lion went away into the forest and found his own supper, and no one ever knew what it was, for he didn't mention it. And the Scarecrow found a tree full of nuts and filled Dorothy's basket with them, so that she would not be hungry for a long time. She thought this was very kind and thoughtful of the Scarecrow, but she laughed heartily at the awkward way in which the poor creature picked up the nuts. His padded hands were so clumsy and the nuts were so small that he dropped almost as many as he put in the basket. But the Scarecrow did not mind how long it took him to fill the basket, for it enabled him to keep away from the fire, as he feared a spark might get into his straw and burn him up. So he kept a good distance away from the flames, and only came near to cover Dorothy with dry leaves when she lay down to sleep. These kept her very snug and warm, and she slept soundly until morning.

When it was daylight, the girl bathed her face in a little rippling brook, and soon after they all started toward the Emerald City.

This was to be an eventful day for the travelers. They had hardly been walking an hour when they saw before them a great ditch that crossed the road and divided the forest as far as they could see on either side. It was a very wide ditch, and when they crept up to the edge and looked into it they could see it was also very deep, and there were many big, jagged rocks at the bottom. The sides were so steep that none of them could climb down, and for a moment it seemed

that their journey must end.

"What shall we do?" asked Dorothy despairingly.

"I haven't the faintest idea," said the Tin Woodman, and the Lion shook his shaggy mane and looked thoughtful.

But the Scarecrow said, "We cannot fly, that is certain. Neither can we climb down into this great ditch. Therefore, if we cannot jump over it, we must stop where we are."

"I think I could jump over it," said the Cowardly Lion, after measuring the distance carefully in his mind.

"Then we are all right," answered the Scarecrow, "for you can carry us all over on your back, one at a time."

"Well, I'll try it," said the Lion. "Who will go first?"

"I will," declared the Scarecrow, "for, if you found that you could not jump over the gulf, Dorothy would be killed, or the Tin Woodman badly dented on the rocks below. But if I am on your back it will not matter so much, for the fall would not hurt me at all."

"I am terribly afraid of falling, myself," said the Cowardly Lion,

"but I suppose there is nothing to do but try it. So get on my back and we will make the attempt."

The Scarecrow sat upon the Lion's back, and the big beast walked to the edge of the gulf and crouched down.

"Why don't you run and jump?" asked the Scarecrow.

"Because that isn't the way we Lions do these things," he replied. Then giving a great spring, he shot through the air and landed safely on the other side. They were all greatly pleased to see how easily he did it, and after the Scarecrow had got down from his back the Lion sprang across the ditch again.

Dorothy thought she would go next; so she took Toto in her arms and climbed on the Lion's back, holding tightly to his mane with one hand. The next moment it seemed as if she were flying through the air; and then, before she had time to think about it, she was safe on the other side. The Lion went back a third time and got the Tin Woodman, and then they all sat down for a few moments to give the beast a chance to rest, for his great leaps had made his breath short, and he panted like a big dog that has been running too long.

They found the forest very thick on this side, and it looked dark and gloomy. After the Lion had rested they started along the road of yellow brick, silently wondering, each in his own mind, if ever they would come to the end of the woods and reach the bright sunshine again. To add to their discomfort, they soon heard strange noises in the depths of the forest, and the Lion whispered to them that it was in this part of the country that the Kalidahs lived.

"What are the Kalidahs?" asked the girl.

"They are monstrous beasts with bodies like bears and heads like tigers," replied the Lion, "and with claws so long and sharp that they could tear me in two as easily as I could kill Toto. I'm terribly afraid of the Kalidahs."

"I'm not surprised that you are," returned Dorothy. "They must be dreadful beasts."

The Lion was about to reply when suddenly they came to another gulf across the road. But this one was so broad and deep that the Lion knew at once he could not leap across it.

So they sat down to consider what they should do, and after serious thought the Scarecrow said:

"Here is a great tree, standing close to the ditch. If the Tin Woodman can chop it down, so that it will fall to the other side, we can walk across it easily."

"That is a first-rate idea," said the Lion. "One would almost suspect you had brains in your head, instead of straw."

The Woodman set to work at once, and so sharp was his axe that the tree was soon chopped nearly through. Then the Lion put his strong front legs against the tree and pushed with all his might, and slowly the big tree tipped and fell with a crash across the ditch, with its top branches on the other side.

They had just started to cross this queer bridge when a sharp growl made them all look up, and to their horror

they saw
running
toward them
two great
beasts with
bodies like bears
and heads like tigers.

"They are the Kalidahs!"
said the Cowardly Lion,
beginning to tremble.

"Quick!" cried the Scarecrow. "Let us
cross over."

So Dorothy went first, holding Toto in her arms, the Tin Woodman followed, and the Scarecrow came next. The Lion, although he was certainly afraid, turned to face the Kalidahs, and then he gave so loud and terrible a roar that Dorothy screamed and the Scarecrow fell over backward, while even the fierce beasts stopped short and looked at him in surprise.

But, seeing they were bigger than the Lion, and remembering that there were two of them and only one of him, the Kalidahs again rushed forward, and the Lion crossed over the tree and turned to see what they would do next. Without stopping an instant the fierce beasts also began to cross the tree. And the Lion said to Dorothy:

"We are lost, for they will surely tear us to pieces with their sharp claws. But stand close behind me, and I will fight them as long as I am alive."

"Wait a minute!" called the Scarecrow. He had been thinking what was best to be done, and now he asked the Woodman to chop away the end of the tree that rested on their side of the ditch. The Tin Woodman began to use his axe at once, and, just as the two Kalidahs were nearly across, the tree fell with a crash into the gulf, carrying the ugly, snarling brutes with it, and both were dashed to pieces on the sharp rocks at the bottom.

"Well," said the Cowardly Lion, drawing a long breath of relief, "I see we are going to live a little while longer, and I am glad of it, for it must be a very uncomfortable thing not to be alive. Those creatures frightened me so badly that my heart is beating yet."

"Ah," said the Tin Woodman sadly, "I wish I had a heart to beat."

This adventure made the travelers more anxious than ever to get out of the forest, and they walked so fast that Dorothy became tired, and had to ride on the Lion's back. To their great joy the trees became thinner the farther they advanced, and in the afternoon they suddenly came upon a broad river, flowing swiftly just before them. On the other side of the water they could see the road of yellow brick running through a beautiful country, with green meadows dotted with bright flowers and all the road bordered with trees hanging full of delicious fruits. They were greatly pleased to see this delightful country before them.

"How shall we cross the river?" asked Dorothy.

The tree fell with a crash into the gulf.

"That is easily done," replied the Scarecrow. "The Tin Woodman must build us a raft, so we can float to the other side."

So the Woodman took his axe and began to chop down small trees to make a raft, and while he was busy at this the Scarecrow found on the riverbank a tree full of fine fruit. This pleased Dorothy, who had eaten nothing but nuts all day, and she made a hearty meal of the ripe fruit.

But it takes time to make a raft, even when one is as industrious and untiring as the Tin Woodman, and when night came the work was not done. So they found a cozy place under the trees where they slept well until the morning; and Dorothy dreamed of the Emerald City, and of the good Wizard Oz, who would soon send her back to her own home again.

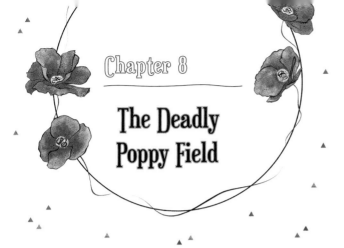

Chapter 8

The Deadly Poppy Field

Our little party of travelers awakened the next morning refreshed and full of hope, and Dorothy breakfasted like a princess off peaches and plums from the trees beside the river. Behind them was the dark forest they had passed safely through, although they had suffered many discouragements; but before them was a lovely, sunny country that seemed to beckon them on to the Emerald City.

To be sure, the broad river now cut them off from this beautiful land. But the raft was nearly done, and after the Tin Woodman had cut a few more logs and fastened them together with wooden pins, they were ready to start. Dorothy sat down in the middle of the raft and held Toto in her arms. When the Cowardly Lion stepped upon the raft it tipped badly, for he was big and heavy; but the Scarecrow and the Tin Woodman stood upon the other end to steady it, and they had long poles in their hands to push the raft through the water.

They got along quite well at first, but when they reached the middle of the river the swift current swept the raft downstream, farther and farther away from the road of yellow brick. And the water grew so deep that the long poles would not touch the bottom.

"This is bad," said the Tin Woodman, "for if we cannot get to the land we shall be carried into the country of the Wicked Witch of the West, and she will enchant us and make us her slaves."

"And then I should get no brains," said the Scarecrow.

"And I should get no courage," said the Cowardly Lion.

"And I should get no heart," said the Tin Woodman.

"And I should never get back to Kansas," said Dorothy.

"We must certainly get to the Emerald City if we can," the Scarecrow continued, and he pushed so hard on his long pole that it stuck fast in the mud at the bottom of the river. Then, before he could pull it out again—or let go—the raft was swept away, and the poor Scarecrow left clinging to the pole in the middle of the river.

"Good-bye!" he called after them, and they were very sorry to leave him. Indeed, the Tin Woodman began to cry,

but fortunately remembered that he might rust, and so dried his tears on Dorothy's apron.

Of course this was a bad thing for the Scarecrow.

"I am now worse off than when I first met Dorothy," he thought. "Then, I was stuck on a pole in a cornfield, where I could make-believe scare the crows, at any rate. But surely there is no use for a Scarecrow stuck on a pole in the middle of a river. I am afraid I shall never have any brains, after all!"

Down the stream the raft floated, and the poor Scarecrow was left far behind. Then the Lion said:

"Something must be done to save us. I think I can swim to the shore and pull the raft after me, if you will only hold fast to the tip of my tail."

So he sprang into the water, and the Tin Woodman caught fast hold of his tail. Then the Lion began to swim with all his might toward the shore. It was hard work, although he was so big; but by and by they were drawn out of the current, and then Dorothy took the Tin Woodman's long pole and helped push the raft to the land.

They were all tired out when they reached the shore at last and stepped off upon the pretty green grass, and they also knew that the stream had carried them a long way past the road of yellow brick that led to the Emerald City.

"What shall we do now?" asked the Tin Woodman, as the Lion lay down on the grass to let the sun dry him.

"We must get back to the road, in some way," said Dorothy.

"The best plan will be to walk along the riverbank until we come to the road again," remarked the Lion.

So, when they were rested, Dorothy picked up her basket and they started along the grassy bank, to the road from which the river had carried them. It was a lovely country, with plenty of flowers and fruit trees and sunshine to cheer them, and had they not felt so sorry for the poor Scarecrow, they could have been very happy.

They walked along as fast as they could, Dorothy only stopping once to pick a beautiful flower; and after a time the Tin Woodman cried out: "Look!"

Then they all looked at the river and saw the Scarecrow perched upon his pole in the middle of the water, looking very lonely and sad.

"What can we do to save him?" asked Dorothy.

The Lion and the Woodman both shook their heads, for they did not know. So they sat down upon the bank and gazed wistfully at the Scarecrow until a Stork flew by, who, upon seeing them, stopped to rest at the water's edge.

"Who are you and where are you going?" asked the Stork.

"I am Dorothy," answered the girl, "and these are my

The stork carried him up into the air.

friends, the Tin Woodman and the Cowardly Lion; and we are going to the Emerald City."

"This isn't the road," said the Stork, as she twisted her long neck and looked sharply at the queer party.

"I know it," returned Dorothy, "but we have lost the Scarecrow, and are wondering how we shall get him again."

"Where is he?" asked the Stork.

"Over there in the river," answered the little girl.

"If he wasn't so big and heavy I would get him for you," remarked the Stork.

"He isn't heavy a bit," said Dorothy eagerly, "for he is stuffed with straw; and if you will bring him back to us, we shall thank you ever and ever so much."

"Well, I'll try," said the Stork, "but if I find he is too heavy to carry I shall have to drop him in the river again."

So the big bird flew into the air and over the water till she came to where the Scarecrow was perched upon his pole. Then the Stork with her great claws grabbed the Scarecrow by the arm and carried him up into the air and back to the bank, where Dorothy and the Lion and the Tin Woodman and Toto were sitting.

When the Scarecrow found himself among his friends again, he was so happy that he hugged them all, even the Lion and Toto; and as they walked along he sang "Tol-de-ri-de-oh!" at every step, he felt so gay.

"I was afraid I should have to stay in the river forever," he said, "but the kind Stork saved me, and if

I ever get any brains I shall find the Stork again and do her some kindness in return."

"That's all right," said the Stork, who was flying along beside them. "I always like to help anyone in trouble. But I must go now, for my babies are waiting in the nest for me. I hope you will find the Emerald City and that Oz will help you."

"Thank you," replied Dorothy, and then the kind Stork flew into the air and was soon out of sight.

They walked along listening to the singing of the brightly colored birds and looking at the lovely flowers which now became so thick that the ground was carpeted with them. There were big yellow and white and blue and purple blossoms, besides great

clusters of scarlet poppies, which were so brilliant in color they almost dazzled Dorothy's eyes.

"Aren't they beautiful?" the girl asked, as she breathed in the spicy scent of the flowers.

"I suppose so," answered the Scarecrow. "When I have brains, I shall probably like them better."

"If I only had a heart, I should love them," added the Tin Woodman.

"I always did like flowers," said the Lion. "They of seem so helpless and frail. But there are none in the forest so bright as these."

They now came upon more and more of the big scarlet poppies, and fewer and fewer of the other flowers; and soon they found themselves in the midst of a great meadow of poppies. Now it is well known that when there are many of these flowers together their odor is so powerful that anyone who breathes it falls asleep, and if the sleeper is not carried away from the scent of the flowers, he sleeps on and on forever. But Dorothy did not know this, nor could she get away from the bright red flowers that were everywhere about; so presently her eyes grew heavy and she felt she must sit down to rest and to sleep.

But the Tin Woodman would not let her do this.

"We must hurry and get back to the road of yellow brick before dark," he said; and the Scarecrow agreed with him. So they kept walking until Dorothy could stand no longer. Her eyes closed in spite of herself and she forgot where she was and fell among the poppies, fast asleep.

"What shall we do?" asked the Tin Woodman.

"If we leave her here she will die," said the Lion. "The smell of the flowers is killing us all. I myself can scarcely keep my eyes open, and the dog is asleep already."

It was true; Toto had fallen down beside his little mistress. But the Scarecrow and the Tin Woodman, not being made of flesh, were not troubled by the scent of the flowers.

"Run fast," said the Scarecrow to the Lion, "and get out of this deadly flower bed as soon as you can. We will bring the little girl with us, but if you should fall asleep you are too big to be carried."

So the Lion aroused himself and bounded forward as fast as he could go. In a moment he was out of sight.

"Let us make a chair with our hands and carry her," said the Scarecrow. So they picked up Toto and put the dog in Dorothy's lap, and then they made a chair with their hands for the seat and their arms for the arms and carried the sleeping girl between them through the flowers.

On and on they walked, and it seemed that the great carpet of deadly flowers that

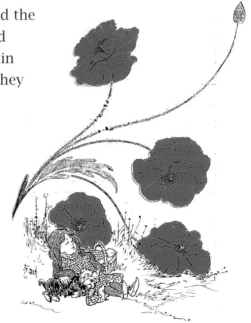

surrounded them would never end. They followed the bend of the river, and at last came upon their friend the Lion, lying fast asleep among the poppies. The flowers had been too strong for the huge beast and he had given up at last, and fallen only a short distance from the end of the poppy bed, where the sweet grass spread in beautiful green fields before them.

"We can do nothing for him," said the Tin Woodman, sadly; "for he is much too heavy to lift. We must leave him here to sleep on forever, and perhaps he will dream that he has found courage at last."

"I'm sorry," said the Scarecrow. "The Lion was a very good comrade for one so cowardly. But let us go on."

They carried the sleeping girl to a pretty spot beside the river, far enough from the poppy field to prevent her breathing any more of the poison of the flowers, and here they laid her gently on the soft grass and waited for the fresh breeze to waken her.

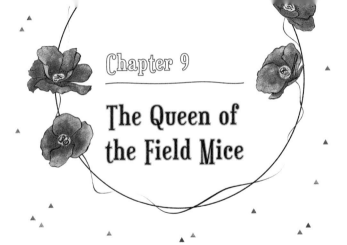

Chapter 9

The Queen of the Field Mice

"We cannot be far from the road of yellow brick, now," remarked the Scarecrow, as he stood beside the girl, "for we have come nearly as far as the river carried us away."

The Tin Woodman was about to reply when he heard a low growl, and turning his head (which worked beautifully on hinges) he saw a strange beast come bounding over the grass toward them. It was, indeed, a great yellow Wildcat, and the Woodman thought it must be chasing something, for its ears were lying close to its head and its mouth was wide open, showing two rows of ugly teeth, while its red eyes glowed like balls of fire. As it came nearer the Tin Woodman saw that running before the beast was a little gray field mouse, and although he had no heart he knew it was wrong for the Wildcat to try to kill such a pretty, harmless creature.

So the Woodman raised his axe, and as the Wildcat ran by he gave it a quick blow that cut the beast's head clean off from its body, and it rolled over at his feet in two pieces.

The field mouse, now that it was freed from its enemy, stopped short; and coming slowly up to the

Woodman it said, in a squeaky little voice:

"Oh, thank you! Thank you ever so much for saving my life."

"Don't speak of it, I beg of you," replied the Woodman. "I have no heart, you know, so I am careful to help all those who may need a friend, even if it happens to be only a mouse."

"Only a mouse!" cried the little animal, indignantly. "Why, I am a Queen—the Queen of all the Field Mice!"

"Oh, indeed," said the Woodman, making a bow.

"Therefore you have done a great deed, as well as a brave one, in saving my life," added the Queen.

At that moment several mice were seen running up as fast as their little legs could carry them, and when they saw their Queen they exclaimed:

"Oh, your Majesty, we thought you would be killed! How did you manage to escape the great Wildcat?" They all bowed so low to the little Queen that they almost stood upon their heads.

"This funny tin man," she answered, "killed the Wildcat and saved my life. So hereafter you must all serve him, and obey his slightest wish."

"We will!" cried all the mice, in a shrill chorus. And then they scampered in all directions, for Toto had awakened from his sleep, and seeing all these mice around him he gave one bark of delight and jumped right into the middle of the group. Toto had always loved to chase mice when he lived in Kansas, and he saw no harm in it.

But the Tin Woodman caught the dog in his arms and held him tight, while he called to the mice, "Come back! Come back! Toto shall not hurt you."

At this the Queen of the Mice stuck her head out from underneath a clump of grass and asked, in a timid voice, "Are you sure he will not bite us?"

"I will not let him," said the Woodman; "so do not be afraid."

One by one the mice came creeping back, and Toto did not bark again, although he tried to get out of the Woodman's arms, and would have bitten him had he not known very well he was made of tin. Finally one of the biggest mice spoke.

"Is there anything we can do," it asked, "to repay you for saving the life of our Queen?"

"Nothing that I know of," answered the Woodman; but the Scarecrow, who had been trying to think, but could not because his head was stuffed with straw, said, quickly, "Oh, yes; you can save our friend, the Cowardly

Lion, who is asleep in the poppy bed."

"A Lion!" cried the little Queen. "Why, he would eat us all up."

"Oh, no," declared the Scarecrow; "this Lion is a coward."

"Really?" asked the Mouse.

"He says so himself," answered the Scarecrow, "and he would never hurt anyone who is our friend. If you will help us to save him I promise that he shall treat you all with kindness."

"Very well," said the Queen, "we trust you. But what shall we do?"

"Are there many of these mice which call you Queen and are willing to obey you?"

"Oh, yes; there are thousands," she replied.

"Then send for them all to come here as soon as possible, and let each one bring a long piece of string."

The Queen turned to the mice that attended her and told them to go at once and get all her people. As soon as they heard her orders they ran away in every direction as fast as possible.

"Now," said the Scarecrow to the Tin Woodman, "you must go to those trees by the riverside and make a truck that will carry the Lion."

So the Woodman went at once to the trees and began to work; and he soon made a truck out of the limbs of trees, from which he chopped away all the leaves and branches. He fastened it together with wooden pegs and made the four wheels out of short pieces of a big tree trunk. So fast and so well did he work that by the time the mice began to arrive the truck was all ready for them.

They came from all directions, and there were thousands of them: big mice and little mice and middle-sized mice; and each one brought a piece of string in his mouth. It was about this time that Dorothy woke from her long sleep and opened her eyes. She was greatly astonished to find herself lying upon the grass, with thousands of mice standing around and looking at her timidly. But the Scarecrow told her about everything, and turning to the dignified little Mouse, he said:

"Permit me to introduce to you her Majesty, the Queen."

"Permit me to introduce to you her
Majesty, the Queen."

Dorothy nodded gravely and the Queen made a curtsy, after which she became quite friendly with the little girl.

The Scarecrow and the Woodman now began to fasten the mice to the truck, using the strings they had brought. One end of a string was tied around the neck of each mouse and the other end to the truck. Of course the truck was a thousand times bigger than any of the mice who were to draw it; but when all the mice had been harnessed, they were able to pull it quite easily. Even the Scarecrow and the Tin Woodman could sit on it, and were drawn swiftly by their queer little horses to the place where the Lion lay asleep.

After a great deal of hard work, for the Lion was heavy, they managed to get him up on the truck. Then the Queen hurriedly gave her people the order to start, for she feared if the mice stayed among the poppies too long they also would fall asleep.

At first the little creatures, many though they were, could hardly stir the heavily loaded truck; but the Woodman and the Scarecrow both pushed from behind, and they got along better. Soon they rolled the Lion out of the poppy bed to the green fields, where he could breathe the sweet, fresh air again, instead of the poisonous scent of the flowers.

Dorothy came to meet them and thanked the little mice warmly for saving her companion from death. She had grown so fond of the big Lion she was glad he had been rescued.

Then the mice were unharnessed from the truck and scampered away through the grass to their homes. The Queen of the Mice was the last to leave.

"If ever you need us again," she said, "come out into the field and call, and we shall hear you and come to your assistance. Good-bye!"

"Good-bye!" they all answered, and away the Queen ran, while Dorothy held Toto tightly lest he should run after her and frighten her.

After this they sat down beside the Lion until he should awaken; and the Scarecrow brought Dorothy some fruit from a tree nearby, which she ate for her dinner.

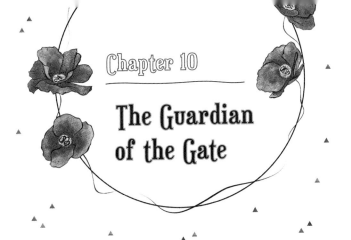

Chapter 10

The Guardian of the Gate

It was some time before the Cowardly Lion awakened, for he had lain among the poppies a long while, breathing in their deadly fragrance; but when he did open his eyes and roll off the truck he was very glad to find himself still alive.

"I ran as fast as I could," he said, sitting down and yawning, "but the flowers were too strong for me. How did you get me out?"

Then they told him of the field mice, and how they had generously saved him from death; and the Cowardly Lion laughed, and said:

"I have always thought myself very big and terrible; yet such little things as flowers came near to killing me, and such small animals as mice have saved my life. How strange it all is! But, comrades, what shall we do now?"

"We must journey on until we find the road of yellow brick again," said Dorothy, "and then we can keep on to the Emerald City."

So, the Lion being fully refreshed, and feeling quite himself again, they all started upon the journey, greatly enjoying the walk through the soft, fresh grass; and it was not long before they reached the road of yellow brick and turned again toward the Emerald City where the Great Oz dwelt.

The road was smooth and well paved, now, and the country about was beautiful, so that the travelers rejoiced in leaving the forest far behind, and with it the many dangers they had met in its gloomy shades. Once more they could see fences built beside the road; but these were painted green, and when they came to a small house, in which a farmer evidently lived, that also was painted green. They passed by several of these houses during the afternoon, and sometimes people came to the doors and looked at them as if they would like to ask questions; but no one came near them nor spoke to them because of the great Lion, of which they were very much afraid. The people were all dressed in clothing of a lovely emerald-green color and wore peaked hats like those of the Munchkins.

"This must be the Land of Oz," said Dorothy, "and we are surely getting near the Emerald City."

"Yes," answered the Scarecrow. "Everything is green here, while in the country of the Munchkins blue was the favorite color. But the people do not seem to be as friendly as the Munchkins, and I'm afraid we shall be unable to find a place to pass the night."

"I should like something to eat besides fruit," said the girl, "and I'm sure Toto is nearly starved. Let us stop at the next house and talk to the people."

So, when they came to a good-sized farmhouse, Dorothy walked boldly up to the door and knocked.

A woman opened it just far enough to look out, and said, "What do you want, child, and why is that great Lion with you?"

"We wish to pass the night with you, if you will allow us," answered Dorothy; "and the Lion is my friend and comrade, and would not hurt you for the world."

"Is he tame?" asked the woman, opening the door a little wider.

"Oh, yes," said the girl,

"and he is a great coward, too. He will be more afraid of you than you are of him."

"Well," said the woman, after thinking it over and taking another peep at the Lion, "if that is the case you may come in, and I will give you some supper and a place to sleep."

So they all entered the house, where there were, besides the woman, two children and a man. The man had hurt his leg, and was lying on the couch in a corner. They seemed greatly surprised to see so strange a company, and while the woman was busy laying the table the man asked:

"Where are you all going?"

"To the Emerald City," said Dorothy, "to see the Great Oz."

"Oh, indeed!" exclaimed the man. "Are you sure that Oz will see you?"

"Why not?" she replied.

"Why, it is said that he never lets anyone come into his presence. I have been to the Emerald City many times, and it is a beautiful and wonderful place; but I have never been permitted to see the Great Oz, nor do I know of any living person who has seen him."

"Does he never go out?" asked the Scarecrow.

"Never. He sits day after day in the great Throne Room of his Palace, and even those who wait upon him do not see him face to face."

"What is he like?" asked the girl.

"That is hard to tell," said the man thoughtfully. "You see, Oz is a Great Wizard, and can take on any form he wishes. So that some say he looks like a bird; and some say he looks like an elephant; and some say he looks like a cat. To others he appears as a beautiful fairy, or a brownie, or in any other form that pleases him. But who the real Oz is, when he is in his own form, no living person can tell."

"That is very strange," said Dorothy, "but we must try, in some way, to see him, or we shall have made our journey for nothing."

"Why do you wish to see the terrible Oz?" asked the man.

"I want him to give me some brains," said the Scarecrow eagerly.

"Oh, Oz could do that easily enough," declared the man. "He has more brains than he needs."

"And I want him to give me a heart," said the Tin Woodman.

"That will not trouble him," continued the man, "for Oz has a large collection of hearts, of all sizes and shapes."

The Lion ate some of the porridge.

"And I want him to give me courage," said the Cowardly Lion.

"Oz keeps a great pot of courage in his Throne Room," said the man, "which he has covered with a golden plate, to keep it from running over. He will be glad to give you some."

"And I want him to send me back to Kansas," said Dorothy.

"Where is Kansas?" asked the man, with surprise.

"I don't know," replied Dorothy sorrowfully, "but it is my home, and I'm sure it's somewhere."

"Very likely. Well, Oz can do anything; so I suppose he will find Kansas for you. But first you must get to see him, and that will be a hard task; for the Great Wizard does not like to see anyone, and he usually has his own way. But what do YOU want?" he continued, speaking to Toto. Toto only wagged his tail; for, strange to say, he could not speak.

The woman now called to them that supper was ready, so they gathered around the table and Dorothy ate some delicious porridge and a dish of scrambled eggs and a plate of nice white bread, and enjoyed her meal. The Lion ate some of the porridge, but did not care for it, saying it was made from oats and oats were food for horses, not for lions. The Scarecrow and the Tin Woodman ate nothing at all. Toto ate a little of everything, and was glad to get a good supper again.

The woman now gave Dorothy a bed to sleep in, and Toto lay down beside her, while the Lion guarded the door of her room so she might not be disturbed. The Scarecrow and the Tin Woodman stood up in a corner and kept quiet all night, although of course they could not sleep.

The next morning, as soon as the sun was up, they started on their way, and soon saw a beautiful green glow in the sky just before them.

"That must be the Emerald City," said Dorothy.

As they walked on, the green glow became brighter and brighter, and it seemed that at last they were nearing the end of their travels. Yet it was afternoon before they came to the great wall that surrounded the City. It was high and thick and of a bright green color.

In front of them, and at the end of the road of yellow brick, was a big gate, all studded with emeralds that glittered so in the sun that even the painted eyes of the Scarecrow were dazzled by their brilliancy.

There was a bell beside the gate, and Dorothy pushed the button and heard a silvery tinkle sound within. Then the big gate swung slowly open, and they all passed through and found themselves in a high arched room, the walls of which glistened with countless emeralds.

Before them stood a little man about the same size as the Munchkins. He was clothed all in green, from his head to his feet, and even his skin was of a greenish tint. At his side was a large green box.

When he saw Dorothy and her companions the man asked, "What do you wish in the Emerald City?"

"We came here to see the Great Oz," said Dorothy.

The man was so surprised at this answer that he sat down to think it over.

"It has been many years since anyone asked me to see Oz," he said, shaking his head in perplexity. "He is powerful and terrible, and if you come on an idle or foolish errand to bother the wise reflections of the Great Wizard, he might be angry and destroy you all in an instant."

"But it is not a foolish errand, nor an idle one," replied the Scarecrow; "it is important. And we have been told that Oz is a good Wizard."

"So he is," said the green man, "and he rules the Emerald City wisely and well. But to those who are not honest, or who approach him from curiosity, he is most terrible, and few have ever dared ask to see his face. I am the Guardian of the Gates, and since you demand to see the Great Oz I must take you to his Palace. But first you must put on the spectacles."

"Why?" asked Dorothy.

"Because if you did not wear spectacles the brightness and glory of the Emerald City would blind you. Even those who live in the City must wear spectacles night and day. They are all locked on, for Oz so ordered it when the City was first built, and I have the only key that will unlock them."

He opened the big box, and Dorothy saw that it was filled with spectacles of every size and shape. All of them had green glasses in them. The Guardian of the Gates found a pair that would just fit Dorothy and put them over her eyes. There were two golden bands fastened to them that passed around the back of her head, where they were locked together by a little key that was at the end of a chain the Guardian of the Gates wore around his neck. When they were on, Dorothy could not take them off had she wished, but of course she did not wish to be blinded by the glare of the Emerald City, so she said nothing.

Then the green man fitted spectacles for the Scarecrow and the Tin Woodman and the Lion, and even on little Toto; and all were locked fast with the key.

Then the Guardian of the Gates put on his own glasses and told them he was ready to show them to the Palace. Taking a big golden key from a peg on the wall, he opened another gate, and they all followed him through the portal into the streets of the Emerald City.

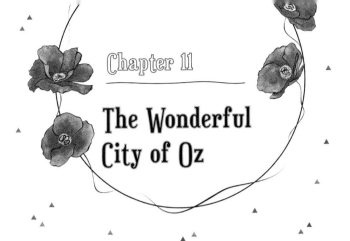

Chapter 11

The Wonderful City of Oz

Even with eyes protected by the green spectacles, Dorothy and her friends were at first dazzled by the brilliancy of the wonderful City. The streets were lined with beautiful houses all built of green marble and studded everywhere with sparkling emeralds. They walked over a pavement of the same green marble, and where the blocks were joined together were rows of emeralds, set closely, and glittering in the brightness of the sun. The window panes were of green glass; even the sky above the City had a green tint, and the rays of the sun were green.

There were many people—men, women, and children—walking about, and these were all dressed in green clothes and had greenish skins. They looked at Dorothy and her strangely assorted company with wondering eyes, and the children all ran away and hid behind their mothers when they saw the Lion; but no one spoke to them. Many shops stood in the street, and Dorothy saw that everything in them was green. Green candy and green popcorn were offered for sale, as well as green shoes, green hats, and green clothes of all sorts. At one place a man was selling green lemonade,

and when the children bought it Dorothy could see that they paid for it with green pennies.

There seemed to be no horses nor animals of any kind; the men carried things around in little green carts, which they pushed before them. Everyone seemed happy and contented and prosperous.

The Guardian of the Gates led them through the streets until they came to a big building, exactly in the middle of the City, which was the Palace of Oz, the Great Wizard. There was a soldier before the door, dressed in a green uniform and wearing a long green beard.

"Here are strangers," said the Guardian of the Gates to him, "and they demand to see the Great Oz."

"Step inside," answered the soldier, "and I will carry your message to him."

So they passed through the Palace Gates and were led into a big room with a green carpet and lovely green furniture set with emeralds. The soldier made them all wipe their feet upon a green mat before entering this room, and when they were seated he said politely:

"Please make yourselves comfortable while I go to the door of the Throne Room and tell Oz you are here."

They had to wait a long time before the soldier returned. When, at last, he came back, Dorothy asked:

"Have you seen Oz?"

"Oh, no," returned the soldier; "I have never seen him. But I spoke to him as he sat behind his screen and gave him your message. He said he will grant you an audience, if you so desire; but each one of you must enter his presence alone, and he will admit but one each day. Therefore, as you must remain in the Palace for several days, I will have you shown to rooms where you may rest in comfort after your journey."

"Thank you," replied the girl; "that is very kind of Oz."

The soldier now blew upon a green whistle, and at once a young girl, dressed in a pretty green silk gown, entered the room. She had lovely green hair and green eyes, and she bowed low before Dorothy as she said, "Follow me and I will show

you your room."

So Dorothy said good-bye to all her friends except Toto, and taking the dog in her arms followed the green girl through seven passages and up three flights of stairs until they came to a room at the front of the Palace. It was the sweetest little room in the world, with a soft comfortable bed that had sheets of green silk and a green velvet counterpane. There was a tiny fountain in the middle of the room, that shot a spray of green perfume into the air, to fall back into a beautifully carved green marble basin. Beautiful green flowers stood in the windows, and there was a shelf with a row of little green books. When Dorothy had time to open these books she found them full of queer green pictures that made her laugh, they were so funny.

In a wardrobe were many green dresses, made of silk and satin and velvet; and all of them fitted Dorothy exactly.

"Make yourself perfectly at home," said the green girl, "and if you wish for anything ring the bell. Oz will send for you tomorrow morning."

She left Dorothy alone and went back to the others. These she also led to rooms, and each one of them found himself lodged in a very pleasant part of the Palace. Of course this politeness was wasted on the Scarecrow; for when he found himself alone in his room he stood stupidly in one spot, just within the doorway, to wait till morning. It would not rest him to lie down, and he could not close his eyes; so he remained all night staring at a little spider which was weaving its web in a corner of the room, just as if it were not one of the most wonderful rooms in the world. The Tin Woodman lay down on his bed from force of habit, for he remembered when he was made of flesh; but not being able to sleep, he passed the night moving his joints up and down to make sure they kept in good working order. The Lion would have preferred a bed of dried leaves in the forest, and did not like being shut up in a room; but he had too much sense to let this worry him, so he sprang upon the bed and rolled himself up like a cat and purred himself asleep in a minute.

The next morning, after breakfast, the green maiden came to fetch Dorothy, and she dressed her in one of the prettiest gowns, made of green brocaded satin. Dorothy put on a green silk apron and tied a green ribbon around Toto's neck, and they started for the Throne Room of the Great Oz.

First they came to a great hall in which were many ladies and gentlemen of the court, all dressed in rich costumes. These people had nothing to do but talk to each other, but they always came to wait outside the Throne Room every morning, although they were never permitted to see Oz. As Dorothy entered they looked at her curiously, and one of them whispered:

"Are you really going to look upon the face of Oz the Terrible?"

"Of course," answered the girl, "if he will see me."

"Oh, he will see you," said the soldier who had taken

her message to the Wizard, "although he does not like to have people ask to see him. Indeed, at first he was angry and said I should send you back where you came from. Then he asked me what you looked like, and when I mentioned your silver shoes he was very much interested. At last I told him about the mark upon your forehead, and he decided he would admit you to his presence."

Just then a bell rang, and the green girl said to Dorothy, "That is the signal. You must go into the Throne Room alone."

She opened a little door and Dorothy walked boldly through and found herself in a wonderful place. It was a big, round room with a high arched roof, and the walls and ceiling and floor were covered with large emeralds set closely together. In the center of the roof was a great light, as bright as the sun, which made the emeralds sparkle in a wonderful manner.

But what interested Dorothy most was the big throne of green marble that stood in the middle of the room. It was shaped like a chair and sparkled with gems, as did everything else. In the center of the

chair was an enormous Head, without a body to support it or any arms or legs whatever. There was no hair upon this head, but it had eyes and a nose and mouth, and was much bigger than the head of the biggest giant.

As Dorothy gazed upon this in wonder and fear, the eyes turned slowly and looked at her sharply and steadily. Then the mouth moved, and Dorothy heard a voice say:

"I am Oz, the Great and Terrible. Who are you, and why do you seek me?"

It was not such an awful voice as she had expected to come from the big Head; so she took courage and answered:

"I am Dorothy, the Small and Meek. I have come to you for help."

The eyes looked at her thoughtfully for a full minute. Then said the voice:

"Where did you get the silver shoes?"

"I got them from the Wicked Witch of the East, when my house fell on her and killed her," she replied.

"Where did you get the mark upon your forehead?" continued the voice.

"That is where the Good Witch of the North kissed me when she bade me good-bye and sent me to you," said the girl.

Again the eyes looked at her sharply, and they saw she was telling the truth. Then Oz asked, "What do you wish me to do?"

"Send me back to Kansas, where my Aunt Em and

The eyes looked at her thoughtfully.

Uncle Henry are," she answered earnestly. "I don't like your country, although it is so beautiful. And I am sure Aunt Em will be dreadfully worried over my being away so long."

The eyes winked three times, and then they turned up to the ceiling and down to the floor and rolled around so queerly that they seemed to see every part of the room. And at last they looked at Dorothy again.

"Why should I do this for you?" asked Oz.

"Because you are strong and I am weak; because you are a Great Wizard and I am only a little girl."

"But you were strong enough to kill the Wicked Witch of the East," said Oz.

"That just happened," returned Dorothy simply; "I could not help it."

"Well," said the Head, "I will give you my answer. You have no right to expect me to send you back to Kansas unless you do something for me in return. In this country everyone must pay for everything he gets. If you wish me to use my magic power to send you home again you must do something for me first. Help me and I will help you."

"What must I do?" asked the girl.

"Kill the Wicked Witch of the West," answered Oz.

"But I cannot!" exclaimed Dorothy, greatly surprised.

"You killed the Witch of the East and you wear the silver shoes, which bear a powerful charm. There is now but one Wicked Witch left in all this land, and when you can tell me she is dead I will send you back to Kansas—

but not before."

The little girl began to weep, she was so much disappointed; and the eyes winked again and looked upon her anxiously, as if the Great Oz felt that she could help him if she would.

"I never killed anything, willingly," she sobbed. "Even if I wanted to, how could I kill the Wicked Witch? If you, who are Great and Terrible, cannot kill her yourself, how do you expect me to do it?"

"I do not know," said the Head; "but that is my answer, and until the Wicked Witch dies you will not see your uncle and aunt again. Remember that the Witch is Wicked—tremendously Wicked -and ought to be killed. Now go, and do not ask to see me again until you have done your task."

Sorrowfully Dorothy left the Throne Room and went back where the Lion and the Scarecrow and the Tin Woodman were waiting to hear what Oz had said to her. "There is no hope for me," she said sadly, "for Oz will not send me home until I have killed the Wicked Witch of the West; and that I can never do."

Her friends were sorry, but could do nothing to help her; so Dorothy went to her own room and lay down on the bed and cried herself to sleep.

The next morning the soldier with the green whiskers came to the Scarecrow and said:

"Come with me, for Oz has sent for you."

So the Scarecrow followed him and was admitted into the great Throne Room, where he saw, sitting in the emerald throne, a most lovely Lady. She was dressed in green silk gauze and wore upon her flowing green locks a crown of jewels. Growing from her shoulders were wings, gorgeous in color and so light that they fluttered if the slightest breath of air reached them.

When the Scarecrow had bowed, as prettily as his straw stuffing would let him, before this beautiful creature, she looked upon him sweetly, and said:

"I am Oz, the Great and Terrible. Who are you, and why do you seek me?"

Now the Scarecrow, who had expected to see the great Head Dorothy had told him of, was much astonished; but he answered her bravely.

"I am only a Scarecrow, stuffed with straw. Therefore I have no brains, and I come to you praying that you will put brains in my head instead of straw, so that I may become as much a

man as any other in your dominions."

"Why should I do this for you?" asked the Lady.

"Because you are wise and powerful, and no one else can help me," answered the Scarecrow.

"I never grant favors without some return," said Oz; "but this much I will promise. If you will kill for me the Wicked Witch of the West, I will bestow upon you a great many brains, and such good brains that you will be the wisest man in all the Land of Oz."

"I thought you asked Dorothy to kill the Witch," said the Scarecrow, in surprise.

"So I did. I don't care who kills her. But until she is dead I will not grant your wish. Now go, and do not seek me again until you have earned the brains you so greatly desire."

The Scarecrow went sorrowfully back to his friends and told them what Oz had said; and Dorothy was surprised to find that the Great Wizard was not a Head, as she had seen him, but a lovely Lady.

"All the same," said the Scarecrow, "she needs a heart as much as the Tin Woodman."

On the next morning the soldier with the green whiskers came to the Tin Woodman and said:

"Oz has sent for you. Follow me."

So the Tin Woodman followed him and came to the great Throne Room. He did not know whether he would find Oz a lovely Lady or a Head, but he hoped it would be the lovely Lady. "For," he said to himself, "if it is the head, I am sure I shall not be given a heart, since a head has no heart of its own and therefore cannot feel for me. But if it is the lovely Lady I shall beg hard for a heart, for all ladies are themselves said to be kindly hearted."

But when the Woodman entered the great Throne Room he saw neither the Head nor the Lady, for Oz had taken the shape of a most terrible Beast. It was nearly as big as an elephant, and the green throne seemed hardly strong enough to hold its weight. The Beast had a head like that of a rhinoceros, only there were five eyes in its face. There were five long arms growing out of its body, and it also had five long, slim legs. Thick, woolly hair covered every part of it, and a more dreadful-looking monster could not be imagined. It was fortunate the Tin Woodman had no heart at that moment,

for it would have beat loud and fast from terror. But being only tin, the Woodman was not at all afraid, although he was much disappointed.

"I am Oz, the Great and Terrible," spoke the Beast, in a voice that was one great roar. "Who are you, and why do you seek me?"

"I am a Woodman, and made of tin. Therefore I have no heart, and cannot love. I pray you to give me a heart that I may be as other men are."

"Why should I do this?" demanded the Beast.

"Because I ask it, and you alone can grant my request," answered the Woodman.

Oz gave a low growl at this, but said, gruffly: "If you indeed desire a heart, you must earn it."

"How?" asked the Woodman.

"Help Dorothy to kill the Wicked Witch of the West," replied the Beast. "When the Witch is dead, come to me, and I will then give you the biggest and kindest and most loving heart in all the Land of Oz."

So the Tin Woodman was forced to return sorrowfully to his friends and tell them of the terrible Beast he had seen. They all wondered greatly at the many forms the Great Wizard could take upon himself, and the Lion said:

"If he is a Beast when I go to see him, I shall roar my loudest, and so frighten him that he will grant all I ask. And if he is the lovely Lady, I shall pretend to spring upon her, and so compel her to do my bidding. And if he is the great Head, he will be at my mercy; for I will roll this head all about the room until he promises to give us what we desire. So be of good cheer, my friends, for all will yet be well."

The next morning the soldier with the green whiskers led the Lion to the great Throne Room and bade him enter the presence of Oz.

The Lion at once passed through the door, and glancing around saw, to his surprise, that before the throne was a Ball of Fire, so fierce and glowing he could scarcely bear to gaze upon it. His first thought was that Oz had by accident caught on fire and was burning up; but when he tried to go nearer, the heat was so intense that it singed his whiskers, and he crept back tremblingly to a spot nearer the door.

Then a low, quiet voice came from the Ball of Fire, and these were the words it spoke:

"I am Oz, the Great and Terrible. Who are you, and why do you seek me?"

And the Lion answered, "I am a Cowardly Lion, afraid of everything. I came to you to beg that you give me courage, so that in reality I may become the King of Beasts, as men call me."

"Why should I give you courage?" demanded Oz.

"Because of all Wizards you are the greatest, and alone have power to grant my request," answered the Lion.

The Ball of Fire burned fiercely for a time, and the voice said, "Bring me proof that the Wicked Witch is dead, and that moment I will give you courage. But as long as the Witch lives, you must remain a coward."

The Lion was angry at this speech, but could say nothing in reply, and while he stood silently gazing at the Ball of Fire it became so furiously hot that he turned tail and rushed from the room. He was glad to find his friends waiting for him, and told them of his terrible interview with the Wizard.

"What shall we do now?" asked Dorothy sadly.

"There is only one thing we can do," returned the Lion, "and that is to go to the land of the Winkies, seek out the Wicked Witch, and destroy her."

"But suppose we cannot?" said the girl.

"Then I shall never have courage," declared the Lion.

"And I shall never have brains," added the Scarecrow.

"And I shall never have a heart," spoke the Tin of Woodman.

"And I shall never see Aunt Em and Uncle Henry," said Dorothy, beginning to cry.

"Be careful!" cried the green girl. "The tears will fall on your green silk gown and spot it."

So Dorothy dried her eyes and said, "I suppose we must try it; but I am sure I do not want to kill anybody, even to see Aunt Em again."

"I will go with you; but I'm too much of a coward to kill the Witch," said the Lion.

"I will go too," declared the Scarecrow; "but I shall not be of much help to you, I am such a fool."

"I haven't the heart to harm even a Witch," remarked the Tin Woodman; "but if you go I certainly shall go with you."

Therefore it was decided to start upon their journey the next morning, and the Woodman sharpened his axe on a green grindstone and had all his joints properly oiled. The Scarecrow stuffed himself with fresh straw and Dorothy put new paint on his eyes that he might see better. The green girl, who was very kind to them, filled Dorothy's basket with good things to eat, and fastened a little bell around Toto's neck with a green ribbon.

They went to bed quite early and slept soundly until daylight, when they were awakened by the crowing of a green cock that lived in the back yard of the Palace, and the cackling of a hen that had laid a green egg.

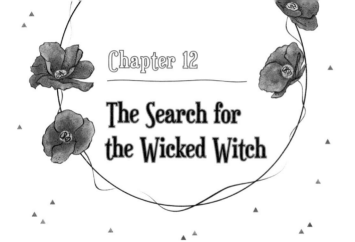

Chapter 12

The Search for the Wicked Witch

The soldier with the green whiskers led them through the streets of the Emerald City until they reached the room where the Guardian of the Gates lived. This officer unlocked their spectacles to put them back in his great box, and then he politely opened the gate for our friends.

"Which road leads to the Wicked Witch of the West?" asked Dorothy.

"There is no road," answered the Guardian of the Gates. "No one ever wishes to go that way."

"How, then, are we to find her?" inquired the girl.

"That will be easy," replied the man, "for when she knows you are in the country of the Winkies she will find you, and make you all her slaves."

"Perhaps not," said the Scarecrow, "for we mean to destroy her."

"Oh, that is different," said the Guardian of the Gates. "No one has ever destroyed her before, so I naturally thought she would make slaves of you, as she has of the rest. But take care; for she is wicked and fierce, and may not allow you to destroy her. Keep to the West, where the sun sets, and you cannot fail to find her."

The soldier with the green whiskers led them through the streets.

They thanked him and bade him good-bye, and turned toward the West, walking over fields of soft grass dotted here and there with daisies and buttercups. Dorothy still wore the pretty silk dress she had put on in the palace, but now, to her surprise, she found it was no longer green, but pure white. The ribbon around Toto's neck had also lost its green color and was as white as Dorothy's dress.

The Emerald City was soon left far behind. As they advanced the ground became rougher and hillier, for there were no farms nor houses in this country of the West, and the ground was untilled.

In the afternoon the sun shone hot in their faces, for there were no trees to offer them shade; so that before night Dorothy and Toto and the Lion were tired, and lay down upon the grass and fell asleep, with the Woodman and the Scarecrow keeping watch.

Now the Wicked Witch of the West had but one eye, yet that was as powerful as a telescope, and could see everywhere. So, as she sat in the door of her castle, she happened to look around and saw Dorothy lying asleep, with her friends all about her. They were a long distance off, but the Wicked Witch was angry to find them in her country; so she blew upon a silver whistle that hung around her neck.

At once there came running to her from all directions a pack of great wolves. They had long legs and fierce eyes and sharp teeth.

"Go to those people," said the Witch, "and tear them

to pieces."

"Are you not going to make them your slaves?" asked the leader of the wolves.

"No," she answered, "one is of tin, and one of straw; one is a girl and another a Lion. None of them is fit to work, so you may tear them into small pieces."

"Very well," said the wolf, and he dashed away at full speed, followed by the others.

It was lucky the Scarecrow and the Woodman were wide awake and heard the wolves coming.

"This is my fight," said the Woodman, "so get behind me and I will meet them as they come."

He seized his axe, which he had made very sharp, and as the leader of the wolves came on the Tin Woodman swung his arm and chopped the wolf's head from its body, so that it immediately died. As soon as he could raise his axe another wolf came up, and he also fell under the sharp edge of the Tin Woodman's weapon.

There were forty wolves, and forty times a wolf was killed, so that at last they all lay dead in a heap before the Woodman.

Then he put down his axe and sat beside the Scarecrow, who said, "It was a good fight, friend."

They waited until Dorothy awoke the next morning. The little girl was quite frightened when she saw the great pile of shaggy wolves, but the Tin Woodman told her all. She thanked him for saving them and sat down to breakfast, after which they started again upon their journey.

Now this same morning the Wicked Witch came to the door of her castle and looked out with her one eye that could see far off. She saw all her wolves lying dead, and the strangers still traveling through her country. This made her angrier than before, and she blew her silver whistle twice.

Straightway a great flock of wild crows came flying toward her, enough to darken the sky.

And the Wicked Witch said to the King Crow, "Fly at once to the strangers; peck out their eyes and tear them to pieces."

The wild crows flew in one great flock toward Dorothy and her companions. When the little girl saw them coming she was afraid.

But the Scarecrow said, "This is my battle, so lie down beside me and you will not be harmed."

So they all lay upon the ground except the Scarecrow, and he stood up and stretched out his arms. And when the crows saw him they were frightened, as these birds always are by scarecrows, and did not dare to come any nearer. But the King Crow said:

"It is only a stuffed man. I will peck his eyes out."

The King Crow flew at the Scarecrow, who caught it by the head and twisted its neck until it died. And then another crow flew at him, and the Scarecrow twisted its neck also.

There were forty crows, and forty times the Scarecrow twisted a neck, until at last all were lying dead beside him. Then he called to his companions to rise, and again they went upon their journey.

When the Wicked Witch looked out again and saw all her crows lying in a heap, she

got into a terrible rage, and blew three times upon her silver whistle.

Forthwith there was heard a great buzzing in the air, and a swarm of black bees came flying toward her.

"Go to the strangers and sting them to death!" commanded the Witch, and the bees turned and flew rapidly until they came to where Dorothy and her friends were walking. But the Woodman had seen them coming, and the Scarecrow had decided what to do.

"Take out my straw and scatter it over the little girl and the dog and the Lion," he said to the Woodman, "and the bees cannot sting them." This the Woodman did, and as Dorothy lay close beside the Lion and held Toto in her arms, the straw covered them entirely.

The bees came and found no one but the Woodman to sting, so they flew at him and broke off all their stings against the tin, without hurting the Woodman at all. And as bees cannot live when their stings are broken that was the end of the black bees, and they lay scattered thick about the Woodman, like little heaps of fine coal.

Then Dorothy and the Lion got up, and the girl helped the Tin Woodman put the straw back into the Scarecrow again, until he was as good as ever. So they started upon their journey once more.

The Wicked Witch was so angry when she saw her black bees in little heaps like fine coal that she stamped her foot and tore her hair and gnashed her teeth. And then she called a dozen of her slaves, who were the Winkies, and gave them sharp spears, telling them to go to the strangers and destroy them.

The Winkies were not a brave people, but they had to do as they were told. So they marched away until they came near to Dorothy. Then the Lion gave a great roar and sprang towards them, and the poor Winkies were so frightened that they ran back as fast as they could.

When they returned to the castle the Wicked Witch beat them well with a strap, and sent them back to their work, after which she sat down to think what she should do next. She could not understand how all her plans to destroy these strangers had failed; but she was a powerful Witch, as well as a wicked one, and she soon made up her mind how to act.

There was, in her cupboard, a Golden Cap, with a circle of diamonds and rubies running round it. This Golden Cap had a charm. Whoever owned it could call three times upon the Winged Monkeys, who would obey any order they were given. But no person could command these strange creatures more than three times. Twice already the Wicked Witch had used the charm of the Cap. Once was when she had made the Winkies her slaves, and set herself to rule over their country. The Winged Monkeys had helped her do this. The second time was when she had fought against the Great Oz himself, and driven him out of the land of the West. The Winged Monkeys had also helped her in doing this. Only once more could she use this Golden Cap, for which reason she did not like to do so until all her other powers were exhausted. But now that her fierce wolves and her wild crows and her stinging bees were gone, and her slaves had been scared away by the Cowardly Lion, she saw there was only one way left to destroy Dorothy and her friends.

So the Wicked Witch took the Golden Cap from her cupboard and placed it upon her head. Then she stood upon her left foot and said slowly:

"Ep-pe, pep-pe, kak-ke!"

Next she stood upon her right foot and said:

"Hil-lo, hol-lo, hel-lo!"

After this she stood upon both feet and cried in a loud voice:

"Ziz-zy, zuz-zy, zik!"

Now the charm began to work. The sky was darkened,

and a low rumbling sound was heard in the air. There was a rushing of many wings, a great chattering and laughing, and the sun came out of the dark sky to show the Wicked Witch surrounded by a crowd of monkeys, each with a pair of immense and powerful wings on his shoulders.

One, much bigger than the others, seemed to be their leader. He flew close to the Witch and said, "You have called us for the third and last time. What do you command?"

"Go to the strangers who are within my land and destroy them all except the Lion," said the Wicked Witch. "Bring that beast to me, for I have a mind to harness him like a horse, and make him work."

"Your commands shall be obeyed," said the leader. Then, with a great deal of chattering and noise, the

Winged Monkeys flew away to the place where Dorothy and her friends were walking.

Some of the Monkeys seized the Tin Woodman and carried him through the air until they were over a country thickly covered with sharp rocks. Here they dropped the poor Woodman, who fell a great distance to the rocks, where he lay so battered and dented that he could neither move nor groan.

Others of the Monkeys caught the Scarecrow, and with their long fingers pulled all of the straw out of his clothes and head. They made his hat and boots and clothes into a small bundle and threw it into the top branches of a tall tree.

The remaining Monkeys threw pieces of stout rope around the Lion and wound many coils about his body and head and legs, until he was unable to bite or scratch or struggle in any way. Then they lifted him up and flew away with him to the Witch's castle, where he was placed in a small yard with a high iron fence around it, so that he could not escape.

But Dorothy they did not harm at all. She stood, with Toto in her arms, watching the sad fate of her comrades and thinking it would soon be her turn. The leader of the Winged Monkeys flew up to her, his long, hairy arms stretched out and his ugly face grinning terribly; but he saw the mark of the Good Witch's kiss upon her forehead and stopped short, motioning the others not to touch her.

"We dare not harm this little girl," he said to them,

The monkeys wound many coils about his body.

"for she is protected by the Power of Good, and that is greater than the Power of Evil. All we can do is to carry her to the castle of the Wicked Witch and leave her there."

So, carefully and gently, they lifted Dorothy in their arms and carried her swiftly through the air until they came to the castle, where they set her down upon the front doorstep. Then the leader said to the Witch:

"We have obeyed you as far as we were able. The Tin Woodman and the Scarecrow are destroyed, and the Lion is tied up in your yard. The little girl we dare not harm, nor the dog she carries in her arms. Your power over our band is now ended, and you will never see us again."

Then all the Winged Monkeys, with much laughing and chattering and noise, flew into the air and were soon out of sight.

The Wicked Witch was both surprised and worried when she saw the mark on Dorothy's forehead, for she knew well that neither the Winged Monkeys nor she, herself, dare hurt the girl in any way. She looked down at Dorothy's feet, and seeing the Silver Shoes, began to tremble with fear, for she knew what a powerful charm belonged to them. At first the Witch was tempted to run away from Dorothy; but she happened to look into the child's eyes and saw how simple the soul behind them was, and that the little girl did not know of the wonderful power the Silver Shoes gave her. So the Wicked Witch laughed to herself, and thought, "I can still make her my slave, for she does not know how to use her power." Then she said to Dorothy, harshly and severely:

"Come with me; and see that you mind everything I tell you, for if you do not I will make an end of you, as I did of the Tin Woodman and the Scarecrow."

Dorothy followed her through many of the beautiful rooms in her castle until they came to the kitchen, where the Witch bade her clean the pots and kettles and sweep the floor and keep the fire fed with wood.

Dorothy went to work meekly, with her mind made up to work as hard as she could; for she was glad the Wicked Witch had decided not to kill her.

With Dorothy hard at work, the Witch thought she would go into the courtyard and harness the Cowardly Lion like a horse; it would amuse her, she was sure, to make him draw her chariot whenever she wished to go to drive. But as she opened the gate the Lion gave a loud roar and bounded at her so fiercely that the Witch was afraid, and ran out and shut the gate again.

"If I cannot harness you," said the Witch to the Lion, speaking through the bars of the gate, "I can starve you. You shall have nothing to eat until you do as I wish."

So after that she took no food to the imprisoned Lion; but every day she came to the gate at noon and asked, "Are you ready to be harnessed like a horse?"

And the Lion would answer, "No. If you come in this yard, I will bite you."

The reason the Lion did not have to do as the Witch wished was that every night, while the woman was asleep, Dorothy carried him food from the cupboard. After he had eaten he would lie down on his bed of straw, and Dorothy would lie beside him and put her head on his soft, shaggy mane, while they talked of their troubles and tried to plan some way to escape. But they could find no way to get out of the castle, for it was constantly guarded by the yellow Winkies, who were the slaves of the Wicked Witch and too afraid of her not to do as she told them.

The girl had to work hard during the day, and often the Witch threatened to beat her with the same old umbrella she always carried in her hand. But, in truth, she did not dare to strike Dorothy, because of the mark upon her forehead. The child did not know this, and was full of fear for herself and Toto. Once the Witch struck Toto a blow with her umbrella and the brave little dog flew at her and bit her leg in return. The Witch did not bleed where she was bitten, for she was so wicked that the blood in her had dried up many years before.

Dorothy's life became very sad as she grew to understand that it would be harder than ever to get back to Kansas and Aunt Em again. Sometimes she would cry bitterly for hours, with Toto sitting at her feet and looking into her face, whining dismally to show how sorry he was for his little mistress. Toto did not really care whether he was in Kansas or the Land of Oz so long as Dorothy was with him; but he knew the little girl was unhappy, and that made him unhappy too.

Now the Wicked Witch had a great longing to have for her own the Silver Shoes which the girl always wore. Her bees and her crows and her wolves were lying in heaps and drying up, and she had used up all the power of the Golden Cap; but if she could only get hold of the Silver Shoes, they would give her more power than all the other things she had lost. She watched Dorothy carefully, to see if she ever took off her shoes, thinking she might steal them. But the child was so proud of her pretty shoes that she never took them off except at night and when she took her bath. The Witch was too much afraid of the dark to dare go in Dorothy's room at night to take the shoes, and her dread of water was greater than her fear of the dark, so she never came near when Dorothy was bathing. Indeed, the old Witch never touched water, nor ever let water touch her in any way.

But the wicked creature was very cunning, and she finally thought of a trick that would give her what she wanted. She placed a bar of iron in the middle of the kitchen floor, and then by her magic arts made the iron invisible to human eyes. So that when Dorothy walked across the floor she stumbled over the bar, not being able to see it, and fell at full length. She was not much hurt, but in her fall one of the Silver Shoes came off; and before she could reach it, the Witch had snatched it away and put it on her own skinny foot.

The wicked woman was greatly pleased with the success of her trick, for as long as she had one of the shoes she owned half the power of their charm, and Dorothy could not use it against her, even had she known how to do so.

The little girl, seeing she had lost one of her pretty shoes, grew angry, and said to the Witch, "Give me back my shoe!"

"I will not," retorted the Witch, "for it is now my shoe, and not yours."

"You are a wicked creature!" cried Dorothy. "You have no right to take my shoe from me."

"I shall keep it, just the same," said the Witch, laughing at her, "and someday I shall get the other one from you, too."

This made Dorothy so very angry that she picked up the bucket of water that stood near and dashed it over the Witch, wetting her from head to foot.

Instantly the wicked woman gave a loud cry of fear, and then, as Dorothy looked at her in wonder, the Witch began to shrink and fall away.

"See what you have done!" she screamed. "In a minute I shall melt away."

"I'm very sorry, indeed," said Dorothy, who was truly frightened to see the Witch actually melting away like brown sugar before her very eyes.

"Didn't you know water would be the end of me?" asked the Witch, in a wailing, despairing voice.

"Of course not," answered Dorothy. "How should I?"

"Well, in a few minutes I shall be all melted, and you will have the castle to yourself. I have been wicked in my day, but I never thought a little girl like you would ever be able to melt me and end my wicked deeds. Look out—here I go!"

With these words the Witch fell down in a brown, melted, shapeless mass and began to spread over the clean boards of the kitchen floor. Seeing that she had really melted away to nothing, Dorothy drew another bucket of water and threw it over the mess. She then swept it all out the door. After picking out the silver shoe, which was all that was left of the old woman, she cleaned and dried it with a cloth, and put it on her foot again. Then, being at last free to do as she chose, she ran out to the courtyard to tell the Lion that the Wicked Witch of the West had come to an end, and that they were no longer prisoners in
a strange land.

Chapter 13

The Rescue

The Cowardly Lion was much pleased to hear that the Wicked Witch had been melted by a bucket of water, and Dorothy at once unlocked the gate of his prison and set him free. They went in together to the castle, where Dorothy's first act was to call all the Winkies together and tell them that they were no longer slaves.

There was great rejoicing among the yellow Winkies, for they had been made to work hard during many years for the Wicked Witch, who had always treated them with great cruelty. They kept this day as a holiday, then and ever after, and spent the time in feasting and dancing.

"If our friends, the Scarecrow and the Tin Woodman, were only with us," said the Lion, "I should be quite happy."

"Don't you suppose we could rescue them?" asked the girl anxiously.

"We can try," answered the Lion.

So they called the yellow Winkies and asked them if they would help to rescue their friends, and the Winkies said that they would be delighted to do all in their power for Dorothy, who had set them free from bondage. So she chose a number of the Winkies who looked as if they knew the most, and they all started away. They traveled that day and part of the next until they came to the rocky plain where the Tin Woodman lay, all battered and bent. His axe was near him, but the blade was rusted and the handle broken off short.

The Winkies lifted him tenderly in their arms, and carried him back to the Yellow Castle again, Dorothy shedding a few tears by the way at the sad plight of her old friend, and the Lion looking sober and sorry. When they reached the castle Dorothy said to the Winkies:

"Are any of your people tinsmiths?"

"Oh, yes. Some of us are very good tinsmiths," they told her.

"Then bring them to me," she said. And when the tinsmiths came, bringing with them all their tools in baskets, she inquired, "Can you straighten out those dents in the Tin Woodman, and bend him back into shape again, and solder him together where he is broken?"

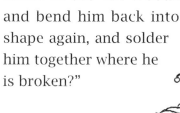

The tinsmiths looked the Woodman over carefully and then answered that they thought they could mend him so he would be as good as ever. So they set to work in one of the big yellow rooms of the castle and worked for three days and four nights, hammering and twisting and bending and soldering and polishing and pounding at the legs and body and head of the Tin Woodman, until at last he was straightened out into his old form, and his joints worked as well as ever. To be sure, there were several patches on him, but the tinsmiths did a good job, and as the Woodman was not a vain man he did not mind the patches at all.

When, at last, he walked into Dorothy's room and thanked her for rescuing him, he was so pleased that he wept tears of joy, and Dorothy had to wipe every tear carefully from his face with her apron, so his joints would not be rusted. At the same time her own tears fell thick and fast at the joy of meeting her old friend again, and these tears did not need to be wiped away. As for the Lion, he wiped his eyes so often with the tip of his tail that it became quite wet, and he was obliged to go out into the courtyard and hold it in the sun till it dried.

"If we only had the Scarecrow with us again," said the Tin Woodman, when Dorothy had finished telling him everything that had happened, "I should be quite happy."

"We must try to find him," said the girl.

So she called the Winkies to help her, and they walked all that day and part of the next until they came to the

The tinsmiths worked for three days and four nights.

tall tree in the branches of which the Winged Monkeys had tossed the Scarecrow's clothes.

It was a very tall tree, and the trunk was so smooth that no one could climb it; but the Woodman said at once, "I'll chop it down, and then we can get the Scarecrow's clothes."

Now while the tinsmiths had been at work mending the Woodman himself, another of the Winkies, who was a goldsmith, had made an axe-handle of solid gold and fitted it to the Woodman's axe, instead of the old broken handle. Others polished the blade until all the rust was removed and it glistened like burnished silver.

As soon as he had spoken, the Tin Woodman began to chop, and in a short time the tree fell over with a crash, whereupon the Scarecrow's clothes fell out of the branches and rolled off on the ground.

Dorothy picked them up and had the Winkies carry them back to the castle, where they were stuffed

with nice, clean straw; and behold! here was the Scarecrow, as good as ever, thanking them over and over again for saving him.

Now that they were reunited, Dorothy and her friends spent a few happy days at the Yellow Castle, where they found everything they needed to make them comfortable. But one day the girl thought of Aunt Em, and said, "We must go back to Oz, and claim his promise."

"Yes," said the Woodman, "at last I shall get my heart."

"And I shall get my brains," added the Scarecrow joyfully.

"And I shall get my courage," said the Lion thoughtfully.

"And I shall get back to Kansas," cried Dorothy, clapping her hands. "Oh, let us start for the Emerald City tomorrow!"

This they decided to do. The next day they called the Winkies together and bade them good-bye. The Winkies were sorry to have them go, and they had grown so fond of the Tin Woodman that they begged him to stay and rule over them and the Yellow Land of the West. Finding they were determined to go, the Winkies gave Toto and the Lion each a golden collar; and to Dorothy they presented a beautiful bracelet studded with diamonds; and to the Scarecrow they gave a gold-headed walking stick, to keep him from stumbling; and to the Tin Woodman they offered a silver oil-can, inlaid with gold and set with precious jewels.

Every one of the travelers made the Winkies a pretty speech in return, and all shook hands with them until their arms ached.

Dorothy went to the Witch's cupboard to fill her basket with food for the journey, and there she saw the Golden Cap. She tried it on her own head and found that it fitted her exactly. She did not know anything about the charm of the Golden Cap, but she saw that it was pretty, so she made up her mind to wear it and carry her sunbonnet in the basket.

Then, being prepared for the journey, they all started for the Emerald City; and the Winkies gave them three cheers and many good wishes to carry with them.

Chapter 14

The Winged Monkeys

You will remember there was no road—not even a pathway—between the castle of the Wicked Witch and the Emerald City. When the four travelers went in search of the Witch she had seen them coming, and so sent the Winged Monkeys to bring them to her. It was much harder to find their way back through the big fields of buttercups and yellow daisies than it was being carried. They knew, of course, they must go straight east, toward the rising sun; and they started off in the right way. But at noon, when the sun was over their heads, they did not know which was east and which was west, and that was the reason they were lost in the great fields. They kept on walking, however, and at night the moon came out and shone brightly. So they lay down among the sweet smelling yellow flowers and slept soundly until morning—all but the Scarecrow and the Tin Woodman.

The next morning the sun was behind a cloud, but they started on, as if they were quite sure which way they were going.

"If we walk far enough," said Dorothy, "I am sure we shall sometime come to some place."

But day by day passed away, and they still saw nothing before them but the scarlet fields. The Scarecrow began to grumble a bit.

"We have surely lost our way," he said, "and unless we find it again in time to reach the Emerald City, I shall never get my brains."

"Nor I my heart," declared the Tin Woodman. "It seems to me I can scarcely wait till I get to Oz, and you must admit this is a very long journey."

"You see," said the Cowardly Lion, with a whimper, "I haven't the courage to keep tramping forever, without getting anywhere at all."

Then Dorothy lost heart. She sat down on the grass and looked at her companions, and they sat down and looked at her, and Toto found that for the first time in his life he was too tired to chase a butterfly that flew past his head. So he put out his tongue and panted and looked at Dorothy as if to ask what they should do next.

"Suppose we call the field mice," she suggested. "They could probably tell us the way to the Emerald City."

"To be sure they could," cried the Scarecrow. "Why didn't we think of that before?"

Dorothy blew the little whistle she had always carried about her neck since the Queen of the Mice had given it to her. In a few minutes they heard the pattering of tiny feet, and many of the small gray mice came running up to her. Among them was the Queen herself, who asked, in her squeaky little voice:

"What can I do for my friends?"

"We have lost our way," said Dorothy. "Can you tell us where the Emerald City is?"

"Certainly," answered the Queen; "but it is a great way off, for you have had it at your backs all this time." Then she noticed Dorothy's Golden Cap, and said, "Why don't you use the charm of the Cap, and call the  Winged Monkeys to you? They will carry you to the City of Oz in less than an hour."

"I didn't know there was a charm," answered Dorothy, in surprise. "What is it?"

"It is written inside the Golden Cap," replied the Queen of the Mice. "But if you are going to call the Winged Monkeys we must run away, for they are full of mischief and think it great fun to plague us."

"Won't they hurt me?" asked the girl anxiously.

"Oh, no. They must obey the wearer of the Cap. Good-bye!" And she scampered out of sight, with all the mice hurrying after her.

Dorothy looked inside the Golden Cap and saw some words written upon the lining. These, she thought, must be the charm, so she read the directions carefully and put the Cap upon her head.

"Ep-pe, pep-pe, kak-ke!" she said, standing on her left foot.

"What did you say?" asked the Scarecrow, who did not know what she was doing.

"Hil-lo, hol-lo, hel-lo!" Dorothy went on, standing this time on her right foot.

"Hello!" replied the Tin Woodman calmly.

"Ziz-zy, zuz-zy, zik!" said Dorothy, who was now standing on both feet. This ended the saying of the charm, and they heard a great chattering and flapping of wings, as the band of Winged Monkeys flew up to them.

The King bowed low before Dorothy, and asked, "What is your command?"

"We wish to go to the Emerald City," said the child, "and we have lost our way."

"We will carry you," replied the King, and no sooner had he spoken than two of the Monkeys caught Dorothy in their arms and flew away with her. Others took the Scarecrow and the Woodman and the Lion, and one little Monkey seized Toto and flew after them, although the dog tried hard to bite him.

The Scarecrow and the Tin Woodman were rather frightened at first, for they remembered how badly the Winged Monkeys had treated them before; but they saw that no harm was intended, so they rode through the

The Monkeys caught
Dorothy in their arms
and flew away with her.

air quite cheerfully, and had a fine time looking at the pretty gardens and woods far below them.

Dorothy found herself riding easily between two of the biggest Monkeys, one of them the King himself. They had made a chair of their hands and were careful not to hurt her.

"Why do you have to obey the charm of the Golden Cap?" she asked.

"That is a long story," answered the King, with a laugh; "but as we have a long journey before us, I will pass the time by telling you about it, if you wish."

"I shall be glad to hear it," she replied.

"Once," began the leader, "we were a free people, living happily in the great forest, flying from tree to tree, eating nuts and fruit, and doing just as we pleased without calling anybody master. Perhaps some of us were rather too full of mischief at times, flying down to pull the tails of the animals that had no wings, chasing birds, and throwing nuts at the people who walked in the forest. But we were careless and happy and full of fun, and enjoyed every minute of the day. This was many years ago, long before Oz came out of the clouds to rule over this land.

"There lived here then, away at the North, a beautiful princess, who was also a powerful sorceress. All her magic was used to help the people, and she was never known to hurt anyone who was good. Her name was Gayelette, and she lived in a handsome palace built from great blocks of ruby. Everyone loved her, but her greatest sorrow was that she could find no one to love in return, since all the men were much too stupid and ugly to mate with one so beautiful and wise. At last, however, she found a boy who was handsome and manly and wise beyond his years. Gayelette made up her mind that when he grew to be a man she would make him her husband, so she took him to her ruby palace and used all her magic powers to make him as strong and good and lovely as any woman could wish. When he grew to manhood, Quelala, as he was called, was said to be the best and wisest man in all the land, while his manly beauty was so great that Gayelette loved him dearly, and hastened to make everything ready for the wedding.

"My grandfather was at that time the King of the Winged Monkeys which lived in the forest near Gayelette's palace, and the old fellow loved a joke better than a good dinner. One day, just before the wedding, my grandfather was flying out with his band when he saw Quelala walking beside the river. He was dressed in a rich costume of pink silk and purple velvet, and my grandfather thought he would see what he could do. At his word the band flew down and

seized Quelala, carried him in their arms until they were over the middle of the river, and then dropped him into the water.

"'Swim out, my fine fellow,' cried my grandfather, 'and see if the water has spotted your clothes.' Quelala was much too wise not to swim, and he was not in the least spoiled by all his good fortune. He laughed, when he came to the top of the water, and swam in to shore. But when Gayelette came running out to him she found his silks and velvet all ruined by the river.

"The princess was angry, and she knew, of course, who did it. She had all the Winged Monkeys brought before her, and she said at first that their wings should be tied and they should be treated as they had treated Quelala, and dropped in the river. But my grandfather pleaded hard, for he knew the Monkeys would drown in the river with their wings tied, and Quelala said a kind word for them also; so that Gayelette finally spared them, on condition that the Winged Monkeys should ever after do three times the bidding of the owner of the Golden Cap. This Cap had been made for a wedding present to Quelala, and it is said to have cost the princess half her kingdom. Of course my grandfather and all the other Monkeys at once agreed to the condition, and that is how it happens that we are three times the slaves of the owner of the Golden Cap, whosoever he may be."

"And what became of them?" asked Dorothy, who had been greatly interested in the story.

"Quelala being the first owner of the Golden Cap," replied the Monkey, "he was the first to lay his wishes upon us. As his bride could not bear the sight of us, he called us all to him in the forest after he had married her and ordered us always to keep where she could never again set eyes on a Winged Monkey, which we were glad to do, for we were all afraid of her.

"This was all we ever had to do until the Golden Cap fell into the hands of the Wicked Witch of the West, who made us enslave the Winkies, and afterward drive Oz himself out of the Land of the West. Now the Golden Cap is yours, and three times you have the right to lay your wishes upon us."

As the Monkey King finished his story Dorothy looked down and saw the green, shining walls of the Emerald City before them. She wondered at the rapid flight of the Monkeys, but was glad the journey was over. The strange creatures set the travelers down carefully before the gate of the City, the King bowed low to Dorothy, and then flew swiftly away, followed by all his band.

"That was a good ride," said the little girl.

"Yes, and a quick way out of our troubles," replied the Lion. "How lucky it was you brought away that wonderful Cap!"

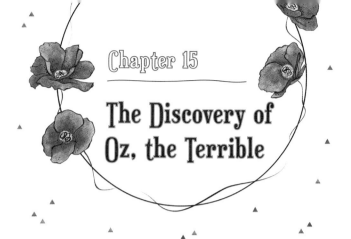

Chapter 15

The Discovery of Oz, the Terrible

The four travelers walked up to the great gate of Emerald City and rang the bell. After ringing several times, it was opened by the same Guardian of the Gates they had met before.

"What! are you back again?" he asked, in surprise.

"Do you not see us?" answered the Scarecrow.

"But I thought you had gone to visit the Wicked Witch of the West."

"We did visit her," said the Scarecrow.

"And she let you go again?" asked the man, in wonder.

"She could not help it, for she is melted," explained the Scarecrow.

"Melted! Well, that is good news, indeed," said the man. "Who melted her?"

"It was Dorothy," said the Lion gravely.

"Good gracious!" exclaimed the man, and he bowed very low indeed before her.

Then he led them into his little room and locked the spectacles from the great box on all their eyes, just as he had done before. Afterward they passed on through the gate into the Emerald City. When the people heard from the Guardian of the Gates that Dorothy had melted the Wicked Witch of the West, they all gathered around the travelers and followed them in a great crowd to the Palace of Oz.

The soldier with the green whiskers was still on guard before the door, but he let them in at once, and they were again met by the beautiful green girl, who showed each of them to their old rooms at once, so they might rest until the Great Oz was ready to receive them.

The soldier had the news carried straight to Oz that Dorothy and the other travelers had come back again, after destroying the Wicked Witch; but Oz made no reply. They thought the Great Wizard would send for them at once, but he did not. They had no word from him the next day, nor the next, nor the next. The waiting was tiresome and wearing, and at last they grew vexed that Oz should treat them in so poor a fashion, after sending them to undergo hardships and slavery. So the Scarecrow at last asked the green girl to take another message to Oz, saying if he did not let them in to see him at once they would call the Winged Monkeys to help them, and find out whether he kept his promises or not. When the Wizard was given this message he was so frightened that he sent word for them to come to the Throne Room at four minutes after nine o'clock the next morning. He had once met the Winged Monkeys in the Land of the West, and he did not wish to meet them again.

The four travelers passed a sleepless night, each thinking of the gift Oz had promised to bestow on him. Dorothy fell asleep only once, and then she dreamed she was in Kansas, where Aunt Em was telling her how glad she was to have her little girl at home again.

Promptly at nine o'clock the next morning the green-whiskered soldier came to them, and four minutes later they all went into the Throne Room of the Great Oz.

Of course each one of them expected to see the Wizard in the shape he had taken before, and all were greatly surprised when they looked about and saw no one at all in the room. They kept close to the door and closer to one another, for the stillness of the empty room was more dreadful than any of the forms they had seen Oz take.

Presently they heard a solemn Voice, that seemed to come from somewhere near the top of the great dome, and it said:

"I am Oz, the Great and Terrible. Why do you seek me?"

They looked again in every part of the room, and then, seeing no one, Dorothy asked, "Where are you?"

"I am everywhere," answered the Voice, "but to the eyes of common mortals I am invisible. I will now seat myself upon my throne, that you may converse with me." Indeed, the Voice seemed just then to come straight from the throne itself; so they walked toward it and stood in a row while Dorothy said:

"We have come to claim our promise, O Oz."

"What promise?" asked Oz.

"You promised to send me back to Kansas when the Wicked Witch was destroyed," said the girl.

"And you promised to give me brains," said the Scarecrow.

"And you promised to give me a heart," said the Tin Woodman.

"And you promised to give me courage," said the Cowardly Lion.

"Is the Wicked Witch really destroyed?" asked the Voice, and Dorothy thought it trembled a little.

"Yes," she answered, "I melted her with a bucket of water."

"Dear me," said the Voice, "how sudden! Well, come to me tomorrow, for I must have time to think it over."

"You've had plenty of time already," said the Tin Woodman angrily.

"We shan't wait a day longer," said the Scarecrow.

"You must keep your promises to us!" exclaimed Dorothy.

The Lion thought it might be as well to frighten the Wizard, so he gave a large, loud roar, which was so fierce and dreadful that Toto jumped away from him in alarm and tipped over the screen that stood in a corner. As it fell with a crash they looked that way, and the next moment all of them were filled with wonder. For they saw, standing in just the spot the screen had hidden, a little old man, with a bald head and a wrinkled face, who seemed to be as much surprised as they were. The Tin Woodman, raising his axe, rushed toward the little man and cried out, "Who are you?"

"I am Oz, the Great and Terrible," said the little man, in a trembling voice. "But don't strike me— please don't— and I'll do anything you want me to."

Our friends looked at him in surprise and dismay.

"I thought Oz was a great Head," said Dorothy.

"And I thought Oz was a lovely Lady," said the Scarecrow.

"And I thought Oz was a terrible Beast," said the Tin Woodman.

"And I thought Oz was a Ball of Fire," exclaimed the Lion.

"No, you are all wrong," said the little man meekly. "I have been making believe."

"Making believe!" cried Dorothy. "Are you not a Great Wizard?"

"Hush, my dear," he said. "Don't speak so loud, or you will be overheard—and I should be ruined. I'm supposed to be a Great Wizard."

"And aren't you?" she asked.

"Not a bit of it, my dear; I'm just a common man."

"You're more than that," said the Scarecrow, in a grieved tone; "you're a humbug."

"Exactly so!" declared the little man, rubbing his hands together as if it pleased him. "I am a humbug."

"But this is terrible," said the Tin Woodman. "How shall I ever get my heart?"

"Or I my courage?" asked the Lion.

"Or I my brains?" wailed the Scarecrow, wiping the tears from his eyes with his coat sleeve.

"My dear friends," said Oz, "I pray you not to speak of these little things. Think of me, and the terrible trouble I'm in at being found out."

"Doesn't anyone else know you're a humbug?" asked Dorothy.

"No one knows it but you four—and myself," replied Oz. "I have fooled everyone so long that I thought I should never be found out. It was a great mistake my ever letting you into the Throne Room. Usually I will not see even my subjects, and so they believe I am something terrible."

"But, I don't understand," said Dorothy, in bewilderment. "How was it that you appeared to me as a great Head?"

"That was one of my tricks," answered Oz. "Step this way, please, and I will tell you all about it."

He led the way to a small chamber in the rear of the

"Exactly so! I am a humbug."

Throne Room, and they all followed him. He pointed to one corner, in which lay the great Head, made out of many thicknesses of paper, and with a carefully painted face.

"This I hung from the ceiling by a wire," said Oz. "I stood behind the screen and pulled a thread, to make the eyes move and the mouth open."

"But how about the voice?" she inquired.

"Oh, I am a ventriloquist," said the little man. "I can throw the sound of my voice wherever I wish, so that you thought it was coming out of the Head. Here are the other things I used to deceive you." He showed the Scarecrow the dress and the mask he had worn when he seemed to be the lovely Lady. And the Tin Woodman saw that his terrible Beast was nothing but a lot of skins, sewn together, with slats to keep their sides out. As for the Ball of Fire, the false Wizard had hung that also from the ceiling. It was really a ball of cotton, but when oil was poured upon it the ball burned fiercely.

"Really," said the Scarecrow, "you ought to be ashamed of yourself for being such a humbug."

"I am—I certainly am," answered the little man sorrowfully; "but it was the only thing I could do. Sit down, please, there are plenty of chairs; and I will tell you my story."

So they sat down and listened while he told the following tale.

"I was born in Omaha—"

"Why, that isn't very far from Kansas!" cried Dorothy.

"No, but it's farther from here," he said, shaking his head at her sadly. "When I grew up I became a ventriloquist, and at that I was very well trained by a great master. I can imitate any kind of a bird or beast." Here he mewed so like a kitten that Toto pricked up his ears and looked everywhere to see where she was. "After a time," continued Oz, "I tired of that, and became a balloonist."

"What is that?" asked Dorothy.

"A man who goes up in a balloon on circus day, so as to draw a crowd of people together and get them to pay to see the circus," he explained.

"Oh," she said, "I know."

"Well, one day I went up in a balloon and the ropes got twisted, so that I couldn't come down again. It went way up above the clouds, so far that a current of air struck it and carried it many, many miles away. For a day and a night I traveled through the air, and on the morning of the second day I awoke and found the balloon floating over a strange and beautiful country.

"It came down gradually, and I was not hurt a bit. But I found myself in the midst of a strange people, who,

seeing me come from the clouds, thought I was a great Wizard. Of course I let them think so, because they were afraid of me, and promised to do anything I wished them to.

"Just to amuse myself, and keep the good people busy, I ordered them to build this City, and my Palace; and they did it all willingly and well. Then I thought, as the country was so green and beautiful, I would call it the Emerald City; and to make the name fit better I put green spectacles on all the people, so that everything they saw was green."

"But isn't everything here green?" asked Dorothy.

"No more than in any other city," replied Oz; "but when you wear green spectacles, why of course everything you see looks green to you. The Emerald City was built a great many years ago, for I was a young man when the balloon brought me here, and I am a very old man now. But my people have worn green glasses on their eyes so long that most of them think it really is an Emerald City, and it certainly is a beautiful place, abounding in jewels and precious metals, and every good thing that is needed to make one happy. I have been good to the people, and they like me; but ever since this Palace was built, I have shut myself up and would not see any of them.

"One of my greatest fears was the Witches, for while I had no magical powers at all I soon found out that the Witches were really able to do wonderful things. There were four of them in this country, and they ruled the people who live in the North and South and East and West. Fortunately, the Witches of the North and South were good, and I knew they would do me no harm; but the Witches of the East and West were terribly wicked, and had they not thought I was more powerful than they themselves, they would surely have destroyed me. As it was, I lived in deadly fear of them for many years; so you can imagine how pleased I was when I heard your house had fallen on the Wicked Witch of the East. When you came to me, I was willing to promise anything if you would only do away with the other Witch; but, now that you have melted her, I am ashamed to say that I cannot keep my promises."

"I think you are a very bad man," said Dorothy.

"Oh, no, my dear; I'm really a very good man, but I'm a very bad Wizard, I must admit."

"Can't you give me brains?" asked the Scarecrow.

"You don't need them. You are learning something every day. A baby has brains, but it doesn't know much. Experience is the only thing that brings knowledge, and the longer you are on earth the more experience you are sure to get."

"That may all be

true," said the Scarecrow, "but I shall be very unhappy unless you give me brains."

The false Wizard looked at him carefully.

"Well," he said with a sigh, "I'm not much of a magician, as I said; but if you will come to me tomorrow morning, I will stuff your head with brains. I cannot tell you how to use them, however; you must find that out for yourself."

"Oh, thank you—thank you!" cried the Scarecrow. "I'll find a way to use them, never fear!"

"But how about my courage?" asked the Lion anxiously.

"You have plenty of courage, I am sure," answered Oz. "All you need is confidence in yourself. There is no living thing that is not afraid when it faces danger. The True courage is in facing danger when you are afraid, and that kind of courage you have in plenty.

"Perhaps I have, but I'm scared just the same," said the Lion. "I shall really be very unhappy unless you give me the sort of courage that makes one forget he is afraid."

"Very well, I will give you that sort of courage tomorrow," replied Oz.

"How about my heart?" asked the Tin Woodman.

"Why, as for that," answered Oz, "I think you are wrong to want a heart. It makes most people unhappy. If you only knew it, you are in luck not to have a heart."

"That must be a matter of opinion," said the Tin Woodman. "For my part, I will bear all the unhappiness without a murmur, if you will give me the heart."

"Very well," answered Oz meekly. "Come to me tomorrow and you shall have a heart. I have played Wizard for so many years that I may as well continue the part a little longer."

"And now," said Dorothy, "how am I to get back to Kansas?"

"We shall have to think about that," replied the little man. "Give me two or three days to consider the matter and I'll try to find a way to carry you over the desert. In the meantime you shall all be treated as my guests, and while you live in the Palace my people will wait upon you and obey your slightest wish. There is only one thing I ask in return for my help—such as it is. You must keep my secret and tell no one I am a humbug."

They agreed to say nothing of what they had learned, and went back to their rooms in high spirits. Even Dorothy had hope that "The Great and Terrible Humbug," as she called him, would find a way to send her back to Kansas, and if he did she was willing to forgive him everything.

Chapter 16

The Magic Art of the Great Humbug

Next morning the Scarecrow said to his friends:

"Congratulate me. I am going to Oz to get my brains at last. When I return I shall be as other men are."

"I have always liked you as you were," said Dorothy simply.

"It is kind of you to like a Scarecrow," he replied. "But surely you will think more of me when you hear the splendid thoughts my new brain is going to turn out." Then he said good-bye to them all in a cheerful voice and went to the Throne Room, where he rapped upon the door.

"Come in," said Oz.

The Scarecrow went in and found the little man sitting down by the window, engaged in deep thought.

"I have come for my brains," remarked the Scarecrow, a little uneasily.

"Oh, yes; sit down in that chair, please," replied Oz. "You must excuse me for taking your head off, but I shall have to do it in order to put your brains in their proper place."

"That's all right," said the Scarecrow. "You are quite welcome to take my head off, as long as it will be a better one when you put it on again."

So the Wizard unfastened his head and emptied out the straw. Then he entered the back room and took up a measure of bran, which he mixed with a great many pins and needles. Having shaken them together thoroughly, he filled the top of the Scarecrow's head with the mixture and stuffed the rest of the space with straw, to hold it in place.

When he had fastened the Scarecrow's head on his body again he said to him, "Hereafter you will be a great man, for I have given you a lot of bran-new brains."

The Scarecrow was both pleased and proud at the fulfillment of his greatest wish, and having thanked Oz warmly he went back to his friends.

Dorothy looked at him curiously. His head was quite bulged out at the top with brains.

"How do you feel?" she asked.

"I feel wise indeed," he answered earnestly. "When I get used to my brains I shall know everything."

"Why are those needles and pins sticking out of your head?" asked the Tin Woodman.

"That is proof that he is sharp," remarked the Lion.

"Well, I must go to Oz and get my heart," said the Woodman. So he walked to the Throne Room and knocked at the door.

"Come in," called Oz, and the Woodman entered and said, "I have come for my heart."

"Very well," answered the little man. "But I shall have to cut a hole in your breast, so I can put your heart in the right place. I hope it won't hurt you."

"Oh, no," answered the Woodman. "I shall not feel it at all."

So Oz brought a pair of tinsmith's shears and cut a small, square hole in the left side of the Tin Woodman's breast. Then, going to a chest of drawers, he took out a pretty heart, made entirely of silk and stuffed with sawdust.

"Isn't it a beauty?" he asked.

"It is, indeed!" replied the Woodman, who was greatly pleased. "But is it a kind heart?"

"Oh, very!" answered Oz. He put the heart in the Woodman's breast and then replaced the square of tin, soldering it neatly together where it had been cut.

"There," said he; "now you have a heart that any man might be proud of. I'm sorry I had to put a patch on your breast, but it really couldn't be helped."

"Never mind the patch," exclaimed the happy Woodman. "I am very grateful to you, and shall never forget your kindness."

"Don't speak of it," replied Oz.

Then the Tin Woodman went back to his friends, who wished him every joy on account of his good fortune.

The Lion now walked to the Throne Room and knocked at the door.

"Come in," said Oz.

"I have come for my courage," announced the Lion, entering the room.

"Very well," answered the little man; "I will get it for you."

He went to a cupboard and reaching up to a high shelf took down a square green bottle, the contents of which he poured into a green-gold dish, beautifully carved. Placing this

before the Cowardly Lion, who sniffed at it as if he did not like it, the Wizard said:

"Drink."

"What is it?" asked the Lion.

"Well," answered Oz, "if it were inside of you, it would be courage. You know, of course, that courage is always inside one; so that this really cannot be called courage until you have swallowed it. Therefore I advise you to drink it as soon as possible."

The Lion hesitated no longer, but drank till the dish was empty.

"How do you feel now?" asked Oz.

"Full of courage," replied the Lion, who went joyfully back to his friends to tell them of his good fortune.

Oz, left to himself, smiled to think of his success in giving the Scarecrow and the Tin Woodman and the Lion exactly what they thought they wanted. "How can I help being a humbug," he said, "when all these people make me do things that everybody knows can't be done? It was easy to make the Scarecrow and the Lion and the Woodman happy, because they imagined I could do anything. But it will take more than imagination to carry Dorothy back to Kansas, and I'm sure I don't know how it can be done."

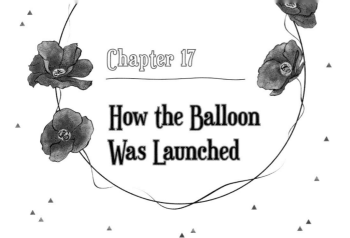

Chapter 17

How the Balloon Was Launched

For three days Dorothy heard nothing from Oz. These were sad days for the little girl, although her friends were all quite happy and contented. The Scarecrow told them there were wonderful thoughts in his head; but he would not say what they were because he knew no one could understand them but himself. When the Tin Woodman walked about he felt his heart rattling around in his breast; and he told Dorothy he had discovered it to be a kinder and more tender heart than the one he had owned when he was made of flesh. The Lion declared he was afraid of nothing on earth, and would gladly face an army or a dozen of the fierce Kalidahs.

Thus each of the little party was satisfied except Dorothy, who longed more than ever to get back to Kansas.

On the fourth day, to her great joy, Oz sent for her, and when she entered the Throne Room he greeted her pleasantly:

"Sit down, my dear; I think I have found the way to get you out of this country."

"And back to Kansas?" she asked eagerly.

"Well, I'm not sure about Kansas," said Oz, "for I haven't the faintest notion which way it lies. But the first thing to do is to cross the desert, and then it should be easy to find your way home."

"How can I cross the desert?" she inquired.

"Well, I'll tell you what I think," said the little man. "You see, when I came to this country it was in a balloon. You also came through the air, being carried by a cyclone. So I believe the best way to get across the desert will be through the air. Now, it is quite beyond my powers to make a cyclone; but I've been thinking the matter over, and I believe I can make a balloon."

"How?" asked Dorothy.

"A balloon," said Oz, "is made of silk, which is coated with glue to keep the gas in it. I have plenty of silk in the Palace, so it will be no trouble to make the balloon. But in all this country there is no gas to fill the balloon with, to make it float."

"If it won't float," remarked Dorothy, "it will be of no use to us."

"True," answered Oz. "But there is another way to make it float, which is to fill it with hot air. Hot air isn't as good as gas, for if the air should get cold the balloon would come down in the desert, and we should be lost."

"We!" exclaimed the girl. "Are you going with me?"

"Yes, of course," replied Oz. "I am tired of being such

a humbug. If I should go out of this Palace my people would soon discover I am not a Wizard, and then they would be vexed with me for having deceived them. So I have to stay shut up in these rooms all day, and it gets tiresome. I'd much rather go back to Kansas with you and be in a circus again."

"I shall be glad to have your company," said Dorothy.

"Thank you," he answered. "Now, if you will help me sew the silk together, we will begin to work on our balloon."

So Dorothy took a needle and thread, and as fast as Oz cut the strips of silk into proper shape the girl sewed them neatly together. First there was a strip of light green silk, then a strip of dark green and then a strip of emerald green; for Oz had a fancy to make the balloon in different shades of the color about them. It took three days to sew all the strips together, but when it was finished they had a big bag of green silk more than twenty feet long.

Then Oz painted it on the inside with a coat of thin glue, to make it airtight, after which he announced that the balloon was ready.

"But we must have a basket to ride in," he said. So he sent the soldier with the green whiskers for a big clothes basket, which he fastened with many ropes to the bottom of the balloon.

When it was all ready, Oz sent word to his people that he was going to make a visit to a great brother Wizard who lived in the clouds. The news spread rapidly throughout the city and everyone came to see the wonderful sight.

Oz ordered the balloon carried out in front of the Palace, and the people gazed upon it with much curiosity. The Tin Woodman had chopped a big pile of wood, and now he made a fire of it, and Oz held the bottom of the balloon over the fire so that the hot air that arose from it would be caught in the silken bag. Gradually the balloon swelled out and rose into the air, until finally the basket just touched the ground.

Then Oz got into the basket and said to all the people in a loud voice:

"I am now going away to make a visit. While I am gone the Scarecrow will rule over you. I command you to obey him as you would me."

The balloon was by this time tugging hard at the rope that held it to the ground, for the air within it was hot, and this made it so much lighter in weight than the air without that it pulled hard to rise into the sky.

"Come, Dorothy!" cried the Wizard. "Hurry up, or the balloon will fly away."

"I can't find Toto anywhere," replied Dorothy, who did not wish to leave her little dog behind. Toto had run into the crowd to bark at a kitten, and Dorothy at last found him. She picked him up and ran towards the balloon.

She was within a few steps of it, and Oz was holding out his hands to help her into the basket, when, crack! went the ropes, and the balloon rose into the air without her.

"Come back!" she screamed. "I want to go, too!"

"I can't come back, my dear," called Oz from the basket. "Good-bye!"

"Good-bye!" shouted everyone, and all eyes were turned upward to where the Wizard was riding in the basket, rising every moment farther and farther into the sky.

And that was the last any of them ever saw of Oz, the Wonderful Wizard, though he may have reached Omaha safely, and be there now, for all we know. But the people remembered him lovingly, and said to one another:

"Oz was always our friend. When he was here he built for us this beautiful Emerald City, and now he is gone he has left the Wise Scarecrow to rule over us."

Still, for many days they grieved over the loss of the Wonderful Wizard, and would not be comforted.

Chapter 18

Away to the South

Dorothy wept bitterly at the passing of her hope to get home to Kansas again; but when she thought it all over she was glad she had not gone up in a balloon. And she also felt sorry at losing Oz, and so did her companions.

The Tin Woodman came to her and said:

"Truly I should be ungrateful if I failed to mourn for the man who gave me my lovely heart. I should like to cry a little because Oz is gone, if you will kindly wipe away my tears, so that I shall not rust."

"With pleasure," she answered, and brought a towel at once. Then the Tin Woodman wept for several minutes, and she watched the tears carefully and wiped them away with the towel. When he had finished, he thanked her kindly and oiled himself thoroughly with his jeweled oil-

can, to guard against mishap.

The Scarecrow was now the ruler of the Emerald City, and although he was not a Wizard the people were proud of him. "For," they said, "there is not another city in all the world that is ruled by a stuffed man." And, so far as they knew, they were quite right.

The morning after the balloon had gone up with Oz, the four travelers met in the Throne Room and talked matters over. The Scarecrow sat in the big throne and the others stood respectfully before him.

"We are not so unlucky," said the new ruler, "for this Palace and the Emerald City belong to us, and we can do just as we please. When I remember that a short time ago I was up on a pole in a farmer's cornfield, and that now I am the ruler of this beautiful City, I am quite satisfied with my lot."

"I also," said the Tin Woodman, "am well-pleased with my new heart; and, really, that was the only thing I wished in all the world."

"For my part, I am content in knowing I am as brave as any beast that ever lived, if not braver," said the Lion modestly.

"If Dorothy would only be contented to live in the Emerald City," continued the Scarecrow, "we might all be happy together."

The Scarecrow sat in the
big throne.

"But I don't want to live here," cried Dorothy. "I want to go to Kansas, and live with Aunt Em and Uncle Henry."

"Well, then, what can be done?" inquired the Woodman.

The Scarecrow decided to think, and he thought so hard that the pins and needles began to stick out of his brains. Finally he said:

"Why not call the Winged Monkeys, and ask them to carry you over the desert?"

"I never thought of that!" said Dorothy joyfully. "It's just the thing. I'll go at once for the Golden Cap."

When she brought it into the Throne Room she spoke the magic words, and soon the band of Winged Monkeys flew in through the open window and stood beside her.

"This is the second time you have called us," said the Monkey King, bowing before the little girl. "What do you wish?"

"I want you to fly with me to Kansas," said Dorothy.

But the Monkey King shook his head.

"That cannot be done," he said. "We belong to this country alone, and cannot leave it. There has never been a Winged Monkey in Kansas yet, and I suppose there never will be, for they don't belong there. We shall be glad to serve you in any way in our power, but we cannot cross the desert. Good-bye."

And with another bow, the Monkey King spread his wings and flew away through the window, followed by all his band.

Dorothy was ready to cry with disappointment. "I have wasted the charm of the Golden Cap to no purpose," she

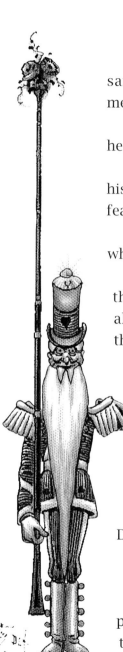

said, "for the Winged Monkeys cannot help me."

"It is certainly too bad!" said the tender-hearted Woodman.

The Scarecrow was thinking again, and his head bulged out so horribly that Dorothy feared it would burst.

"Let us call in the soldier with the green whiskers," he said, "and ask his advice."

So the soldier was summoned and entered the Throne Room timidly, for while Oz was alive he never was allowed to come farther than the door.

"This little girl," said the Scarecrow to the soldier, "wishes to cross the desert. How can she do so?"

"I cannot tell," answered the soldier, "for nobody has ever crossed the desert, unless it is Oz himself."

"Is there no one who can help me?" asked Dorothy earnestly.

"Glinda might," he suggested.

"Who is Glinda?" inquired the Scarecrow.

"The Witch of the South. She is the most powerful of all the Witches, and rules over the Quadlings. Besides, her castle stands on the edge of the desert, so she may know a way to cross it."

"Glinda is a Good Witch, isn't she?" asked the child.

"The Quadlings think she is good," said the soldier, "and she is kind to everyone. I have heard that Glinda is a beautiful woman, who knows how to keep young in spite of the many years she has lived."

"How can I get to her castle?" asked Dorothy.

"The road is straight to the South," he answered, "but it is said to be full of dangers to travelers. There are wild beasts in the woods, and a race of queer men who do not like strangers to cross their country. For this reason none of the Quadlings ever come to the Emerald City."

The soldier then left them and the Scarecrow said:

"It seems, in spite of dangers, that the best thing Dorothy can do is to travel to the Land of the South and ask Glinda to help her. For, of course, if Dorothy stays here she will never get back to Kansas."

"You must have been thinking again," remarked the Tin Woodman.

"I have," said the Scarecrow.

"I shall go with Dorothy," declared the Lion, "for I am tired of your city and long for the woods and the country again. I am really a wild beast, you know. Besides, Dorothy will need someone to protect her."

"That is true," agreed the Woodman. "My axe may be of service to her; so I also will go with her to the Land of the South."

"When shall we start?" asked the Scarecrow.

"Are you going?" they asked, in surprise.

"Certainly. If it wasn't for Dorothy I should never have

had brains. She lifted me from the pole in the cornfield and brought me to the Emerald City. So my good luck is all due to her, and I shall never leave her until she starts back to Kansas for good and all."

"Thank you," said Dorothy gratefully. "You are all very kind to me. But I should like to start as soon as possible."

"We shall go tomorrow morning," returned the Scarecrow. "So now let us all get ready, for it will be a long journey."

Chapter 19

Attacked by the Fighting Trees

The next morning Dorothy kissed the pretty green girl good-bye, and they all shook hands with the soldier with the green whiskers, who had walked with them as far as the gate. When the Guardian of the Gate saw them again he wondered greatly that they could leave the beautiful City to get into new trouble. But he at once unlocked their spectacles, which he put back into the green box, and gave them many good wishes to carry with them.

"You are now our ruler," he said to the Scarecrow; "so you must come back to us as soon as possible."

"I certainly shall if I am able," the Scarecrow replied; "but I must help Dorothy to get home, first."

As Dorothy bade the good-natured Guardian a last farewell she said:

"I have been very

kindly treated in your lovely City, and everyone has been good to me. I cannot tell you how grateful I am."

"Don't try, my dear," he answered. "We should like to keep you with us, but if it is your wish to return to Kansas, I hope you will find a way." He then opened the gate of the outer wall, and they walked forth and started upon their journey.

The sun shone brightly as our friends turned their faces toward the Land of the South. They were all in the best of spirits, and laughed and chatted together. Dorothy was once more filled with the hope of getting home, and the Scarecrow and the Tin Woodman were glad to be of use to her. As for the Lion, he sniffed the fresh air with delight and whisked his tail from side to side in pure joy at being in the country again, while Toto ran around them and chased the moths and butterflies, barking merrily all the time.

"City life does not agree with me at all," remarked the Lion, as they walked along at a brisk pace. "I have lost much flesh since I lived there, and now I am anxious for a chance to show the other beasts how courageous I have grown."

They now turned and took a last look at the Emerald City. All they could see was a mass of towers and steeples behind the green walls, and high up above everything the spires and dome of the Palace of Oz.

"Oz was not such a bad Wizard, after all," said the Tin Woodman, as he felt his heart rattling around in his breast.

"He knew how to give me brains, and very good brains, too," said the Scarecrow.

"If Oz had taken a dose of the same courage he gave me," added the Lion, "he would have been a brave man."

Dorothy said nothing. Oz had not kept the promise he made her, but he had done his best, so she forgave him. As he said, he was a good man, even if he was a bad Wizard.

The first day's journey was through the green fields and bright flowers that stretched about the Emerald City on every side. They slept that night on the grass, with nothing but the stars over them; and they rested very well indeed.

In the morning they traveled on until they came to a thick wood. There was no way of going around it, for it seemed to extend to the right and left as far as they could see; and, besides, they did not dare change the direction of their journey for fear of getting lost. So they looked for the place where it would be easiest to get into the forest.

The Scarecrow, who was in the lead, finally discovered a big tree with such wide-spreading branches that there was room for the party to pass underneath. So he walked forward to the tree, but just as he came under the first branches they bent down and twined around him, and the next minute he was raised from the ground and flung headlong among his fellow travelers.

This did not hurt the Scarecrow, but it surprised him, and he looked rather dizzy when Dorothy picked him up.

"Here is another space between the trees," called the Lion.

The branches bent down and twined around him.

"Let me try it first," said the Scarecrow, "for it doesn't hurt me to get thrown about." He walked up to another tree, as he spoke, but its branches immediately seized him and tossed him back again.

"This is strange," exclaimed Dorothy. "What shall we do?"

"The trees seem to have made up their minds to fight us, and stop our journey," remarked the Lion.

"I believe I will try it myself," said the Woodman, and shouldering his axe, he marched up to the first tree that had handled the Scarecrow so roughly. When a big branch bent down to seize him the Woodman chopped at it so fiercely that he cut it in two. At once the tree began shaking all its branches as if in pain, and the Tin Woodman passed safely under it.

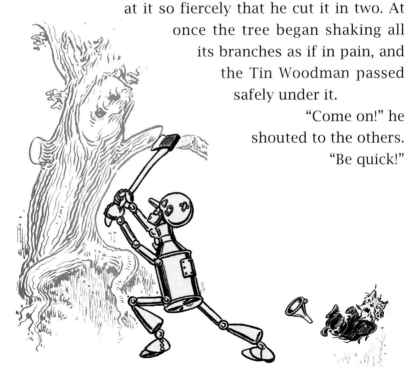

"Come on!" he shouted to the others. "Be quick!"

They all ran forward and passed under the tree without injury, except Toto, who was caught by a small branch and shaken until he howled. But the Woodman promptly chopped off the branch and set the little dog free.

The other trees of the forest did nothing to keep them back, so they made up their minds that only the first row of trees could bend down their branches, and that probably these were the policemen of the forest, and given this wonderful power in order to keep strangers out of it.

The four travelers walked with ease through the trees until they came to the farther edge of the wood. Then, to their surprise, they found before them a high wall which seemed to be made of white china. It was smooth, like the surface of a dish, and higher than their heads.

"What shall we do now?" asked Dorothy.

"I will make a ladder," said the Tin Woodman, "for we certainly must climb over the wall."

Chapter 20

The Dainty China Country

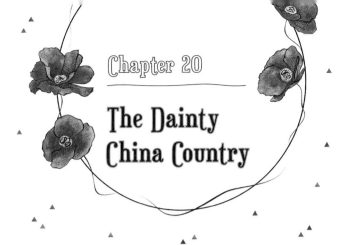

While the Woodman was making a ladder from wood which he found in the forest Dorothy lay down and slept, for she was tired by the long walk. The Lion also curled himself up to sleep and Toto lay beside him.

The Scarecrow watched the Woodman while he worked, and said to him:

"I cannot think why this wall is here, nor what it is made of."

"Rest your brains and do not worry about the wall," replied the Woodman. "When we have climbed over it, we shall know what is on the other side."

After a time the ladder was finished. It looked clumsy, but the Tin Woodman was sure it was strong and would answer their purpose. The Scarecrow waked Dorothy and the Lion and Toto, and told them that the ladder was ready. The Scarecrow climbed up the ladder first, but he was so awkward that Dorothy had to follow close behind and keep him from falling off. When he got his head over the top of the wall the Scarecrow said, "Oh, my!"

"Go on," exclaimed Dorothy.

So the Scarecrow climbed farther up and sat down on the top of the wall, and Dorothy put her head over and cried, "Oh, my!" just as the Scarecrow had done.

Then Toto came up, and immediately began to bark, but Dorothy made him be still.

The Lion climbed the ladder next, and the Tin Woodman came last; but both of them cried, "Oh, my!" as soon as they looked over the wall. When they were all sitting in a row on the top of the wall, they looked down and saw a strange sight.

Before them was a great stretch of country having a floor as smooth and shining and white as the bottom of a big platter. Scattered around were many houses made entirely of china and painted in the brightest colors. These houses were quite small, the biggest of them reaching only as high as Dorothy's waist. There were also pretty little barns, with china fences around them; and many cows and sheep and horses and pigs and chickens, all made of china, were standing about in groups.

But the strangest of all were the people who lived in this queer country. There were milkmaids and shepherdesses, with brightly colored bodices and golden spots all over their gowns; and princesses with most gorgeous frocks of silver and gold and purple; and shepherds dressed in knee breeches with pink and yellow and blue stripes down them, and golden buckles

on their shoes; and princes with jeweled crowns upon their heads, wearing ermine robes and satin doublets; and funny clowns in ruffled gowns, with round red spots upon their cheeks and tall, pointed caps. And, strangest of all, these people were all made of china, even to their clothes, and were so small that the tallest of them was no higher than Dorothy's knee.

No one did so much as look at the travelers at first, except one little purple china dog with an extra-large head, which came to the wall and barked at them in a tiny voice, afterwards running away again.

"How shall we get down?" asked Dorothy.

They found the ladder so heavy they could not pull it up, so the Scarecrow fell off the wall and the others jumped down upon him so that the hard floor would not hurt their feet. Of course they took pains not to light on his head and get the pins in their feet. When all were safely down they picked up the Scarecrow, whose body was quite flattened out, and patted his straw into shape again.

"We must cross this strange place in order to get to the other side," said Dorothy, "for it would be unwise for us to go any other way except due South."

They began walking through the country of the china people, and the first thing they came to was a china milkmaid milking a china cow. As they drew near, the cow suddenly gave a kick and kicked over the stool, the pail, and even the milkmaid herself, and all fell on the china ground with a great clatter.

Dorothy was shocked to see that the cow had broken her leg off, and that the pail was lying in several small pieces, while the poor milkmaid had a nick in her left elbow.

"There!" cried the milkmaid angrily. "See what you have done! My cow has broken her leg, and I must take her to the mender's shop and have it glued on again. What do you mean by coming here and frightening my cow?"

"I'm very sorry," returned Dorothy. "Please forgive us."

But the pretty milkmaid was much too vexed to make any answer. She picked up the leg sulkily and led her cow away, the poor animal limping on three legs. As she left them the milkmaid cast many reproachful glances over her shoulder at the clumsy strangers, holding her nicked elbow close to her side.

Dorothy was quite grieved at this mishap.

"We must be very careful here," said the kind-hearted Woodman, "or we may hurt these pretty little people so they will never get over it."

A little farther on Dorothy met a most beautifully dressed young Princess, who stopped short as she saw the strangers and started to run away.

Dorothy wanted to see more of the Princess, so she ran after her. But the china girl cried out:

"Don't chase me! Don't chase me!"

She had such a frightened little voice that Dorothy stopped and said, "Why not?"

"Because," answered the Princess, also stopping, a safe distance away, "if I run I may fall down and break myself."

"But could you not be mended?" asked the girl.

"Oh, yes; but one is never so pretty after being mended, you know," replied the Princess.

"I suppose not," said Dorothy.

"Now there is Mr. Joker, one of our clowns," continued the china lady, "who is always trying to stand upon his head. He has broken himself so often that he is mended in a hundred places, and doesn't look at all pretty. Here he comes now, so you can see for yourself."

Indeed, a jolly little clown came walking toward them, and Dorothy could see that in spite of his pretty clothes of red and yellow and green he was completely covered with cracks, running every which way and showing plainly that he had been mended in many places.

The Clown put his hands in his pockets, and after puffing out his cheeks and nodding his head at them saucily, he said:

"My lady fair,
Why do you stare
At poor old Mr. Joker?
You're quite as stiff
And prim as if
You'd eaten up a poker!"

"Be quiet, sir!" said the Princess. "Can't you see these are strangers, and should be treated with respect?"

"Well, that's respect, I expect," declared the Clown, and immediately stood upon his head.

"Don't mind Mr. Joker," said the Princess to Dorothy. "He is considerably cracked in his head, and that makes him foolish."

"Oh, I don't mind him a bit," said Dorothy. "But you are so beautiful," she continued, "that I am sure I could love you dearly. Won't you let me carry you back to Kansas, and stand you on Aunt Em's mantel? I could carry you in my basket."

"That would make me very unhappy," answered the china Princess. "You see, here in our country we live contentedly, and can talk and move around as we please. But whenever any of us are taken away our joints at once stiffen, and we can only stand straight and look pretty. Of course that is all that is expected of us when we are on mantels and cabinets and drawing-room tables, but our lives are much pleasanter here in our own country."

"I would not make you unhappy for all the world!" exclaimed Dorothy. "So I'll just say good-bye."

"Good-bye," replied the Princess.

They walked carefully through the china country. The little animals and all the people scampered out of their way, fearing the strangers would break them, and after an hour or so the travelers reached the other side of the country and came to another china wall.

It was not so high as the first, however, and by standing upon the Lion's back they all managed to scramble to the top. Then the Lion gathered his legs under him and jumped on the wall; but just as he jumped, he upset a china church with his tail and smashed it all to pieces.

"That was too bad," said Dorothy, "but really I think we were lucky in not doing these little people more harm than breaking a cow's leg and a church. They are all so brittle!"

"They are, indeed," said the Scarecrow, "and I am thankful I am made of straw and cannot be easily damaged. There are worse things in the world than being a Scarecrow."

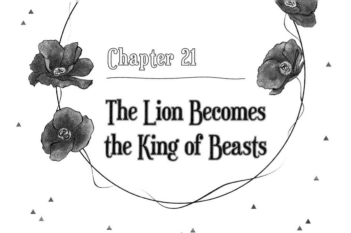

Chapter 21

The Lion Becomes the King of Beasts

After climbing down from the china wall the travelers found themselves in a disagreeable country, full of bogs and marshes and covered with tall, rank grass. It was difficult to walk without falling into muddy holes, for the grass was so thick that it hid them from sight. However, by carefully picking their way, they got safely along until they reached solid ground. But here the country seemed wilder than ever, and after a long and tiresome walk through the underbrush they entered another forest, where the trees were bigger and older than any they had ever seen.

"This forest is perfectly delightful," declared the Lion, looking around him with joy. "Never have I seen a more beautiful place."

"It seems gloomy," said the Scarecrow.

"Not a bit of it," answered the Lion. "I should like to live here all my life. See how soft the dried leaves are under your feet and how rich and green the moss is that clings to these old trees. Surely no wild beast could wish a pleasanter home."

"Perhaps there are wild beasts in the forest now," said Dorothy.

"I suppose there are," returned the Lion, "but I do not see any of them about."

They walked through the forest until it became too dark to go any farther. Dorothy and Toto and the Lion lay down to sleep, while the Woodman and the Scarecrow kept watch over them as usual.

When morning came, they started again. Before they had gone far they heard a low rumble, as of the growling of many wild animals. Toto whimpered a little, but none of the others was frightened, and they kept along the well-trodden path until they came to an opening in the wood, in which were gathered hundreds of beasts of every variety. There were tigers and elephants and bears and wolves and foxes and all the others in the natural history, and for a moment Dorothy was afraid. But the Lion explained that the animals were holding a meeting, and he judged by their snarling and growling that they were in great trouble.

As he spoke several of the beasts caught sight of him, and at once the great assemblage hushed as if by magic. The biggest of the tigers came up to the Lion and bowed, saying:

"Welcome, O King of Beasts! You have come in good time to fight our enemy and bring peace to all the animals of the forest once more."

"What is your trouble?" asked the Lion quietly.

"We are all threatened," answered the tiger, "by a fierce enemy which has lately come into this forest. It is a most tremendous monster, like a great spider, with a body as

big as an elephant and legs
as long as a tree trunk.
It has eight of these
long legs, and
as the monster
crawls
through
the forest
he seizes
an animal with a
leg and drags it to his mouth, where he
eats it as a spider does a fly. Not one of us
is safe while this fierce creature is alive, and we
had called a meeting to decide how to take
care of ourselves when you came among us."

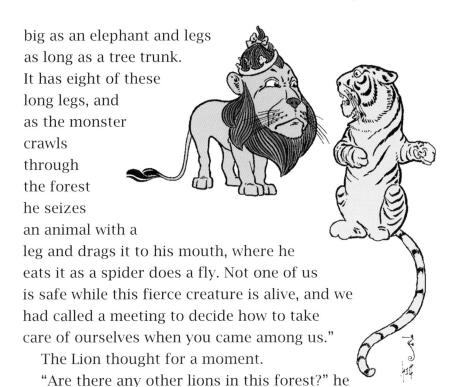

The Lion thought for a moment.

"Are there any other lions in this forest?" he
asked.

"No; there were some, but the monster has eaten
them all. And, besides, they were none of them nearly
so large and brave as you."

"If I put an end to your enemy, will you bow down
to me and obey me as King of the Forest?" inquired the
Lion.

"We will do that gladly," returned the tiger; and all
the other beasts roared with a mighty roar: "We will!"

"Where is this great spider of yours now?" asked the
Lion.

"Yonder, among the oak trees," said the tiger,

pointing with his forefoot.

"Take good care of these friends of mine," said the Lion, "and I will go at once to fight the monster."

He bade his comrades good-bye and marched proudly away to do battle with the enemy.

The great spider was lying asleep when the Lion found him, and it looked so ugly that its foe turned up his nose in disgust. Its legs were quite as long as the tiger had said, and its body covered with coarse black hair. It had a great mouth, with a row of sharp teeth a foot long; but its head was joined to the pudgy body by a neck as slender as a wasp's waist. This gave the Lion a hint of the best way to attack the creature, and as he knew it was easier to fight it asleep than awake, he gave a great spring and landed directly upon the monster's back. Then, with one blow of his heavy paw, all armed with sharp claws, he knocked the spider's head from its body. Jumping down, he watched it until the long legs stopped wiggling, when he knew it was quite dead.

The Lion went back to the opening where the beasts of the forest were waiting for him and said proudly:

"You need fear your enemy no longer."

Then the beasts bowed down to the Lion as their King, and he promised to come back and rule over them as soon as Dorothy was safely on her way to Kansas.

Chapter 22

The Country of the Quadlings

The four travelers passed through the rest of the forest in safety, and when they came out from its gloom saw before them a steep hill, covered from top to bottom with great pieces of rock.

"That will be a hard climb," said the Scarecrow, "but we must get over the hill, nevertheless."

So he led the way and the others followed. They had nearly reached the first rock when they heard a rough voice cry out, "Keep back!"

"Who are you?" asked the Scarecrow.

Then a head showed itself over the rock and the same voice said, "This hill belongs to us, and we don't allow anyone to cross it."

"But we must cross it," said the Scarecrow. "We're going to the country of the Quadlings."

"But you shall not!" replied the voice, and there stepped from behind the rock the strangest man the travelers had ever seen.

He was quite short and stout and had a big head, which was flat at the top and supported by a thick neck full of wrinkles. But he had no arms at all, and, seeing this, the Scarecrow did not fear that so helpless a creature could prevent them from climbing the hill. So he said, "I'm sorry not to do as you wish, but we must pass over your hill whether you like it or not," and he walked boldly forward.

As quick as lightning the man's head shot forward and his neck stretched out until the top of the head, where it was flat, struck the Scarecrow in the middle and sent him tumbling, over and over, down the hill. Almost as quickly as it came the head went back to the body, and the man laughed harshly as he said, "It isn't as easy as you think!"

A chorus of boisterous laughter came from the other rocks, and Dorothy saw hundreds of the armless Hammer-Heads upon the hillside, one behind every rock.

The Lion became quite angry at the laughter caused by the Scarecrow's mishap, and giving a loud roar that echoed like thunder, he dashed up the hill.

Again a head shot swiftly out, and the great Lion went rolling down the hill as if he had been struck by a cannon ball.

Dorothy ran down and helped the Scarecrow to his feet, and the Lion came up to her, feeling rather bruised and sore, and said, "It is useless to fight people with shooting heads; no one can withstand them."

"What can we do, then?" she asked.

"Call the Winged Monkeys," suggested the Tin Woodman. "You have still the right to command them once more."

"Very well," she answered, and putting on the Golden

The Head shot forward and struck the Scarecrow.

The Country of the Quadlings   Chapter 22

Cap she uttered the magic words. The Monkeys were as prompt as ever, and in a few moments the entire band stood before her.

"What are your commands?" inquired the King of the Monkeys, bowing low.

"Carry us over the hill to the country of the Quadlings," answered the girl.

"It shall be done," said the King, and at once the Winged Monkeys caught the four travelers and Toto up in their arms and flew away with them. As they passed over the hill the Hammer-Heads yelled with vexation, and shot their heads high in the air, but they could not reach the Winged Monkeys, which carried Dorothy and her comrades safely over the hill and set them down in the beautiful country of the Quadlings.

"This is the last time you can summon us," said the leader to Dorothy; "so good-bye and good luck to you."

"Good-bye, and thank you very much," returned the girl; and the Monkeys rose into the air and were out of sight in a twinkling.

The country of the Quadlings seemed rich and happy. There was field upon field of ripening grain, with well-paved roads running between, and pretty rippling brooks with strong bridges across them. The fences and houses and bridges were all painted bright red, just as they had been painted yellow in the country of the Winkies and blue in the country of the Munchkins. The Quadlings themselves, who were short and fat and looked chubby and good-natured, were dressed all

197

in red, which showed bright against the green grass and the yellowing grain.

The Monkeys had set them down near a farmhouse, and the four travelers walked up to it and knocked at the door. It was opened by the farmer's wife, and when Dorothy asked for something to eat the woman gave them all a good dinner, with three kinds of cake and four kinds of cookies, and a bowl of milk for Toto.

"How far is it to the Castle of Glinda?" asked the child.

"It is not a great way," answered the farmer's wife. "Take the road to the South and you will soon reach it.

Thanking the good woman, they started afresh and walked by the fields and across the pretty bridges until they saw before them a very beautiful Castle. Before the gates were three young girls, dressed in handsome red uniforms trimmed with gold braid; and as Dorothy

approached, one of them said to her:

"Why have you come to the South Country?"

"To see the Good Witch who rules here," she answered. "Will you take me to her?"

"Let me have your name, and I will ask Glinda if she will receive you." They told who they were, and the girl soldier went into the Castle. After a few moments she came back to say that Dorothy and the others were to be admitted at once.

Chapter 23

Glinda The Good Witch Grants Dorothy's Wish

Before they went to see Glinda, however, they were taken to a room of the Castle, where Dorothy washed her face and combed her hair, and the Lion shook the dust out of his mane, and the Scarecrow patted himself into his best shape, and the Woodman polished his tin and oiled his joints.

When they were all quite presentable they followed the soldier girl into a big room where the Witch Glinda sat upon a throne of rubies.

She was both beautiful and young to their eyes. Her hair was a rich red in color and fell in flowing ringlets over her shoulders. Her dress was pure white but her eyes were blue, and they looked kindly upon the little girl.

"What can I do for you, my child?" she asked.

Dorothy told the Witch all her story: how the cyclone had brought her to the Land of Oz, how she had found her companions, and of the wonderful adventures they had met with.

"My greatest wish now," she added, "is to get back to Kansas, for Aunt Em will surely think something dreadful has happened to me, and that will make her put on mourning; and unless the crops are better this year than they were last, I am sure Uncle Henry cannot afford it."

Glinda leaned forward and kissed the sweet, upturned face of the loving little girl.

"Bless your dear heart," she said, "I am sure I can tell you of a way to get back to Kansas." Then she added, "But, if I do, you must give me the Golden Cap."

"Willingly!" exclaimed Dorothy; "indeed, it is of no use to me now, and when you have it you can command the Winged Monkeys three times."

"And I think I shall need their service just those three times," answered Glinda, smiling.

Dorothy then gave her the Golden Cap, and the Witch said to the Scarecrow, "What will you do when Dorothy has left us?"

"I will return to the Emerald City," he replied, "for Oz has made me its ruler and the people like me. The only thing that worries me is how to cross the hill of the Hammer-Heads."

"By means of the Golden Cap I shall command the Winged Monkeys to carry you to the gates of the Emerald City," said Glinda, "for it would be a shame to deprive the people of so wonderful a ruler."

You must give me
the Golden Cap.

"Am I really wonderful?" asked the Scarecrow.

"You are unusual," replied Glinda.

Turning to the Tin Woodman, she asked, "What will become of you when Dorothy leaves this country?"

He leaned on his axe and thought a moment. Then he said, "The Winkies were very kind to me, and wanted me to rule over them after the Wicked Witch died. I am fond of the Winkies, and if I could get back again to the Country of the West, I should like nothing better than to rule over them forever."

"My second command to the Winged Monkeys," said Glinda "will be that they carry you safely to the land of the Winkies. Your brain may not be so large to look at as those of the Scarecrow, but you are really brighter than he is—when you are well polished—and I am sure you will rule the Winkies wisely and well."

Then the Witch looked at the big, shaggy Lion and asked, "When Dorothy has returned to her own home, what will become of you?"

"Over the hill of the Hammer-Heads," he answered, "lies a grand old forest, and all the beasts that live there have made me their King. If I could only get back to this forest, I would pass my life very happily there."

"My third command to the Winged Monkeys," said Glinda, "shall be to carry you to your forest. Then, having used up the powers of the Golden Cap, I shall give it to the King of the Monkeys, that he and his band may thereafter be free for evermore."

The Scarecrow and the Tin Woodman and the Lion

now thanked the Good Witch earnestly for her kindness; and Dorothy exclaimed:

"You are certainly as good as you are beautiful! But you have not yet told me how to get back to Kansas."

"Your Silver Shoes will carry you over the desert," replied Glinda. "If you had known their power you could have gone back to your Aunt Em the very first day you came to this country."

"But then I should not have had my wonderful brains!" cried the Scarecrow. "I might have passed my whole life in the farmer's cornfield."

"And I should not have had my lovely heart," said the Tin Woodman. "I might have stood and rusted in the forest till the end of the world."

"And I should have lived a coward forever," declared the Lion, "and no beast in all the forest would have had a good word to say to me."

"This is all true," said Dorothy, "and I am glad I was of use to these good friends. But now that each of them has had what he most desired, and each is happy in having a kingdom to rule besides, I think I should like to go back to Kansas."

"The Silver Shoes," said the Good Witch, "have wonderful powers. And one of the most curious things about them is that they can carry you to any place in the world in three steps, and each step will be made in the wink of an eye. All you have to do is to knock the heels together three times and command the shoes to carry you wherever you wish to go."

"If that is so," said the child joyfully, "I will ask them to carry me back to Kansas at once."

She threw her arms around the Lion's neck and kissed him, patting his big head tenderly. Then she kissed the Tin Woodman, who was weeping in a way most dangerous to his joints. But she hugged the soft, stuffed body of the Scarecrow in her arms instead of kissing his painted face, and found she was crying herself at this sorrowful parting from her loving comrades.

Glinda the Good stepped down from her ruby throne to give the little girl a good-bye kiss, and Dorothy thanked her for all the kindness she had shown to her friends and herself.

Dorothy now took Toto up solemnly in her arms, and having said one last good-bye she

205

clapped the heels of her shoes together three times, saying:

"Take me home to Aunt Em!"

Instantly she was whirling through the air, so swiftly that all she could see or feel was the wind whistling past her ears.

The Silver Shoes took but three steps, and then she stopped so suddenly that she rolled over upon the grass several times before she knew where she was.

At length, however, she sat up and looked about her.

"Good gracious!" she cried.

For she was sitting on the broad Kansas prairie, and just before her was the new farmhouse Uncle Henry built after the cyclone had carried away the old one. Uncle Henry was milking the cows in the barnyard, and Toto had jumped out of her arms and was running toward the barn, barking furiously.

Dorothy stood up and found she was in her stocking-feet. For the Silver Shoes had fallen off in her flight through the air, and were lost forever in the desert.

Chapter 24

Home Again

Aunt Em had just come out of the house to water the cabbages when she looked up and saw Dorothy running toward her.

"My darling child!" she cried, folding the little girl in her arms and covering her face with kisses. "Where in the world did you come from?"

"From the Land of Oz," said Dorothy gravely. "And here is Toto, too. And oh, Aunt Em! I'm so glad to be at home again!"

The Wizard of Oz

綠野仙蹤

序

　　民間傳奇和神話故事伴隨著孩子們走過童年，每個健康的孩子，相信都對神奇有趣又虛幻的故事愛不釋手。就像格林童話和安徒生童話，帶給孩子的心靈許多歡笑，絕非其他作品可比。

　　然而，在兒童的圖書館中，代代相傳的老式童話已經被分類成「老故事」了，現在的「奇幻故事」已不再需要刻板印象中的精靈、侏儒和仙女。而且，以往的童話作者為了在童話中達到教化目的，所設計的血腥駭人故事，現在也已經不適用了。因為現代教育已經納入道德倫理，兒童想從神奇的童話故事中得到的是趣味，而不樂見令人感到不適的情節。

　　有了這樣的想法，我寫了《綠野仙蹤》這本書來取悅現代的兒童。我想讓這本書成為一種現代童話，讓孩子們能在這本書中獲得趣味與喜悅，而不會感到憂傷，或是留下夢魘。

法蘭克・巴姆
一九〇〇年四月於芝加哥

Chapter 1

龍捲風

桃樂絲和亨利叔叔，還有愛姆嬸嬸，一起住在堪薩斯州中部的大草原裡。亨利叔叔和愛姆嬸嬸是對夫妻，務農為生。因為建房子的木材要從好幾哩外用卡車運來，所以他們的房子就蓋得小小的。房子的結構就四面牆、一層地板和一個屋頂。屋內有一個已經生鏽的煮飯爐灶、一個碗櫃、一張桌子、三四把椅子和床。亨利叔叔和愛姆嬸嬸的大床放在一個角落，桃樂絲的小床則擺在另一頭。房子裡沒有閣樓，也沒有地下室，不過地上挖了一個小洞，他們稱作「龍捲風地洞」。當大型龍捲風來襲時，它行進路徑上的任何建築物都會被摧毀，這時，他們就可以躲進地洞。地板中央有一扇活動的門，從梯子下去，就是又小又暗的地洞。

每當桃樂絲站在門口，往四面八方望去，舉目所及，都是一望無際的灰色大草原。這一大片寬闊平坦的草原，從四方綿延到天際，其間看不到半棵樹或半間房子。太陽把犁過的田，曬成大片大片的灰色，細細的龜裂痕跡，交錯其上。這裡連草也不是綠色的，太陽曬烤著長長的草葉，把它們烘曬得和四周的顏色一樣地灰。他們的房子曾經粉刷過一次，不過油漆被太陽曬得發泡，之後又經過雨水的沖刷，現在，房子跟所有東西一樣，也是灰壓壓一片暗沉。

想當初，愛姆嬸嬸初來乍到時，還是個美麗的少婦。不過，陽光和風也改變了她的容貌。太陽和風帶走她眼裡的光彩，只留下黯然的灰色；也帶走了她臉頰和嘴唇上的紅潤色澤，一樣只剩灰色。如今，愛姆嬸嬸消瘦憔悴，不再微笑。成了孤兒的桃樂絲剛來到這裡的時候，愛姆嬸嬸對她的笑聲感到很吃驚。每次她一聽到桃樂絲開懷大笑，就震驚得禁不住尖叫，把手摀住胸口。現在，她看著這個小女孩時，依舊感到驚奇，因為她還能發現令自己開懷大笑的事情。

亨利叔叔從來不笑。他從早工作到晚，根本不知喜悅為何物。從他的大鬍子到靴子，他一身也都是灰的。他看起來很嚴肅，一臉正經，不太講話。

會讓桃樂絲笑開懷的，就是托托了。還好有托托，

才沒讓桃樂絲像其他東西一樣，變成了灰色的。托托不是灰的，牠是隻小黑狗，有一身光滑的長毛，和一對小小的黑眼睛。牠的眼睛擺在古怪的滑稽鼻頭兩旁，眼神快活而閃爍。托托整天都在嬉戲，桃樂絲跟牠玩在一塊兒。牠是桃樂絲的心肝寶貝。

不過今天，他們沒跑出去玩。亨利叔叔坐在門前的階梯上，憂心地望著灰得不太尋常的天空。桃樂絲站在門邊，抱著托托，也盯著天空看，愛姆嬸嬸則在洗著碗盤。

他們聽到風聲低吼，從北方遠處呼嘯而來。亨利叔叔和桃樂絲望見，遠方的長草叢被即將襲來的風暴吹得彎下腰，如波浪般起伏。南方也傳來呼呼的尖銳風聲，他們轉過頭，看見南方的草叢也如波浪般搖擺著。

突然，亨利叔叔站了起來。

「愛姆，龍捲風來了！」他對妻子大喊道：「我去看一下家畜！」他說罷，就跑向畜房，去巡視他所養的牛馬。

愛姆嬸嬸停下手邊的工作，走到門口，一看就看出了會有危險。

她扯開喉嚨，喊道：「桃樂絲！快！快躲到地洞裡去！」

托托掙開桃樂絲，躲進床底下，桃樂絲跑去捉牠。

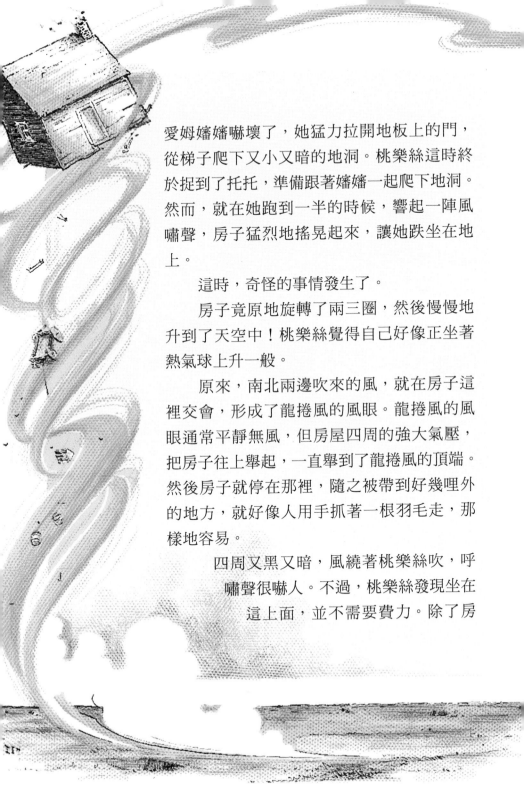

愛姆嬸嬸嚇壞了，她猛力拉開地板上的門，從梯子爬下又小又暗的地洞。桃樂絲這時終於捉到了托托，準備跟著嬸嬸一起爬下地洞。然而，就在她跑到一半的時候，響起一陣風嘯聲，房子猛烈地搖晃起來，讓她跌坐在地上。

這時，奇怪的事情發生了。

房子竟原地旋轉了兩三圈，然後慢慢地升到了天空中！桃樂絲覺得自己好像正坐著熱氣球上升一般。

原來，南北兩邊吹來的風，就在房子這裡交會，形成了龍捲風的風眼。龍捲風的風眼通常平靜無風，但房屋四周的強大氣壓，把房子往上舉起，一直舉到了龍捲風的頂端。然後房子就停在那裡，隨之被帶到好幾哩外的地方，就好像人用手抓著一根羽毛走，那樣地容易。

四周又黑又暗，風繞著桃樂絲吹，呼嘯聲很嚇人。不過，桃樂絲發現坐在這上面，並不需要費力。除了房

She caught Toto
by the ear.

　子一開始時轉的那幾圈，和一次房子傾斜很大時的旋轉
之外，桃樂絲覺得自己像是躺在搖籃裡的小嬰兒，被輕
輕地搖著。

　　可托托不喜歡這樣子搖晃，牠在房子裡跑來跑去，
大聲地吠著。但桃樂絲只是靜靜地坐在地板上，靜觀其
變。有一次，托托因太靠近那扇開著的活動地板門，所
以掉下去了。桃樂絲原以為再也見不到牠了，但她很快
就看到洞口探出了一隻狗耳朵。原來是強大的氣壓托住

了牠，讓牠不至於摔下去。桃樂絲爬近洞口，抓住托托的耳朵，把牠拉回房內，關上小門，以免再發生意外。

　　時間一個小時一個小時地過去，桃樂絲也不再那麼害怕。只不過，她開始覺得孤單，而且四周尖銳的風嘯聲，大得讓她震耳欲聾。一開始她想，等房子掉落時，自己會不會摔得粉碎，然而幾個鐘頭過去了，也沒有什麼可怕的事情發生。於是她不再擔心，決定靜觀事情的演變。最後，她爬過搖晃不已的地板，來到她的床邊，躺了上去。托托也跟著爬過去，躺在一旁。

　　她再也管不了東搖西晃的房子，或是呼呼作響的風聲了。她才一闔上眼，就沉沉地睡去了。

Chapter 2

遇見芒奇金
的居民

————陣猛烈而突然的震動，震醒了桃樂絲，要不是她躺在柔軟的床上，可能就受傷了。強烈的晃動，令她屏息，她心忖發生了什麼事。托托把冰冷的小鼻子靠在桃樂絲的臉上，哀哀叫著。桃樂絲坐起來，發現房子不再移動，四周也不是一片漆黑。明亮的陽光從窗戶射進來，照亮了小房子。她從床上一躍而起，跑向門口，打開門，後面跟著托托。

小女孩放眼環顧四周，驚叫了一聲。眼前的奇妙景象，讓她眼睛越睜越大。

龍捲風把房屋輕輕放下——噢，以一個龍捲風來說，這樣算是很輕的了——放在一個奇異而美麗的地方。這裡綠草如茵，高大筆直的樹上，掛滿甜美碩大的水果。一叢叢嬌美艷麗的花朵，隨處可見。鳥兒們一身罕見華麗的羽毛，在樹林和灌木叢裡振翅歌唱。在遠一點的地方，有一條小溪流，在兩岸綠意之間奔流閃耀。

淙淙的流水聲，聽在這個久住灰色乾草原的小女孩耳裡，煞是悅耳。

正當桃樂絲站著，熱切地望著眼前奇異而美麗的景象時，她看到有一群人，正朝她這個方向走來。那群人長得很奇特，是她前所未見的。他們沒有她平常看到的大人那般高大，但也不是很矮小。事實上，他們跟桃樂絲差不多高，而桃樂絲以她的年齡來說，算是個發育良好的小孩。不過，他們的年紀，看起來要比桃樂絲大多了。

那群人共有三個男人和一個婦人，穿著都很古怪。他們戴著圓帽，帽子中間突起一個一呎高的尖頂，旁邊掛了小鈴鐺。他們一走路，悅耳的鈴鐺聲就叮噹作響。男人的帽子是藍色的，婦人的則是白色的。婦人穿了件肩部以下打褶的白色長袍，上面鑲著亮晶晶的小星星，在陽光下閃閃發光，就像鑽石一樣。男人身著跟帽子顏色差不多的藍衣，穿著擦得發亮的靴子，靴子上端是一大圈深藍色。桃樂絲心想，這些男人大概跟亨利叔叔差不多年紀，因為其中兩人留了鬍子。至於那個矮小的女人，她的年紀一定更大了，因為她的臉上布滿了皺紋，頭髮幾

乎全白，走起路來也不很靈活。

　　這群人走近桃樂絲的房子，桃樂絲正站在門口。他們停下腳步，竊竊私語了起來，似乎不敢再向前走近。但那位老婦人還是走了過來，向桃樂絲深深鞠了個躬，很和氣地說道：「偉大的魔法師啊，歡迎您來到芒奇金之地，我們太感激您了，您除掉了東方邪惡女巫，讓我們人民不用再受她奴役！」

　　桃樂絲聽得莫名其妙，這個矮小的婦人稱她是魔法師，說她除掉了東方的邪惡女巫，是什麼意思呢？她只是個不懂事、也不會害人的小女孩，剛被龍捲風帶到這個離家數百哩的地方，況且她這輩子都還沒殺害過任何生命呢。

　　不過老婦人顯然在等她開口回答，她只好支支吾吾地說：「噢，謝謝你，不過你一定是哪裡搞錯了，我沒有殺害過什麼啊。」

　　老婦人笑著答道：「喔！是你的房子殺了她，反正都差不多啦。你看！」老婦人指著房屋的一角，繼續說道：「那個從木板下面伸出來的，就是女巫的兩隻腳！」

　　桃樂絲一看，嚇得叫了一聲。房屋的屋腳下果然伸出了兩隻腳，還套著一雙銀色的尖頭鞋。「天啊！天啊！」桃樂絲叫道，驚慌得兩手緊緊地揪在一起：「一定是房子壓到她了，怎麼辦呀？」

　　「不怎麼辦呀。」老婦人冷靜地說。

　　「她是誰呀？」桃樂絲問。

　　「她就是我所說的東方邪惡女巫。」老婦人說：「她奴役芒奇金的人民好些年了，要他們從早到晚替她做牛做馬。如今，他們自由了，他們很感謝你所做的事。」

　　「芒奇金人民是誰啊？」桃樂絲問。

　　「就是住在東方之地的人民，這裡本來是受邪惡女巫所統治的。」

　　「那你是芒奇金人嗎？」桃樂絲問。

　　「我不是，不過我是他們的友人，我住在北方。他們看到東方女巫死了，就差了一個動作迅速的信使來找我，所以我就來了。我是北方女巫。」

　　「哇！天呀！」桃樂絲大喊：「你是貨真價實的女

I am the Witch of the North.

巫嗎？」

「是的，沒錯。」矮小的婦人回答：「不過我可是個好女巫，大家都很喜歡我。只可惜，我的法力沒有統治這裡的邪惡女巫那麼高強，不然我就自己把她除掉，解放人民了。」

「我還以為女巫都是壞蛋呢！」小女孩說。面對著一個真正的女巫，她其實是有點害怕的。

「喔，這可真是個天大的誤會啊。在奧茲王國裡，總共只有四位女巫，住在北方和南方的那兩位，是善良的女巫。這種事問我準沒錯，因為我就是其中一個，不會搞錯的。至於住在東方和西方的那兩個，可真的就是壞女巫了。不過，現在你已經除掉了一個，整個奧茲王國就只剩一個壞女巫，也就是住在西方的那個。」

桃樂絲想了一下，說：「可是，愛姆嬸嬸告訴我說，在很多很多年以前，女巫就已經都消失了。」

「誰是愛姆嬸嬸啊？」矮小的老婦人問。

「她是我的嬸嬸，住在堪薩斯，我就是從那裡來的。」

北方女巫低下頭，看著地上，一副沉思的樣子。一會兒後，她抬起頭來，說道：「我不知道堪薩斯在哪裡，也從沒聽說過這個地方。你倒說說看，那是一個文明的地方嗎？」

「啊，是呀。」桃樂絲回答。

「這就對了。我想，在文明的地方的確是沒有女巫、巫師、術士或魔法師了。不過，你看，因為我們奧茲王國和世界的其他地方是分隔開來的，沒那麼文明，所以我們還有女巫和巫師。」

「誰是巫師啊？」桃樂絲問。

「奧茲本人就是一位偉大的巫師。」女巫回答，她壓低音量小聲地說：「他的力量，比我們全部的巫師加起來都還要大。他就住在翡翠城。」

桃樂絲打算繼續追問，但靜靜站在一旁的芒奇金人卻忽然大吼了一聲，指著壞女巫躺著的那個屋角。

「什麼事？」老婦人問。她一看，便笑了起來。原來是壞女巫的腳整個化為烏有，只剩一雙銀色鞋子還留在那裡。

「她太老了！」老婦人解釋道：「所以在太陽底下一下子就乾枯蒸發了——這就是她的下場了。這雙銀鞋是你的了，穿上它們吧。」她走過去撿起銀鞋，抖一抖上面的灰塵，把鞋子交給了桃樂絲。

「這雙銀鞋可是讓東方女巫非常引以為傲的。」其中一位芒奇金人說：「而且這雙鞋子具有魔力，不過到

底是什麼魔力，我們就不知道了。」

　　桃樂絲把鞋子拿進房子放在桌上，又走出來問這群人說：「我好想回去叔叔和嬸嬸那裡，我知道他們一定會很擔心我的。你們能幫我找到回去的路嗎？」

　　芒奇金人和女巫互相看了幾眼後，望著桃樂絲，最後都搖了搖頭。

　　「離這裡不遠的東方，是一片大沙漠，從來沒有人能活著走過沙漠。」其中一個芒奇金人說。

　　另一個說：「南方也是一片大沙漠，我曾在那裡親眼目睹過，那裡是垮德林人的領土。」

　　第三個人說：「有人跟我說過，西方也是一大片沙漠。那裡的人民叫做維奇人，為西方邪惡女巫所統治。只要有人經過她的領土，就會被抓去當奴隸。」

　　「北方是我的家鄉。」老婦人說：「那裡的邊界也和奧茲王國的其他邊界一樣，都是一大片沙漠。親愛的小女孩，恐怕你得和我們一起生活了。」

　　聽到這裡，桃樂絲哭了起來。與這群奇怪的人在一起，她覺得很孤單。她的眼淚似乎感染了這群好心的芒奇金人，他們隨即拿出手帕，也開始哭了起來。老婦人把帽子拿下來，用帽子的尖端頂在自己的鼻子上，認真地數著「一，二，三」。忽然間，帽子變成一塊大石板，上面寫著大大的粉筆字：「叫桃樂絲往翡翠城去」。

　　老婦人把石板從鼻子上拿下來，讀完上面的字後，問道：「親愛的，你就是桃樂絲嗎？」

「是的。」小女孩回答道，一邊抬起頭來擦乾眼淚。

「那麼，你就該往翡翠城去，或許奧茲國王可以幫你。」

「翡翠城在哪裡啊？」桃樂絲問。

「它就在奧茲王國的正中央，由奧茲國王所統治，他就是我跟你提過那個力量最強的巫師。」

「他是個好心的人嗎？」小女孩擔憂地問。

「他是個好心的巫師。只不過，他是不是人類，我就沒辦法告訴你了，因為我也沒見過他。」

「那我要怎麼去那裡呢？」桃樂絲問。

「你得用走的。那是一條很遠很遠的路，一路上會經過美麗的地方，也會經過黑暗又恐怖的地方。不過，我會用我所知道的一切魔法，來幫助你避免災禍。」

「你不跟我一起去嗎？」小女孩懇求道。現在，她已經把這位老婦人視為唯一的朋友了。

「不，我沒辦法跟你一起去。」她回答：「不過我會給你一個親吻，在這裡，只要是北方女巫所親吻過的人，是沒人敢傷害的。」

她走近桃樂絲，在她額頭上輕輕地吻了一下。桃樂絲後來發現，她額頭上被吻過的地方，有了一個圓圓亮亮的標記。

「通往翡翠城的那條路，都鋪上了黃色的磚塊，你不會走丟的。」女巫說：「當你見到奧茲國王的時候，別害怕，只管告訴他你的來歷，然後請他幫助你。再見

了，親愛的孩
子。」

　　三個芒奇金人
對她深深鞠了躬，祝她旅途
一切平安後，就穿越樹林離
開。女巫親切地向她點了點
頭，然後用左腳跟旋轉三次，
人就消失了。這讓托托很驚訝，
女巫走後，牠大聲吠叫。剛剛
女巫在的時候，牠怕得都不敢吭
聲。

　　桃樂絲因為知道她是個女巫，
早料到她會這樣憑空消失，所以也就
不覺得詫異了。

Chapter 3

救出稻草人

那一群人走了以後，獨自一人的桃樂絲，開始感到飢餓。她走去櫥櫃，切了點麵包，抹上奶油，並分了一些給托托。隨後，她從架子上拿了一個桶子，走到小溪旁去打了一桶清澈閃亮的水。托托跑到林子裡，對著樹上的鳥兒吠叫，桃樂絲去找牠時，發現枝頭結滿美味的果實，便摘了一些，搭配早餐吃正好。

她回到房子裡，和托托喝過清澈冰涼的溪水後，就準備動身前往翡翠城。

桃樂絲只有一件洋裝可以更換，不過還好是洗乾淨了的，就掛在她床邊的釘子上。那是一件藍白相間的格子棉布洋裝，雖然藍格子的部分因為洗刷太多次，已經有點褪色了，不過仍是件漂亮的洋裝。桃樂絲仔細梳洗，換上乾淨的洋裝，戴上粉紅色的遮陽圓帽。她拿了一個小籃子，把櫥櫃裡的麵包放進去裝滿，再蓋上一塊白布。她低下頭，看看自己的腳，腳下是一雙已經磨得很舊的鞋子。

「托托呀，這雙鞋子一定撐不了長途跋涉的。」她說。托托用牠小小的黑眼睛看著她，搖搖尾巴，表示牠明白桃樂絲的意思。

這時，桃樂絲瞥見了放在桌上的那雙東方女巫的銀鞋。

「不知道這雙鞋合不合腳？」她對托托說：「這很耐穿，適合用來走遠路。」

她脫下腳上的舊皮鞋，換上銀鞋，而銀鞋就像是特別訂做的，很合她的腳。

最後，她拿起籃子。

「托托，要跟上喔。」她說：「我們要去翡翠城，請教偉大的奧茲，要怎樣才能回堪薩斯。」

她關上門，把門鎖上，小心地將鑰匙放進洋裝的口袋裡。就這樣，她展開了她的旅程，托托跟在她後面，莊重地跑著。

附近有好幾條路，不過沒多久，她就找到了那條

鋪著黃磚塊的路。她立刻輕快地走向翡翠城，一雙銀鞋踩在堅硬的黃磚路上，發出叮叮咚咚的悅耳聲響。陽光閃耀，鳥兒吱啾，桃樂絲一個小女孩雖然突然被吹離家鄉，來到陌生的國度，但她並沒有想像中那樣的哀傷。

她一路走著，沿途的美景，令她訝異不已。沿路兩旁，盡是又整齊又乾淨的圍籬。圍籬漆著清爽的藍色，圍著一塊塊生長良好的穀物田和菜園。毫無疑問，芒奇金人長於農事，農收豐稔。她路過一旁的住家時，時而有居民跑出來盯著她看，並向她鞠躬致意。他們都知道，就是她把邪惡女巫除掉，解放了大家。芒奇金的房子都是圓形的，看起來很特別，屋頂也是圓形的，房子都漆成藍色。在這個東方國裡，藍色是最受人喜愛的顏色。

桃樂絲走了好長一段路，到了向晚時分，她走得累了，便開始想要去哪裡過夜。她走向其中一棟最大的房子，房子前的綠地上，有許多男男女女在跳舞，還有五位小提琴手正卯足勁拉出最響亮的樂音；人們歡笑歌唱，一旁的大桌子上擺滿美味的水果、堅果、派餅、蛋糕，和一大堆令人垂涎三尺的食物。

他們熱忱地招呼桃樂絲，邀她一塊吃晚餐，並留下來過夜。這戶人家是芒奇金人的大富翁，他們一夥人歡聚在此，慶祝脫離了邪惡女巫的奴役。

富有的主人叫做波克，他親自招待桃樂絲享用豐盛的晚餐。飯後，她坐在長椅上欣賞人們跳舞。

You must be a great sorceress.

看到她的銀鞋，波克說道：「你一定是位偉大的魔法師！」

「怎麼說？」她問。

「因為你穿著銀鞋，又除掉了邪惡女巫，而且你的衣服上有白色格子，只有女巫或魔法師才會穿白色的。」

「我的洋裝是藍白相間的格子。」桃樂絲一邊說，一邊把起皺的洋裝撫平。

「你這樣穿就對了。」波克說：「藍色是芒奇金人的顏色，白色是女巫的顏色，所以我們就知道，你是一個友善的女巫！」

桃樂絲不知道該怎麼回答。所有人都以為她是個女巫，但她很清楚自己只是一個普通的小女孩，恰巧被龍捲風吹來這個奇異的國度罷了。

她舞看得倦了，波克就帶她進屋子。屋內有一間房間，擺著一張美麗的床，床的被單也是藍色的。桃樂絲躺上床，一直酣睡到天亮，托托則蜷著身子，睡在一旁的藍地毯上。

桃樂絲用過豐盛的早餐後，看著一個芒奇金小嬰兒和托托在玩耍。小嬰兒拉著托托的尾巴，又叫又笑，讓桃樂絲看得津津有味。這裡的人對托托很好奇，他們還沒見過狗這種動物呢。

「翡翠城離這裡有多遠？」小女孩問。

「這我不知道。」波克沉重地回答：「我也沒去過那裡。除非有什麼特別的事，不然還是離奧茲國遠一點比較好。不管怎麼說，翡翠城離這裡有一段距離，要走好多天才到得了。我們這裡土地豐饒，環境宜人，去翡翠城卻要經過險惡的路途。」

波克的一番話，讓桃樂絲有點憂心。不過，既然只有奧茲能助她一臂之力重回堪薩斯，她就決心一往直前，不折回頭。

她向朋友道過別，又再度踏上黃磚路。走了幾哩路後，她想歇一下腳，就爬到路旁的圍籬上坐下。圍籬外是一大片玉米田，田裡不遠處有個被高高綁在竹竿上的稻草人，用來嚇阻鳥類啄食玉米。

桃樂絲雙手托著腮，若有所思地盯著稻草人看。稻草人的頭是用塞滿稻草的小袋子做成的，上面畫上眼睛、鼻子和嘴巴，裝成一張臉，頭上戴了一頂不知是哪個芒奇金人的舊尖頂藍帽；身體的部分也是稻草綁成的，還套著一件又破又舊的藍色衣服，腳上跟這裡的居民一樣，穿著一雙藍色的老舊靴子；它的背部被綁上一根竿子，好把它豎立起來。

當桃樂絲目不轉睛盯著稻草人那張古怪的臉時，稻草人竟對她緩緩地眨了一下眼睛，令她很訝異。她起先想，一定是自己眼花了，因為堪薩斯的稻草人是不會眨眼睛的。不過她隨即又發現，稻草人竟然還向她頷首致意！她爬下圍籬，走向稻草人，托托也跑向稻草人，吠個沒停。

Dorothy gazed thoughtfully at the Scarecrow.

「你好。」稻草人用他粗嘎的聲音說。

「你會說話呀？」小女孩好奇地問。

「當然囉。」稻草人回答：「你好嗎？」

「我很好，謝謝你。」小女孩禮貌地回答：「那你呢？」

「我有點不舒服。」稻草人微笑著說：「日日夜夜被綁在這裡嚇烏鴉，很無聊。」

「你不能下來嗎？」桃樂絲問。

「沒辦法，我和背上的竹竿綁在一起。如果你能幫我把竹竿拿下來，那就感激不盡了。」

桃樂絲伸出雙手，把稻草人抱了下來。稻草人是稻草做的，所以很輕。

「真的很感謝你。」稻草人下到地面時說：「我感覺煥然一新。」

桃樂絲覺得怪怪的，聽一個稻草人講話，還在一旁走動，真是件怪事。

「你叫什麼名字？」稻草人伸伸懶腰，打了個呵欠，問道：「要去什麼地方？」

「我叫桃樂絲。」小女孩回答：「我要去翡翠城，請求偉大的奧茲巫師送我回堪薩斯。」

「翡翠城在哪裡啊？」稻草人問：「奧茲又是什麼來頭？」

「什麼？你不知道啊！」她驚訝地反問稻草人。

「不知道，我一無所知。你看，我是稻草做的，根本沒有腦子。」稻草人傷心地回答。

桃樂絲回答：「噢，這真是太可憐了！」

稻草人問：「你想，我要是也跟你去翡翠城，那位奧茲先生會不會給我一些腦子？」

「這我不知道。」她回答：「不過你想去，我們就一起去吧！反正就算奧茲不給你腦子，你也沒什麼損失。」

「這倒是。」稻草人說。他向桃樂絲傾吐心事，繼續說道：「你看，我的手腳和身體都是稻草綁成的，不過這樣也沒什麼不好，因為這樣一來我就不會受傷了。就算有人踩到我的腳趾，或是拿針刺我，也無所謂，反正我不痛不癢。可是，我不希望被叫笨蛋！我的頭要是一直塞著稻草，而不是像你一樣有腦子，那我怎麼懂得了事情？」

「我可以體會你的感覺。」小女孩說，她真是為稻草人感到悲哀。「如果你跟我一起走，我就去求奧茲盡他所能來幫你。」

「謝謝你。」他充滿感激地說。

他們走回路上，桃樂絲幫稻草人翻過圍籬，然後沿著黃磚路往翡翠城前進。

一開始，托托並不喜歡這個新夥伴，老是對著他東聞西嗅，好像他的稻草裡有老鼠窩一樣，常毫不客氣對著他吠。

「別管托托。」桃樂絲對這位新朋友說：「牠不會

咬人的。」

　　「我不怕啦。」稻草人回答：「牠傷害不了稻草的。對了，讓我幫你提籃子吧，不要客氣，我不會累。」稻草人一邊走，一邊說道：「告訴你一個祕密，在這個世界上，我只怕一樣東西。」

　　「什麼東西？」桃樂絲問：「是不是把你做出來的那個芒奇金人？」

　　「不是。」稻草人回答：「是點燃的火柴。」

Chapter 4

穿越森林的路

走了幾個小時後，路越來越崎嶇難行，稻草人常常被絆倒，黃磚塊變得很不平整，有時還破裂，甚至根本就缺了一塊，留下一個窟窿在那裡。托托碰到了會跳過去，桃樂絲會繞過去，但是稻草人因為沒有腦子，只會直直走，所以老是踩到窟窿，整個人跌在堅硬的磚路上，還好他不會受傷。桃樂絲會把他拉起來，幫他重新站直，他就一邊跟上桃樂絲，一邊為自己的摔跤感到莞爾。

沿路上，農田不比之前那樣受到細心照料，屋舍果樹也越來越少。他們愈走下去，四周就愈顯得荒涼冷清。

到了中午，他們坐在沿著一條小溪的路邊。桃樂絲打開籃子，拿出一些麵包。她遞給稻草人一塊麵包，但稻草人沒有拿。

「我是不會餓的。」他說：「我不會餓，是件好事。因為我的嘴巴是畫上去的，如果把它割個洞，用來吃東西，那裡面的稻草就會跑出來，我的頭就會變形了。」

桃樂絲立刻了解這是實話，就點點頭，繼續吃她的麵包。

　　「跟我說說你的故事，還有你家鄉的事情。」桃樂絲吃完晚餐後，稻草人問道。桃樂絲就把堪薩斯的一切都告訴他，說那裡的東西都是灰色的啦，還有龍捲風如何把她帶來這個奇異的奧茲王國。稻草人專心聽著，問道：「我不懂你為什麼想離開這個美麗的地方，回去那個叫堪薩斯、又乾燥又灰暗的地方呢？」

　　「就是因為你沒有腦子，所以才不懂。」小女孩回答：「不論自己的家鄉多麼枯燥陰沉，我們有血有肉的人，都寧願待在自己的家鄉，也不願意住在其他美麗的地方。沒有一個地方，能比得上自己的家。」

　　稻草人嘆了口氣。

　　「當然我是不懂啦。」他說：「如果你們的頭也像我一樣塞著稻草，那你們應該都會選擇住在美麗的地方吧，然後堪薩斯就會毫無人煙了。還好你們有腦子，堪薩斯才會有人住。」

　　「趁我們現在
休息，講一個故事
給我聽如何？」小
女孩問。

　　稻草人責難地
看著她，回答道：
「我的生命才剛開
始，什麼都不懂。

我是前天才被人做出來的。在那之前，世界上所發生的事我都不知道。還好的是，農夫在做我的頭的時候，先畫我的耳朵，讓我聽得到發生了什麼事。當時，有另一個芒奇金人跟他在一起。我聽到的第一句話是，農夫說：『你覺得這對耳朵如何？』

『耳朵不是很正。』另一個人說。

『沒關係啦。』農夫說：『不就耳朵嘛。』他說得倒也沒錯啦。

『現在我要來畫眼睛。』農夫說。然後他就開始畫我的右眼，等畫完的時候，我發現自己正滿心好奇地盯著農夫和周遭瞧，這是我第一次見到這世界。

『這眼睛畫得很不錯。』芒奇金人一邊瞧著，一邊說道：『藍色最適合用來畫眼睛了。』

『我打算把另外一個眼睛畫大一些。』農夫說。等他畫完了我的左眼，我立刻看得更清楚了。後來他又畫了鼻子和嘴巴，不過我沒說話，因為那時我還不清楚嘴巴是用來做什麼的。我饒富興味地看他們束起我的身體、手臂和腳，最後他們綁好我的頭時，我覺得非常驕傲，因為我認為我跟其他人一樣的完好了。

『這傢伙一定可以把烏鴉嚇得遠遠的。』農夫說：『他看起來簡直跟真人沒有兩樣。』

『當然囉，他就是個人呀。』另一個人說。這一點我很同意。農夫把我夾在手臂下，帶到玉米田裡，把我綁在長竿上，也就是你發現我的那個地方。隨後農夫和

"I was only made day before yesterday," said the Scarecrow.

他的友人就離開，留下我一個人。

「我不喜歡這樣被丟下，我想跟他們一起走，可是我的腳碰不到地，只好待在長竿上。那種生活是很孤單的，我才剛來到這世上，連可以思考的事情都少得可憐。很多烏鴉和鳥飛來這片玉米田，不過牠們以為我是個芒奇金人，所以一看到我就飛走了。我看了覺得很過癮，好像自己很重要。但後來有一隻老烏鴉飛過來仔細打量我之後，就停在我的肩膀上叫道：『農夫竟然想用這種笨法子來騙我。只要是有見識的烏鴉，都會知道你只是稻草做的呀。』然後牠就跳到我的腳上，隨心所欲地啄食玉米。其他的鳥看到烏鴉安然無事，也飛過來啄玉米。沒多久，我旁邊就聚集了一大堆鳥兒了。

「我很難過，因為這表示我不是一個優秀的稻草人。不過老烏鴉安慰我說：『如果你有腦子，那你就會跟其他人一樣優秀，甚至比某些人更棒。不管是對烏鴉或是對人來說，腦子都是這世界上最值得擁有的東西。』

「那些烏鴉飛走了以後，我把牠的話想了又想，決定要努力得到腦子。算我幸運，你把我從長竿上放下來，而且如你所說的，我想只要我們到翡翠城，偉大的奧茲一定能給我腦子的。」

「我也希望。」桃樂絲真誠地說：「而且你又真的那麼想要腦子。」

「噢，對呀，我是很想。」稻草人回答：「知道自己是個笨蛋,可不好受。」

小女孩說:「嗯。我們走吧。」說著便把籃子交給稻草人。

現在,道路兩旁已經完全看不到圍籬,地面高低不平,一片荒蕪。接近傍晚時,他們走近一片大森林,高聳的樹木緊緊毗鄰,黃磚道上枝葉交疊。濃密的樹蔭阻擋了陽光,樹下幾乎一片漆黑。不過,他們沒有停下腳步,仍繼續往森林裡走去。

「既然可以從這條路走進森林,一定也可以從這條路走出森林的。」稻草人說:「而且既然翡翠城在路的另一頭,我們就要沿著這條路走。」

「這人盡皆知。」桃樂絲說。

「當然囉,所以我才會知道。」稻草人回答:「如果需要用到腦筋想才知道,那我就不會懂得要這樣說了。」

約莫又走了一個小時後,天色漸漸暗了,他們只能摸黑地蹣跚前進。桃樂絲完全看不到路,不過托托還看得見,有些狗在黑暗中可以看得很清楚。稻草人也說他可以看得跟白天一樣清楚,所以她挽著稻草人的手走,這樣

就不成問題了。

　　「如果你有看到房子，或是什麼可以讓我們過夜的地方，你一定要跟我說。」她說：「因為在黑暗中趕路實在很不方便。」

　　沒多久，稻草人停下了腳步。

　　「我們右手邊有一間小農舍。」他說：「是用圓木和樹枝搭的，要去嗎？」

　　「當然要呀，我已經筋疲力竭了。」孩子回答。

　　於是稻草人帶桃樂絲穿過樹叢，走到小農舍。桃樂絲走進屋內，在角落裡發現一張枯葉鋪成的床，就立刻躺了上去，進入夢鄉。托托也在一旁躺著，而不會疲倦的稻草人就站在另一個角落，耐心地等候天亮。

Chapter 5

拯救鐵錫樵夫

當桃樂絲醒來時，陽光已經照進樹叢，而托托早就出去追逐鳥兒和松鼠了。她坐起來看看四周，稻草人還是耐心地站在角落裡，等她醒來。

「我們要去找一些水來。」她告訴稻草人。

「要水做什麼啊？」他問。

「我要洗臉，這一路上灰塵不少，而且我還要喝水，乾麵包才不會卡在喉嚨裡。」

「用肉做成的身體想必很不方便。」稻草人一邊想，一邊說道：「要睡，要吃，還要喝。不過你們有腦子能好好思考，就算有這麼多不方便，也是值得的吧。」

他們離開農舍，穿越樹林，直到找到一處清澈的泉水。桃樂絲在那裡喝水、清洗、吃早餐。她心想，還好稻草人不用吃東西，因為籃子裡的麵包所剩不多，只夠她和托托今天吃。

吃完早餐，就在準備啟程回到黃磚路時，她聽到附近傳來一聲深沉的低吟聲，嚇了一跳。

「那是什麼？」她害怕地問道。

稻草人回答：「我想不出來那是什麼，不過我們可以過去看看。」

　　這時，又傳來另一聲低吟，聲音似乎是從他們後方傳來的。他們轉過身，走進樹林幾步後，桃樂絲發現在陽光的照耀下，樹林間有個東西，被照得反光。她往那個地方跑過去，突然又停下腳步，驚叫了一聲。

　　她看到有一棵大樹被砍到一半，樹旁站了一個手舉著斧頭、全身都是用錫做的人。那個人的頭、手臂和腳，都有連接到身體上，可是卻動也不動地站著，好像無法動彈。

　　桃樂絲吃驚地看著他，稻草人也是。托托更對他大叫，還咬了錫人的腿一口，結果咬得自己牙齒痛。

　　「是你在呻吟嗎？」桃樂絲問。

　　錫人答道：「是的，是我在呻吟。我已經在這裡叫了一年多了，可是一直都沒有人聽見，也沒有人過來幫我。」

　　「要怎樣做才能幫你呢？」桃樂絲輕聲地問。錫人悲傷的聲音令她不忍。

　　「拿油罐來，幫我把關節上油。」他回答：「我的關節鏽得很厲害，完全不能動了。不過只要上了油，很快就可以恢復正常。油罐就放在我農舍裡的一個架子上。」

　　桃樂絲旋即跑回農舍，找到油罐，回來後著急地問：「哪裡的關節？」

　　「先幫我的脖子上油。」鐵錫樵夫回答。她便將脖子上油，可是因為脖子鏽得很嚴重，還得稻草人捧著他的頭，把頭輕輕地左右來回轉動，一直到轉順了，錫人才能自己轉動頭部。

　　「現在幫我手臂的關節上油。」他說。桃樂絲也幫他上了油，稻草人小心翼翼幫忙彎曲手臂，直到手臂像新做的一樣，沒有再被鏽住。

　　錫人發出一聲滿意的嘆息，放下那把一直靠在樹幹上的斧頭。

　　「真是太好了。」他說：「自從我生鏽以後，我就一直舉著這把斧頭，真高興現在終於可以把它放下來了。如果你可以再幫我把腿關節也上油，那我就可以再次活動自如了。」

　　於是他們再幫他的腿關節上了油，直到關節可以自由轉動。他再三感謝桃樂絲和稻草人解救他，看來他是很懂得禮貌和感恩的。

　　「如果不是你們來，我就要永遠站在這了。」他說：「你們真的是救了我一命。你們怎麼會剛好來這裡呢？」

　　「我們正要去翡翠城找偉大的奧茲。」她回答：「我們還在你的農舍借宿了一夜。」

"This is a great comfort," said the Tin Woodman.

「你們為什麼想要去找奧茲？」他問。

「我要請他送我回堪薩斯，稻草人則希望他能在他的頭裡放一點腦子。」她回答。

鐵錫樵夫一副深思的樣子，一會兒後，說道：「你想，奧茲能不能給我一顆心呢？」

「嗯，我想可以吧。」桃樂絲回答：「就像給稻草人腦子一樣的容易。」

「這倒是。」鐵錫樵夫回答：「那如果你們願意讓我加入，我也要去翡翠城請求奧茲幫助我。」

「那就一起來吧。」稻草人衷心地說。桃樂絲也表示很高興有錫人可以作伴。於是錫人扛起斧頭，一夥人穿越樹林，回到黃磚路上。

錫人拜託桃樂絲把油罐放進籃子裡，說道：「萬一我被雨淋到，又生鏽了，那我就非得要有這罐油不可。」

他們有這位新夥伴加入算是很幸運的，因為出發不久，他們就走到了一個枝葉叢生的地方，路被擋住，無法通行。多虧鐵錫樵夫拿著他的斧頭，熟練地砍著，很快就清出了一條路讓人走了。

一路走著，桃樂絲走得出神，沒注意到稻草人被地上的坑洞給絆倒，摔到了路邊。稻草人只好出聲，叫她幫忙把自己拉起來。

「你為什麼不繞過去？」鐵錫樵夫問。

「因為我不懂呀。」稻草人興高采烈地說：「你也知道，我的頭是稻草塞成的，所以我才要去求奧茲給我

一些腦子。」

「噢，我懂了。」錫人說：「不過呀，到頭來，腦子並不是世界上最好的東西。」

「你有腦子嗎？」稻草人問。

「沒有，我的頭是空的。」錫人回答：「不過我曾經有過腦子和心，兩個都用過以後，我寧願要心。」

「為什麼？」稻草人問。

「我跟你說我的故事，你就知道了。」

於是在穿越森林的路上，錫人就說了自己的故事：

「我的父親是一位樵夫，在森林中伐木，賣柴維生。我長大了以後，也成了樵夫。自從父親去世之後，我就照顧我母親，直到她離開人世。後來我決定要結婚，不要一個人生活，才不會孤單。

那時，有一位長得很美的芒奇金女孩，令我一見傾心。她答應我，只要我賺到足夠的錢，為她建造一間更舒適的房子，她就嫁給我。所以，我就更加努力工作。但是，那位女孩和一個老婦人住在一起，老婦人很懶惰，她不希望女孩出嫁，想把她留在身邊，好幫她煮飯做家事。為此，老婦人就跑去找東方邪惡女巫，並答應只要女巫能阻止我們結婚，就會送上兩隻羊和一頭牛。於是邪惡女巫就對我的斧頭下咒。有一天，當我正全力砍著柴，希望可以早點蓋新房、娶新娘的時候，斧頭滑了下來，砍斷我的左腿。

　　一開始，我覺得這是一個很大的災難，因為我知道，缺一條腿的人是不可能成為一個出色的樵夫的。所以我就去找錫匠，要他幫我用錫做一條新的腿。新的腿功能很好，我也漸漸習慣了。可是我這個舉動觸怒了東方邪惡女巫，因為她承諾過老婦人，不會讓我娶那位美麗的芒奇金女孩。所以當我再去砍柴時，斧頭又掉了下來，砍斷我的右腿。我再度去找錫匠，他又幫我做了一隻錫腿。後來被下咒的斧頭連續砍斷我的雙臂。但我不氣餒，改用錫手臂來代替。後來，邪惡女巫又讓斧頭砍落我的頭。起初我以為自己必死無疑，好在錫匠剛好路過，又幫我用錫做了一個頭。

　　我本來以為我打敗邪惡女巫了，就更加努力工作。

但我未察自己的敵人，究竟有多麼殘暴不仁。女巫又想到別的方法，要讓我對女孩死心。她再一次讓我的斧頭掉落，砍中我的身體，把我劈成兩半。又幸虧錫匠再次來解救我，幫我做了一個錫製的身體，還把錫做的手、腿和頭，用零件連接起來，讓我可以依舊活動自如。但是，唉！我現在沒有了心，對那位芒奇金女孩的愛也就蕩然無存，一點也不在乎能不能娶到她了。我猜，她大概還是和那個老婦人住在一起，等著我去找她吧。

我的身體在太陽下會閃閃發亮，我覺得很神氣，而且現在斧頭再掉下來也不打緊了，反正傷不了我。我唯一的危險就是關節會生鏽，不過我農舍裡都會放油罐，隨時幫自己上油。只是有一天，我忘了上油，而且又遇上暴風雨，在我意識到危險之前，我的關節就生鏽了，我就一直站在樹林中，直到你們來幫我。這實在很悽慘，不過在我站在那裡的這一年當中，也讓我有時間去思考。我明白到，我這一生中最大的損失，就是失去了我的心。當我戀愛時，我是世上最快樂的人。然而沒有了心的人，是沒辦法去愛的。所以我決心要拜託奧茲給我一顆心，如果我成功了，我就要回去找那位芒奇金女孩，娶她為妻。」

鐵錫樵夫的故事，讓桃樂絲和稻草人聽得入迷，他們現在明白他為什麼渴望一顆新的心了。

稻草人說：「雖說如此，我還是要腦子，而不是心，因為一個傻子就算有了心，也不會懂得心要怎麼使用。」

「我要心。」鐵錫樵夫回答：「因為腦子無法使人快樂，但快樂是世上最重要的東西。」

桃樂絲沒作聲，她搞不清楚這兩個朋友誰說的對。不過她認為，只要能回到堪薩斯和愛姆嬸嬸身邊，那不管是樵夫沒有腦，還是稻草人沒有心，或者他們都能如願以償，都沒那麼重要了。

最讓她擔心的是，麵包快要吃完了。等她和托托吃完下一餐後，籃子就空了。她確定錫人和稻草人都不需要吃東西，可是她不是錫或稻草做的，如果沒有東西吃，她就活不下去了。

Chapter 6

膽小的獅子

桃樂絲一行人在蓊鬱的森林中不斷前進，路面上雖然仍舖著黃磚，但因為上面覆蓋了一層枯枝落葉，所以很不好走。

在這一帶的森林裡，鳥類不多，因為鳥喜歡開闊的地方，陽光比較充足。但樹林裡有野獸，不時會傳來低吼的聲音，讓桃樂絲心驚膽戰，不知道是什麼動物在吼叫。不過托托知道是誰在叫，所以牠跟緊在桃樂絲腳邊，不敢吠回去。

「還要多久，我們才能走出這片森林？」孩子問鐵錫樵夫。

「我不知道，我也沒去過翡翠城。」他回答：「不過在我小時候，我父親曾去過一次。他說，奧茲所居住的地方雖然很美麗，可是去那裡要經過很多危險的地方。不過，我呢，只要有油罐在手，就不怕了；稻草人呢，他不會受傷；而你，額頭上有善良女巫親吻的印記，可以保護你不受到傷害。」

「那托托怎麼辦？」桃樂絲緊張地說道：「誰來保護托托？」

「如果牠遭遇危險，我們必須自己保護牠。」鐵錫樵夫回答。

就在他說話的這當時，森林裡傳來了一聲可怕的吼叫聲。接著，路上就跳出了一隻大獅子。獅子腳掌一揮，把稻草人打得團團轉，滾到了路邊。接著牠用尖爪攻擊錫人，卻吃了一驚，因為牠的爪子傷不了錫人，儘管錫人也被打得跌在馬路上不動。

這一刻，小托托得面對這個敵人了。牠跑上前，對著獅子大聲吠叫。這頭大野獸張開嘴巴要咬小狗，桃樂絲怕托托會被咬死，便不顧危險地衝到獅子面前，使盡力氣摳獅子的鼻子，一邊叫道：「你竟敢咬托托！你應該為自己感到可恥，像你這樣一頭大野獸，竟然想欺負可憐的小狗！」

「我沒有咬牠！」獅子一邊說，一邊用腳掌揉著剛被桃樂絲打到的鼻子。

「你是還沒有咬牠，不過你想呀。」桃樂絲回嘴道：「你只是一個長得又高又大的懦夫罷了。」

「這我知道。」獅子羞愧地低下頭，說道：「我一直都知道呀，可是能怎麼辦呢？」

「我哪知道啊。你想想，你竟然還攻擊稻草人這種用稻草塞成的人！」

You ought to be ashamed of yourself!

「他是用稻草塞成的嗎？」獅子驚訝地問，一邊看著桃樂絲把稻草人拉起來扶正，拍一拍他，讓他恢復原來的形狀。

「他當然是稻草做的呀！」還氣呼呼的桃樂絲回答。

「難怪他那麼容易就翻倒。看他那樣團團轉，還真嚇了我一跳。那另一個也是稻草做的嗎？」獅子說。

桃樂絲回答：「不是，他是錫做的。」說著，她就去扶錫人起來。

「難怪他快把我的爪子給弄鈍了。」獅子說：「我抓到錫皮的時候，背上打了個冷顫。那隻小動物又是什麼，你這麼保護牠？」

「牠是我的狗，叫托托。」桃樂絲回答。

「牠是錫做的嗎？還是稻草？」獅子問。

「都不是。牠是……嗯……是……一隻有血有肉的狗。」小女孩說。

「噢，牠真是隻奇怪的動物，我現在看牠，牠長得可真小，除了像我這樣一個懦夫之外，沒人會想咬這樣一個小東西的。」獅子一臉悲哀地說。

「你怎麼會這麼膽小？」桃樂絲問道，納悶地看著眼前這個和一匹小馬差不多大的大野獸。

「這是個謎。」獅子回答：「我猜我一出生就是這個樣子了。獅子不管走到哪裡，都被尊為萬獸之王，森林裡所有的動物自然都認為我很勇敢。我發現只要我大吼一聲，所有動物就會嚇得半死，然後躲得遠遠的。每當我碰到人類，我就怕得要命，不過我還是對他吼，然後他就會一溜煙逃走。如果有大象、老虎或是熊想要跟我挑戰，我會逃之夭夭──我就是這麼一個膽小鬼。還好的是，牠們只要聽到我的吼聲，就會想離我遠一點，當然啦，我就會任牠們溜掉。」

「可是這樣是不對的，萬獸之王不應該是個懦夫。」稻草人說。

獅子一邊用尾巴的末端擦著眼淚，一邊說道：「這我知道，這是我最難過的事了，讓我活得很悶。可是，只要一遇到危險，我的心就會跳得很快。」

「搞不好你有心臟病。」鐵錫樵夫說。

「有可能。」獅子說。

鐵錫樵夫繼續說：「如果你有心臟病，那你應該感到高興，因為這證明了你有一顆心。像我就沒有心，所以根本不可能有心臟病。」

「大概是吧。」獅子想了想，說道：「如果我沒有心，我就不會是懦夫了。」

「那你有腦子嗎？」稻草人問。

「我猜是有，不過我自己

也沒看過。」獅子回答。

「我要去找偉大的奧茲，請他給我腦子。」稻草人說：「因為我的頭是用稻草紮成的。」

「我要請他給我一顆心。」錫人說。

「我要請他送我和托托回堪薩斯。」桃樂絲補充道。

「你覺得奧茲會給我勇氣嗎？」膽小的獅子問。

「那會像給我腦子一樣地簡單吧。」稻草人說。

「或是像給我心一樣地簡單。」錫人說。

「或是像送我回堪薩斯一樣地簡單。」桃樂絲說。

「那如果你們不介意，我就跟你們一起走。」獅子說：「如果沒有勇氣，我簡直無法忍受我的這一生。」

「我們很歡迎你，你能嚇走其他的野獸。」桃樂絲回答：「不過，我覺得如果牠們這麼容易就被你唬住了，那牠們應該比你還膽小吧。」

「牠們是很膽小。」獅子說：「不過即使如此，我也沒有變得比較勇敢。我只要一想到自己是個懦夫，就很鬱悶。」

這幾個夥伴於是繼續啟程。獅子威風凜凜地走在桃樂絲旁邊，托托起初不贊成這個新夥伴加入，牠很難忘掉自己差一點命喪獅口。不過一段時間後，牠就比較放鬆自在了。現在，托托和膽小的獅子逐漸成了好朋友。

這一天接下來沒有發生什麼事，一路平安。但有一次，錫人踩到一隻在地上爬行的甲蟲，踏死了這個可憐小生命。錫人為此感到難過，因為他一向很小心不要去傷害任何的生命。他一邊走著，流下了幾滴傷心後悔的眼淚。眼淚慢慢從他臉上滑落，流到了下巴的關節，結果關節就生鏽了。下巴因為生鏽而緊緊合住，所以桃樂絲問他問題時，他沒辦法開口回答。他很慌張，比手劃腳要桃樂絲幫他解圍，但是桃樂絲沒有意會出來，獅子也摸不著頭腦，不知道出了什麼問頭。只有稻草人從桃樂絲的籃子裡拿出油罐，幫他的下巴上油。沒多久，他才又說話自如了。

「我學到一個教訓，那就是要注意腳下。」他說：「如果我又殺了小蟲或甲蟲，我鐵定又要哭，而我一哭，下巴就會生鏽，然後就不能說話了。」

之後，他走起路來格外小心，眼睛緊盯著路面，他看到有小螞蟻在爬行，就繞過去，免得傷到牠。錫人很清楚自己沒有心，所以他就更加小心，千萬不要殘忍粗暴地對待了什麼東西。

他說：「你們有心的人，是有指引的，所以不會做錯事。可是我沒有，所以一定要加倍小心。當然，在奧茲給我一顆心以後，我就不用這樣地小心翼翼了。」

Chapter 7

驚險的旅程

當晚，因為附近找不到房子，他們就在森林中的一棵大樹下野營過夜。大樹枝葉繁密，讓他們不會被露水沾濕。錫人用斧頭砍了一大堆木柴，桃樂絲升了火，火很旺，讓她覺得暖和，不那麼冷清。她和托托吃完了籃子裡僅剩的麵包後，就不知道要吃什麼來當明天的早餐了。

「如果你想，我可以去森林裡殺一隻鹿來給你。」獅子說：「你們的口味很特別，喜歡吃煮熟的東西，你可以把鹿烤來吃，這樣你就有豐盛的早餐了。」

「不，請不要這樣做。」錫人懇求道：「如果你殺了可憐的鹿，我一定會哭的，那我的下巴又要生鏽了。」

獅子只管逕自走進樹林，去尋找牠自己的晚餐。至於牠吃了些什麼，牠沒提起，我們也不得而知。稻草人找到一棵結滿堅果的樹，他把桃樂絲的籃子裝滿堅果，這樣她就有好長一段時間不必挨餓。她覺得稻草人好心又體貼，只不過，看到稻草人採集堅果的怪樣子，她還是忍不住打從心底笑了起來。他那稻草紮的手實在笨拙，堅果又很小，所以掉落在地上的堅果，和裝進籃子裡的一樣多。但稻草人倒不介意花時間來裝滿籃子，因為這樣他也可以遠離營火。他怕火星濺到身上，會把他燒成灰燼，所以總是跟火堆保持安全距離。只有當桃樂絲躺下睡著時，他才會過去幫她蓋  上乾燥的樹葉，讓她睡得舒適溫暖，一覺到天亮。

　　天亮時，小女孩在小溪流中洗過臉。不久，大家就一起出發前往翡翠城。

　　對這些旅人來說，今天是多事的一天。走不到一個小時，他們就碰到一個深谷。道路被中斷，森林一分為二，遠遠望過去，只能看到對崖。深谷很寬，他們爬到崖邊往下看，發現谷也很深。谷底有很多巨大的尖石，谷壁也非常陡峭，爬不下去。眼前看來，他們的旅程似乎要告一段落了。

　　「怎麼辦呢？」桃樂絲失望地問。

　　「我一點主意也沒有。」錫人說。獅子搖搖鬃毛，似乎陷入了沉思。

　　但稻草人說：「我們不會飛，這是可以確定的，而且我們也沒辦法爬下大深谷。所以如果我們不跳過去，就得在這裡結束了。」

「我想我可以跳得過去。」膽小的獅子仔細評估了距離後說道。

「那就沒問題了。」稻草人回答：「你可以把我們帶過去，一次一個。」

「好，我來試試看。」獅子問道：「誰要先來？」

「我先來。」稻草人說：「你要是跳不過去，桃樂絲會摔死，錫人掉到下面的岩石上會撞壞，但我坐在你的背上不會有這些顧慮，就算掉下去，我也毫髮無傷。」

「我自己也很怕會掉下去。」膽小的獅子說：「不過我想除了試試看，也沒有其他辦法了。上來吧，我們試看看。」

稻草人坐上獅子的背之後，這隻大野獸走到崖邊蹲伏了下來。

「你怎麼不助跑，然後跳過去？」稻草人問。

「那不是我們獅子的作風。」牠回答。獅子一躍而起，躍過空中，平安到達對崖。大夥看到獅子輕而易舉地跳過去，歡喜不已。稻草人從獅背上下來之

後，獅子
又再度跳過山
谷回到這一邊。

　　桃樂絲想下一個應該
是她，便抱起托托，爬到獅子
背上，一隻手緊緊抓住獅子的鬃毛。接
著，她簡直像是在空中飛翔一樣，但她還來不及想些什
麼，就已經安全到達另一邊了。獅子又第三次跳回去，
把錫人接過來。之後，他們坐下來休息了一會兒，讓獅
子喘口氣。接連著幾次的大跳躍，讓獅子很喘，就像一
隻跑了很久的狗一樣。

　　他們發現這邊的森林非常茂密，望過去又黑又陰
森。等獅子休息過後，他們又踏上黃磚路。他們每個人
都暗自心忖，不知能否走出這片森林，重見燦爛的陽
光。讓他們感到更不安的是，他們不久就聽到了從森林
深處傳出的怪聲音。獅子小聲地向大家說，這附近是
「喀力靶」的勢力範圍。

　　「什麼是『喀力靶』？」女孩問。

　　「喀力靶是一種殘暴的野獸，身體像熊，頭像老
虎。」獅子回答：「爪子又長又利，可以輕易地把我撕

成兩半，就像我殺托托那樣地簡單。我怕死喀力鞑了。」

「也難怪你會怕，牠們一定是很可怕的怪獸。」桃樂絲說。

獅子正要說話時，他們不期又碰到了另一個谷溝，道路又被中斷。這個谷溝又寬又深，獅子立刻知道自己是跳不過去的。

他們坐了下來，思索對策。稻草人仔細考慮後說道：「谷邊有一棵大樹，如果錫人可以把它砍倒，它就會倒向谷的另一邊，那我們要走過去就容易了。」

「這真是個一流的點子。」獅子說：「別人會以為你的頭殼裡有腦子，而不是稻草。」

錫人立刻動手。他的斧頭很利，樹一下子就幾乎整個被砍斷。隨後，獅子用牠強而有力的前肢，使勁推著樹幹，大樹慢慢傾斜，最後砰一聲，樹幹橫過谷溝，樹梢落在谿谷的另一端。

就在他們正準備走過這座不尋常的橋時，一陣尖銳的吼聲，讓他們抬頭張望了起來。接著，只見兩隻身體像熊、頭像老虎的大怪獸朝他們奔過來，把他們給嚇壞了。

「那就是喀力鞑！」膽小的獅子說罷，便開始發抖。

「快！」稻草人喊道：「我們快過去！」

於是桃樂絲抱起托托走在最前面，後面跟著錫人，再來是稻草人。獅子雖然心裡著實害怕，但還是轉過身去面對喀力軛。獅子發出又大聲又可怕的吼叫聲，嚇得桃樂絲尖叫，稻草人往後翻了過去，而凶猛的野獸也突然愣住，吃驚地看著獅子。

不過，野獸發現自己的體型比獅子大，而且又是二對一，便又衝了上來。獅子走過樹幹，轉身看喀力軛有什麼動靜。喀力軛沒有緩下腳步，牠們也開始走上樹幹做成的橋。獅子對桃樂絲說：「我們輸了，牠們一定會用尖銳的爪子把我們撕成碎片的。不過站在我身後吧，只要我還有一口氣在，我就一定跟牠們拚到底。」

「等一下！」稻草人叫道。他一直在思索怎麼做最好，現在，他叫錫人把這一端的樹幹砍斷。錫人立刻拿起斧頭砍樹，就在兩隻喀力軛快要通過橋時，樹幹斷落，連同兩隻咆哮的可怕野獸掉進深谷。野獸就在尖石林立的谷底，摔得粉碎了。

膽小的獅子呼出長長的一口氣，放心地說道：「好了，真慶幸我們可以再活久一些。我想，死掉的感覺一定很難受。那些怪物真把我嚇壞了，我的心臟到現在還在跳。」

錫人悲傷地說：「啊！我希望我也有一顆心可以跳。」

這場經歷，讓他們更一心想走出森林。他們加緊腳步走得很快，讓桃樂絲覺得很累，只好騎在獅子的背上。讓他們很高興的是，他們愈往前走，森林就愈沒那麼濃密。到了下午，他們看到一條寬闊的河流橫在前

The tree fell with a crash into the gulf.

面，河水滔滔。在河的另一岸，可以看見黃磚路在美麗的大地上蜿蜒著，鮮綠的草地上點綴著鮮豔的花朵，路旁都是長滿豐碩果實的果樹。看到眼前這個宜人地方，他們的心情為之一振。

「我們要怎麼過河呢？」桃樂絲問。

稻草人說：「這簡單，錫人做一個木筏，我們就能漂到對岸。」

於是錫人拿起斧頭，砍了一些小樹來做木筏。就在他忙著進行時，稻草人看到岸邊有一棵樹，長滿鮮美的水果。桃樂絲很高興，因為她今天一整天只吃了堅果，便給自己來了一頓豐盛的水果大餐。

就算鐵錫樵夫很勤奮，又不會累，但做木筏還是需要一些時間。當夜幕降臨，木筏還沒造好，於是他們就在樹下找了個舒適的地方，休息到天亮。夢裡，桃樂絲見到了翡翠城，還有即將送她回家的好心奧茲巫師。

Chapter 8

致命的罌粟花田

隔天早晨，這一群人醒來時，回復了精神，也充滿了希望。桃樂絲摘下河邊樹上的桃子和李子當早餐，就像公主所吃的一樣。他們歷經千辛萬苦，平安通過身後的黑暗森林，如今眼前這塊美麗地方，陽光一片燦爛，彷彿在召喚他們走向翡翠城。

的確大河把他們和那塊美麗的地方隔了開來，不過木筏就快完成了，只要錫人再砍一些木柴，用木釘接起來，他們就可以啟程出發。桃樂絲坐在木筏中央，將托托抱在懷裡；膽小的獅子踏上木筏時，因為牠又大又重，木筏傾斜得很厲害，還好有稻草人和錫人站在另一頭，才穩住木筏。他們兩人手拿長竿，撐筏前進。

一開始，他們前進得很順利，但到了河中央時，急流把木筏往下游推，愈來愈偏離黃磚路，而且河水也愈來愈深，長竿也搆不到河底。

錫人說：「糟了，如果我們不能到對岸，就會被帶到西方邪惡女巫的國土，她會對我們下咒，把我們都變成她的奴隸。」

「那我就得不到腦子了。」稻草人說。

「那我就得不到勇氣了。」膽小的獅子說。

「那我就得不到心了。」鐵錫樵夫說。

「那我就永遠回不了堪薩斯了。」桃樂絲說。

「如果可以，我們一定要到翡翠城。」稻草人說。他撐筏撐得很用力，結果長竿牢牢卡在河底的污泥裡。接著，在他還來不及把長竿拔出來或放開之前，木筏被水流給沖開去，可憐的稻草人就被留在河中的長竿上了。

「再見了！」稻草人在他們的身後喊著。把稻草人拋在後面，大家感到非常難過。錫人已經哭了起來，還好他意識到自己會生鏽，就用桃樂絲的圍裙把眼淚擦掉。

當然，這對稻草人來說是件悽慘的事。

「我現在的樣子，比我初遇桃樂絲時，來得更加悲慘了。」他想：「那時我被綁在玉米田裡的竹竿上，至少還可以裝裝樣子嚇唬烏鴉。可是，一個稻草人待在河中的一根竹竿上，是一點作用也沒有的。我恐怕永遠都得不到腦子了！」

木筏漂流而下，把可憐的稻草人遠遠地留在後面。獅子說：「我們必須想辦法自救。你們在木筏上抓住我的尾巴，我想我可以拖著木筏游到岸邊。」

　　獅子躍入水中，錫人立刻牢牢抓住牠的尾巴，然後獅子開始使勁游向岸邊。雖然獅子體型很大，但這對牠來說還是很費力的。慢慢地，他們脫離了急流，桃樂絲也拿起錫人的長竿，幫忙把木筏撐向岸邊。

　　終於，他們上了岸，踏上美麗的綠草地，但每個人也都筋疲力竭了。他們很清楚，水流把他們遠遠沖離了通往翡翠城的黃磚路。

　　「我們現在該怎麼辦？」錫人問。獅子則躺在草地上，讓太陽把牠的毛曬乾。

　　「我們一定要想辦法回到黃磚路上。」桃樂絲說。

　　「最好的辦法，就是沿著河岸走回黃磚路。」獅子說。

　　他們休息過後，桃樂絲提起籃子，大家便一齊沿著長滿青草的河岸，走回河流把他們沖走的地方。這個地方景色宜人，遍地花草果樹，還有令人振奮的陽光。要不是大家還在為可憐的稻草人感到難過，那他們一定很快樂。

他們用最快的速度往前走。途中，桃樂絲只停過一次腳步，去摘一朵漂亮的花。過了一會兒，錫人叫道：「看！」

大家一齊望向河流，看到了稻草人就攀在河中的長竿上，一副孤單又傷心的模樣。

「有什麼方法能救他？」桃樂絲問。

獅子和錫人搖搖頭，想不出好主意，就坐在岸邊悲傷地望著稻草人。後來，有一隻鸛鳥飛過，看到他們，便在岸邊停了下來。

「你們是誰？要往哪裡去？」鸛鳥問。

女孩回答：「我叫桃樂絲，他們是我的朋友，鐵錫樵夫和膽小的獅子。我們正要去翡翠城。」

鸛鳥扭著長頸，目光銳利地看著這群奇怪的組合，說道：「那不是走這條路。」

桃樂絲回答：「我知道，可是我們失去了稻草人，正在想著要怎麼把他救回來。」

「他在哪裡？」鸛鳥問。

「就在河那裡。」小女孩回答。

「要是他沒那麼大又那麼重的話，我可以幫你們把他帶過來。」鸛鳥說。

「他一點也不重，他是用稻草紮成的。」桃樂絲急切地說：「如果你把他帶過來，我們會非常非常感激你的！」

「好吧，我試試看。」鸛鳥說：「可是如果我發現他

The stork carried him up into the air.

太重，提不動，那我就只好把他扔回河裡了。」

於是這隻大鳥飛到空中，往河中稻草人抱住長竿的地方飛去。接著，鸛鳥用她的大爪子抓住稻草人的手臂，提著他飛到空中，回到河岸邊，桃樂絲、獅子、錫人和托托都坐在那裡。

稻草人發現自己又回到這群朋友的身邊，高興得抱住每一個人，連獅子和托托也不例外。他興奮不已，大夥往前走時，他每走一步，就高唱一句「多──得──力──的──悠！」，非常雀躍。

「我很害怕要永遠待在河裡。」他說：「不過好心的鸛鳥救了我，要是我真的得到腦子，我一定要回來找牠，報答牠。」

在他們一旁飛著的鸛鳥說道：「這沒什麼，我很樂意幫助有難的人。不過現在我得走了，我的寶寶還在巢裡等我。希望你們能找到翡翠城，也希望奧茲能幫助你們。」

「謝謝你。」桃樂絲說完，好心的鸛鳥便飛入天際，很快就不見蹤影。

他們一路向前走，聽著豔麗的鳥兒啁啾歌唱，欣賞著鋪滿大地的美麗花朵。那些大朵大朵的花，有黃色的啊，白色的啊，藍色的啊，還有紫色的。另外還有一大叢一大叢的緋色罌粟花，顏色亮麗奪目，讓桃樂絲幾乎睜不開眼睛。

「它們真是漂亮啊，不是嗎？」桃樂絲一邊說道，一邊聞著花的香氣。

　　「我想是的。」稻草人回答：「等我有腦子了，我可能會更加喜愛它們。」

　　「如果我有了心，一定會愛上它們。」錫人說道。

　　「我一向都喜歡花，它們看起來那麼嬌弱。」獅子說：「不過，森林裡的花沒有這麼鮮豔的。」

　　路旁深紅色的大罌粟花愈來愈多，其他的花愈來愈少。不久，他們就發現自己站在一大片罌粟花田之中。

　　大家現在都知道，很多罌粟花叢聚在一起時，香味會很濃，濃到人一聞到，就會昏睡過去。而如果不把昏睡的人帶離有香味的地方，他們就會一直昏睡下去。但桃樂絲並不知道這件事，況且這裡到處都是緋紅的罌粟花，也沒辦法離開。這時，她的眼皮越來越重，覺得自己一定要坐下來休息，睡上一覺。

但是錫人不會任她這麼做。

　　「我們得趕路，趁天黑之前，走回黃磚路。」他說。稻草人也表示同意。於是他們繼續趕路，直到桃樂絲再也站不住。她的眼睛不由自主地闔上，忘了自己身在何處，就這樣栽進罌粟田中睡著了。

　　「我們該怎麼辦？」錫人問。

　　「如果我們把她留在這裡，她一定會沒命的。」獅子說：「花的香味會取走我們所有人的性命。我已經快要張不開眼睛了，而托托早就睡著了。」

　　的確，托托已經在牠小主人的身旁睡著了。但稻草人和錫人不是血肉之軀，所以不會被花香影響。

　　「快跑，你趕快離開這片致命的花田。」稻草人對獅子說：「我們會帶小女孩一起走，但假如你也睡著，我們是扛不動你的。」

　　獅子打起精神，使勁向前跑去。沒多久，牠便跑得不見蹤跡了。

　　「我們用手圍成一張椅子帶她走。」稻草人說。他們抱起托托，放在桃樂絲的膝上，然後用手圍成椅子，手臂形成扶手，讓昏睡的女孩坐在上面，帶她穿越花田。

　　他們一路走下去，周圍這一大片致命的花田，彷彿無邊無際。他們沿著彎曲的河道前進，最後遇到了他們的獅子朋友，獅子已經在花田中倒頭大睡了。因為香味太濃，這隻大野獸終於撐不住，在距罌粟田盡頭咫尺之遙的地方倒了下來，而前方就是長滿鮮嫩青草的綠色原野了。

錫人悲傷地說：「我們沒辦法為牠做什麼，牠太重了，我們扛不動，只能讓牠永遠昏睡在這裡。也許牠最後會在夢裡找到勇氣。」

　　稻草人說：「我很傷心。以這麼膽小的動物來說，獅子是個很好的夥伴。但是我們必須繼續往前走。」

　　他們帶著昏睡的小女孩，走到河邊。河邊景致優美，離罌粟田也夠遠，不會再讓她吸入有毒的花香。他們輕輕地把她放在柔軟的草皮上，等待新鮮的微風吹醒她。

Chapter 9

田鼠皇后

「 現在，我們離黃磚路應該不遠了。」稻草人站在小女孩旁邊說：「我們往回走的路，和我們被流水沖離的距離，已經差不多遠了。」

就在錫人正要說話時，傳來了一聲低吼。錫人轉過頭（關節運作自如），看見一隻奇怪的野獸，正跳過草地，向他們跑來。那是——沒錯，是一隻黃色的大野貓。錫人猜想牠一定是在追逐什麼東西，因為牠的耳朵壓得很低，緊貼著頭顱，而且嘴巴張得很大，露出兩排可怕的牙齒，赤紅的眼睛像火球一樣發亮。等牠跑得更接近時，錫人發現有一隻小小的灰田鼠正跑在牠前面。錫人雖然沒有心，但他也知道，野貓要殺害這樣一隻可愛又無害的小生物，是沒有道理的。

錫人於是舉起斧頭，在野貓經過時，飛快地一砍，把野貓劈得身首分離，貓頭滾到他的腳邊。

田鼠不再受敵，就停了下來。牠慢慢走向錫人，小聲地吱吱說：

「噢，謝謝你！非常感謝你救了我一命。」

「請別這麼說。」錫人回答：「你要知道，我是沒有心的，所以就格外留神去幫助所有需要幫助的人，就算只是一隻老鼠，也要拔刀相助。」

「只是一隻老鼠！」小動物憤慨地叫道：「什麼，我可是貴為皇后的，我是所有田鼠的皇后！」

「噢，真的！」錫人邊說，邊鞠了個躬。

「你救我，算是立了大功一件，十足地英勇。」皇后補充道。

這時，飛快地跑來了幾隻老鼠。牠們一看到皇后，就大喊：

「噢！皇后陛下，我們還以為您會遇難！您是怎麼逃過那隻大野貓的？」牠們的腰躬得很低，簡直像是用頭在站立。

「這個可笑的錫人，殺了野貓，救了我一命。」她回答：「今後，你們都要服從他，對他不得稍有違令。」

「遵命！」所有老鼠用尖銳的聲音喊道。就在這時，托托醒了過來。牠看到周圍那麼多的老鼠，興奮地

吠了一聲之後，就跳進鼠群中，所有老鼠立刻往四面八方竄逃。在堪薩斯的時候，托托就很喜歡追逐老鼠，牠覺得這種事無傷大雅。

但錫人把狗逮住，緊緊夾在手臂下，一面向老鼠們說：「回來！回來吧！托托不會傷害你們的。」

田鼠皇后聽到這話，就從地上的草叢探出頭來，緊張地問：「你確定牠不會咬我們嗎？」

「我不會讓牠咬你們的。」錫人說：「別害怕。」

老鼠們一隻一隻爬回來。托托不再吠叫，只是想掙開錫人的手臂。要不是知道錫人是錫做的話，托托就把他咬下去了。最後，其中最大的老鼠說話了。

牠問：「你救了皇后，我們該如何相報？」

「我想沒有可報的事。」錫人回答。稻草人一直在努力思索，但是他的頭是用稻草紮成的，所以沒辦法思考。稻草人很快地說：「噢，有了。你們可以救膽小的獅子，牠是我們的朋友，正昏睡在罌粟田裡。」

「一隻獅子！」小皇后叫道：「噢，牠會把我們都吃掉的！」

「噢，不會的。」稻草

人說：「這隻獅子很膽小。」

「真的嗎？」老鼠問。

「牠自己是這樣說的。」稻草人回答：「而且他不會傷害我們的朋友。如果您幫我們救牠，我敢保證，牠一定對你們非常友善。」

「好，我們相信你。」皇后說：「但是我們要怎麼做？」

「是不是有很多老鼠稱您為皇后，願意服從您呢？」

「噢，是的，有好幾千隻呢。」她回答。

「那就盡快把牠們召集過來，並要牠們都帶一條長繩子來。」

皇后轉向隨侍的老鼠，要牠們立刻去召集所有的老鼠子民。隨從一聽到命令，便用最快的速度往四面八方跑去。

稻草人對錫人說：「現在，你到河邊的樹林裡去做一輛要載獅子用的推車。」

錫人立刻前往樹林，開始動手工作。他把樹幹的枝葉削去，很快就用樹枝做成一輛推車。他把材料用木釘組合起來，並用一根大樹幹做了四個輪子。他做得又快又好，等老鼠都到齊時，推車也已經大功告成了。

數千隻老鼠從四面八方趕來，不管是大隻的、小隻的、中型的，都趕來了，而且牠們每一隻嘴裡，都叼了一段繩子。就在這時，昏睡已久的桃樂絲也甦醒過來，

"Permit me to introduce to you her
Majesty, the Queen."

睜開了眼睛。當她發現自己躺在草地上，周圍有數千隻老鼠緊張地盯著她看時，她甚是詫異。稻草人向她說明事情的始末，然後轉身向高貴的老鼠皇后說道：

「允許我把尊貴的皇后陛下介紹給你。」

桃樂絲嚴肅地點了點頭，皇后回了個禮之後，也對這個小女孩友善了起來。

稻草人和錫人開始用老鼠叼來的繩子，把老鼠和推車綁在一起。繩子的一端綁在老鼠的脖子上，另一端綁在推車上。不消說，推車要比任何一隻拉車的老鼠，都還要大上千倍。然而，只要所有老鼠一起綁上繩子，就可以輕易地拉動車子。即使稻草人和錫人坐在推車上面，這些奇特的小馬，也很快就把車子拉到了獅子躺著昏睡的地方。

獅子很重，但經過一番努力後，終於把牠架上了推車。接著，皇后立即命令她的子民開始行動，她擔心老鼠在罌粟田裡待太久，也會昏睡過去。

這些小動物數量雖多，但一開始時，還是很難抬動這個負載沉重的推車。還好錫人和稻草人也在後面幫忙推，才進行得順利了些。不久，牠們把獅子抬出罌粟田，來到綠野上，好讓獅子可以再次呼吸新鮮甜美的空氣，而不要再聞到有毒的花香。

桃樂絲前來迎接牠們，並熱忱感謝這些小老鼠救了她同伴的性命。她很高興救回了獅子，因為她現在愈來愈喜歡獅子了。

老鼠們卸下推車，快速穿越草地，回到各自的家。田鼠皇后最後才離開。

　　「如果你還需要我們，就來這片田野找我們。」她說：「我們一聽到你們的聲音，就會前來相助。再會了！」

　　「再會了！」他們齊聲回答。皇后隨後便離開。桃樂絲緊緊抱住托托，以免牠會去追逐皇后，把她嚇著了。

　　之後，他們坐在獅子旁邊，等牠醒來，而稻草人在附近的一棵樹上，摘了一些水果，讓桃樂絲當晚餐。

Chapter 10

大門守衛

膽小的獅子因為在罌粟田裡躺了很久,吸進致命的香氣,所以過了好一段時間才甦醒過來。當牠睜開眼睛,從推車上躍下時,牠真高興自己還活著。

「我當時全速奔跑,無奈花香實在太濃了。」牠坐著,邊打呵欠說:「你們是怎麼把我救出來的?」

他們便告訴牠田鼠的事情,還有牠們如何慷慨相助,救了牠的性命。獅子笑說:

「我一直以為自己巨大又可怕,卻差一點被花朵這種小東西給害死了,而像田鼠這樣的小動物,卻又救了我。這真是奇怪啊!不過,夥伴們,我們現在有什麼打算?」

桃樂絲說:「我們要啟程了。回到黃磚路上,繼續往翡翠城前進。」

獅子養足了精神之後,他們便又一齊上路,興高采烈地走在柔嫩的草地上。不久,他們就找到了黃磚路,繼續向偉大奧茲所住的翡翠城邁進。

黃磚路現在變得很平坦,而且四周景色宜人。他們很慶幸已經遠離了後面那片森林,以及在那幽暗樹蔭下所遭遇過的許多危險。他們又看到路旁築起圍籬，只不過圍籬現在是綠色的。他們看到一間小屋，顯然是個農夫的住家，那屋子也是綠色的。這天下午，他們途經了幾棟這樣的房子。有時候，居民會跑到門口，對他們張望，一副想要探問的樣子。不過，由於大家害怕那頭大獅子，也就沒人敢走近攀談。此地居民的穿著，都是一身悅目的翡翠綠，還戴著芒奇金人那種尖頂帽。

「這裡一定是奧茲王國。」桃樂絲說：「我們一定離翡翠城越來越近了。」

稻草人回答：「沒錯，在芒奇金國，藍色最常見；在這裡，什麼都是綠色的。不過，這裡的人好像沒有芒奇金人那麼友善，我擔心我們會找不到地方過夜。」

「我真想吃一點水果以外的東西，而且我想托托一

定餓壞了。」女孩說：「走到下一戶人家時，我們就停下來問問看吧。」

於是當他們走到一間大戶農家時，桃樂絲大膽走向前敲門。

一個婦人開了點門縫往外看，說道：「孩子，你要什麼？你旁邊怎麼會有一隻大獅子？」

「如果可以，我們想在你這裡借住一宿。」桃樂絲說：「這隻獅子是我的朋友，也是同行的夥伴，牠絕不會傷害你的。」

「牠溫馴嗎？」婦人問道，並把門開大了一點。

「噢，是的。」女孩說：「而且他非常膽小，你怕牠，牠還更怕你呢。」

婦人想了一會兒，又瞄了獅子一眼，說道：「好吧，這樣的話，你們可以進來，我會給你們晚餐吃，還有睡覺的地方。」

他們一行人走進了房子。屋子裡除了婦人，還有兩個孩子和一個男人。男人的腿受了傷，正躺在角落的躺椅上。他們看到這樣奇怪的一群組合，都露出一副詫異的表情。婦人在一旁忙著擺設餐桌時，男人問道：

「你們一夥要去哪裡呀？」

「去翡翠城。」桃樂絲說：「去找偉大的奧茲。」

「噢，天啊！」男人喊道：「你們確定奧茲會見你們嗎？」

「為什麼不？」她回答。

「聽說呀，他從不讓人見他的。我自己去過翡翠城好幾次，那裡美如仙境，不過我從未能見奧茲一面，也沒聽說有誰見過他了。」

「他從不出來嗎？」稻草人問。

「從不出來。他每天都待在皇宮中宏偉的王室裡，連服侍他的人都沒有面對面見過他。」

「他長得什麼樣呀？」女孩問。

「這就難說了。」男人沉思地說道：「你看，奧茲是個偉大的巫師，可以隨心所欲地變化外形。有人說他長得像鳥，有人說他長得像大象，也有人說他長得像貓。有時，他又會現身成美麗的仙女、淘氣的精靈，或任何他覺得有趣的樣子。不過奧茲的廬山真面目究竟如何，無人知曉。」

「真是怪透了。」桃樂絲說：「不過我們一定要想辦法見到他，不然我們這一趟就白來了。」

「你們為什麼想見令人敬畏的奧茲？」男人問。

「我想要他給我一些腦子。」稻草人急切地說。

「噢，這對奧茲來說再簡單也不過了。」男人說道：「他擁有的腦子，比他需要的還多。」

「我想要他給我一顆心。」錫人說。

「這也不成問題。」男人繼續說：「奧茲收集了很多心，各種大小和形狀的都有。」

「我想要他給我勇氣。」膽小的獅子說。

「奧茲的王室裡有一大罐勇氣，還用一個金盤子蓋著，免得勇氣漏掉了。」男人說：「他會很樂意給你一些的。」

「我想要他送我回堪薩斯。」桃樂絲說。

「堪薩斯在哪兒？」男人驚訝地問。

「我不知道。」桃樂絲傷心地回答：「但那是我的家鄉，我很確定一定有這個地方。」

「很可能吧。奧茲啊，是無所不能的，我想他會幫你找到堪薩斯的。只是你們得先見到他才行，而這就很難了，因為偉大的巫師不喜歡見人，而且總是自行其是。那你想要什麼呢？」他對著托托繼續說道。托托只是搖搖尾巴。說也奇怪，托托竟不會說話。

這時，婦人說晚餐已經張羅好，大夥便圍在餐桌旁。桃樂絲大塊朵頤了一番，享用美味的燕麥粥、一盤

The Lion ate some of the porridge.

炒蛋和好吃的白麵包。獅子吃了一些燕麥粥，不過牠不大喜歡。牠說那是燕麥做的，而燕麥是給馬吃的，不該給獅子吃。稻草人和錫人什麼也沒吃。托托每一樣都嚐一點，牠很高興又吃到了一頓好晚餐。

婦人給桃樂絲一張床睡覺，托托躺在她旁邊，獅子守著她的房門，以免她被打擾。稻草人和錫人當然是不用睡覺的，於是便整夜不作聲地站在角落裡。

隔天早上，太陽一升起，他們便上路。不久，他們就看到前方的天空上，出現了一道美麗的綠色光芒。

「那一定就是翡翠城了。」桃樂絲說。

他們繼續往前走，綠色光芒越來越亮。看來，他們似乎終於抵達了旅程的終點站。在他們來到環城的高牆下之前，已經是下午時刻。那道城牆又高又厚，漆著明亮的綠色。

在他們面前，黃磚路的盡頭處是一扇鑲滿綠寶石的大門，大門在陽光下閃閃發光，連稻草人那雙畫上去的眼睛，也被光芒照得眩目。

在大門旁邊有一個鈴，桃樂絲按下按鈕，聽見裡面傳來銀鈴般的聲響。隨後，大門緩緩開啟，他們一起走了進去。大門內是一間有高拱頂的房間，房間四壁嵌著無數的綠寶石，閃耀奪目。

在他們面前，站了一個矮小的男人。男人的個頭跟芒奇金人差不多，從頭到腳一身綠色，連皮膚也有點帶綠。在他旁邊，有一個綠色的大箱子。

他看到桃樂絲一行人，就問道：「你們來到翡翠城，有何貴事？」

　　「我們來這裡，是想求見偉大的奧茲。」桃樂絲說。

　　男人一聽，很吃驚。他坐了下來，反覆思量。

　　「已經有好幾年都沒有人來求見奧茲了。」他不解地搖搖頭，一邊說道：「他法力強大，令人生畏，如果你們是為了什麼無聊或愚蠢的事，來打擾這位偉大巫師的冥想，他可能會勃然大怒，立刻把你們殺掉。」

　　「我們的事情既不愚蠢，也不無聊。」稻草人回答：「我們是為很重要的事情而來的。而且有人跟我們說，奧茲是個善良的巫師。」

　　綠色的人說：「的確，奧茲是個好巫師，而且治國賢明。不過，對於不老實的人，或是出於好奇而想見他的人，那他可是非常恐怖的，所以很少人敢斗膽求見他一面。我是大門守衛，而既然你們想求見奧茲國王，我就必須帶你們到他的宮殿。不過，你們要先戴上眼鏡。」

　　「為什麼？」桃樂絲問。

　　「假如你們不戴上眼鏡，會被翡翠城的光輝和燦爛弄瞎眼睛。即使是這裡的居民，也必須日夜戴著眼鏡。這個城市剛建立時，奧茲就下令眼鏡都要上鎖，而唯一能開鎖的鑰匙，就在我這裡。」

　　他打開大箱子，桃樂絲看見裡面有各種大小和形狀的眼鏡，而且每一副眼鏡的鏡片都是綠色。大門守衛找了一副合適桃樂絲大小的眼鏡，幫她戴上，把兩條金色的帶子繞到她腦後，然後用掛在頸鍊上的小鑰匙，把它鎖上。戴上眼鏡之後，桃樂絲就沒辦法隨意拿下。不過她當然不希望被翡翠城的光芒弄瞎，所以也沒說什麼話。

　　一身綠色的門衛，也為稻草人、錫人、獅子戴上合適的眼鏡，連小托托也戴上了，然後再用鑰匙鎖上。

　　接著，大門守衛也戴上他自己的眼鏡，然後宣布要領他們進宮殿了。他從牆上的一個木釘上，取下一把金色的大鑰匙，打開另一扇大門，他們跟著他一起穿過門，走進了翡翠城的街道。

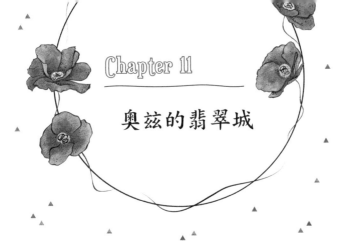

Chapter 11

奧茲的翡翠城

儘管戴上了綠色的眼鏡,這座奇妙城市的閃耀光芒,一開始時還是讓桃樂絲一行人感到眩目不已。街道兩旁的房子,都是用綠色大理石所蓋成,上面鑲滿閃亮的綠寶石,美侖美奐。他們走在以同樣的綠色大理石舖設的人行道上,每塊大理石之間都鑲著成行的綠寶石,排列緊密,在陽光下閃閃發亮。一塊塊的窗戶,也嵌著綠色的玻璃。就連城市上方的天空,也帶著一抹淡淡的綠,連太陽的光線也是綠色。

街道上行人雜遝,男女老少皆有,人人都穿著綠色的衣服,皮膚也略帶綠色。人們盯著桃樂絲和她奇特的夥伴們瞧,一臉好奇。小孩子們一看到獅子,就全躲到媽媽的背後,不過,沒有人前來跟他們攀談。街道上商店林立,桃樂絲發現,店家所販賣的東西也都是綠色的。有綠色的糖果、綠色的爆米花,還有各式各樣綠色的鞋子、帽子和衣服。有個男人在一處賣綠色的檸檬水,桃樂絲注意到,孩子們所付的錢幣也是綠色的。

這個地方看起來好像沒有馬或其他動物。人們用綠色的兩輪小貨車運送物品,他們把小貨車推在身前。人人一副快樂富足的樣子。

　　大門守衛帶他們穿越街道，來到一座大建築物前，那裡就是偉大巫師奧茲的宮殿，座落於城市的中央。宮殿門前，立著一個士兵，他穿著綠色制服，留著長長的綠鬍鬚。

　　大門守衛對他說：「這些外地人想求見奧茲國王。」

　　「進來吧。」士兵回答：「我去稟報。」

　　他們走進宮殿大門，被帶到一個大房間裡。房間內鋪著綠色地毯，還有鑲著綠寶石的成套綠色精巧家具。進入房間前，士兵要他們在一張綠色的踏墊上，把鞋子揩乾淨。待他們坐定，士兵恭敬地說：

　　「請自便，我現在要去王室門前，向奧茲稟報你們來訪一事。」

　　他們等了許久之後，才見士兵回來。見士兵終於回來，桃樂絲問道：

「你有見到奧茲了嗎？」

「噢，沒有。」士兵回答：「我從沒見過他，他坐在布幔後面，我向他稟報，轉呈你們的話。奧茲說，如果你們真的想求見他，那他就接見你們。不過，你們得一個一個單獨去見他，而且他一天只接見一位。所以呢，既然你們勢必要在宮中停留數天，我就帶你們到房間去，讓你們可以在一路跋涉之後好好休息一下。」

「謝謝你。」女孩回答：「奧茲真是體貼呀。」

士兵吹響綠哨子之後，房內隨即走進來一名身穿綠色絲袍的少女。少女有一頭美麗的綠髮和漂亮的綠色眼睛，她向桃樂絲深深一鞠躬後，說道：「請跟我來，我帶你去寢房。」

桃樂絲便向朋友們道別，除了托托。她抱起托托，尾隨綠色少女，穿過七個走廊，走上三段樓梯後，來到了宮殿正面的一個房間裡。這真是世上最溫馨的小房間了，房間裡有一張柔軟舒適的床，鋪著綠色的絲質薄被和絲絨床單；房間中央有一個小型噴泉，往空中噴出綠色的香水，香水再接著落回到雕刻精細的綠色大理石池子裡；窗戶旁，擺著美麗的綠色花朵，還有一個書架，上面擺了一排綠色的小書。在桃樂絲趁暇翻閱這些書時，發現書中盡是令她發噱的古怪綠色圖片。

衣櫃裡有很多綠色洋裝，有絲質的，有錦緞的，也有絲絨的，而且每一件桃樂絲穿起來都剛好合身。

「請當在自己家裡吧。」綠色少女說：「有什麼需要，儘管按鈴。明天早上，奧茲就會派人來叫你。」

說罷，她就讓桃樂絲獨自留在房間裡，回去帶領其他人。她領每個人到各自的房間去，大家都被安置在宮殿某個舒適的房間裡。不過，這對稻草人當然是白費工夫了。稻草人被獨自留在房間裡後，就傻呼呼地站在門口，等待天亮。要他躺在床上，他又不能休息，況且他的眼睛也沒辦法闔上，所以他就整晚盯著一隻小蜘蛛，看牠在房間的角落裡織網，好像這個房間不太值得一顧似的。錫人因為還有血肉之軀時的記憶，就出於習慣躺上床，不過他也無法入睡。他整夜上上下下地移動關節，以確保運轉順暢。

獅子比較喜歡樹林裡的乾葉床，而不喜歡被關在房間裡面。不過牠夠聰明，不會以此自擾。牠跳到床上，像隻貓一樣踡縮起來，發出咕嚕聲，霎時就睡著了。

隔天清晨，吃過早餐後，綠色少女來接桃樂絲，幫她穿上一件最漂亮的繡花錦緞綠袍，然後圍上綠色的絲質圍裙，並在托托的脖子綁上綠絲巾後，就前往奧茲國王的宮室。

一開始，他們來到一個寬廣的大廳，大廳裡有很多身著華服的宮廷紳士和仕女。他們無事可做，只是閒聊。雖然他們沒被恩准過可以見奧茲，但還是每天早上都來宮室外面等候。桃樂絲走進大廳時，他們好奇地看著她，其中一人低聲道：

「你真的要當面去見可怕的奧茲嗎？」

女孩回答：「當然。如果他肯接見我的話。」

「噢，他會接見你的，儘管他不喜歡有人求見。」那位稟報過奧茲巫師的士兵說：「他一開始是很生氣，還叫我把你送回你來的地方。後來，他問我你的長相，當我提到你的銀鞋子之後，他就感興趣了。最後，我稟報說，你額頭上有記號，他就決定准你見他了。」

這時，鈴響了。綠色少女孩對桃樂絲說：「這是信號，你得自己一個人進去宮室。」

少女打開一個小門，桃樂絲勇敢地走進去。門內是一間奇特的圓形大房間，有高高的拱頂，四周的牆壁、天花板和地板，都緊密地鋪著大顆綠寶石。在屋頂中央，有一盞明亮如太陽的大燈，照得綠寶石閃爍不已。

不過讓桃樂絲最感興趣的，還是房間中

央用綠色大理石做成的寶座。寶座的形狀做得像椅子，上面的寶石也是閃閃發光。在椅子中央，有一個巨大的頭顱，卻沒有身體撐著，也沒有手或腿。頭顱上沒有頭髮，但有眼睛、鼻子和嘴巴。這個頭顱，比最大的巨人的頭還要大上很多。

當桃樂絲驚奇又害怕地盯著頭顱看時，頭顱上的眼睛緩緩地轉動了起來，並且目光銳利地定睛看著她。接著，那一張嘴巴也動了起來，桃樂絲聽見一個聲音說：

「我就是偉大而可怕的奧茲。你是誰，為什麼要來求見我？」

從大頭顱所發出來的聲音，並沒有桃樂絲所想的那麼恐怖，她便鼓起勇氣，回答道：「我是渺小而溫和的桃樂絲。我是來這裡請求您幫忙的。」

那對眼睛若有所思地看著她足足有一分鐘，說道：「你那雙銀鞋是哪裡來的？」

「那是東方邪惡女巫的鞋子，我的房子壓到她，把她給壓死了。」她回答。

「你額頭上的記號，又是怎麼來的？」聲音繼續問道。

「那是北方善良女巫親吻我時所留下來的，她向我道別，要我來找您。」女孩說。

那雙眼睛又銳利地盯著她，看得出來她所言不假。奧茲問：「你希望我做什麼？」

「送我回堪薩斯，回到愛姆嬸嬸和亨利叔叔住的地

The eyes looked at her
thoughtfully.

方。」她急切地回答：「雖然您的國家很美麗，可是我不喜歡。而且我消失那麼久了，愛姆嬸嬸一定會很著急的。」

那雙眼睛眨了三下，往上看看天花板，又往下看看地板，怪異地轉著眼珠子，好像在打量房間裡的每個角落。最後，眼神又轉向桃樂絲。

「我為什麼要幫你做這件事？」奧茲問。

「因為您很強大，而我很弱小；因為您是偉大的巫師奧茲，而我只是個小女孩。」

「可是你強大得足以殺掉東方邪惡女巫啊。」奧茲說。

「那只是恰巧發生的事。」桃樂絲簡單地回答：「我也沒辦法。」

頭顱回答道：「好吧，那我告訴你，除非你有所回報，否則你就沒有權利叫我送你回堪薩斯。在這個國家，人必有付出，才能有所得。如果你希望我用魔法送你回家，你就得先為我效命。你助我，我便助你。」

「您要我做什麼呢？」女孩問。

「除掉西方邪惡女巫。」奧茲回答。

「不行，我做不到！」桃樂絲吃驚地喊道。

「你殺了東方邪惡女巫，又穿著有神奇魔力的銀鞋。如今，在這個國家境內，就只剩一個邪惡女巫了。等到你跟我說她已經被除掉了，我就送你回堪薩斯，不然免談。」

小女孩很失望，便啜泣了起來。那一雙眼睛又眨了眨，迫切地看著她，偉大的奧茲好像覺得，只要桃樂絲肯，就能幫他這個忙似的。

　　「我從不樂意殺任何人。」她哭道：「就算我想，我又怎麼殺得掉邪惡女巫呢？如果，連偉大又可怕的您，都無法親自殺掉她了，又怎能期望我呢？」

　　頭顱說道：「這我不管，我的回答就是這樣了。除非除掉邪惡女巫，不然你就無法再見到叔叔和嬸嬸。記住，那個女巫是很邪惡的，她罪大惡極，應該被除掉。現在你走吧，任務沒有達成，就不要回來找我。」

　　桃樂絲傷心地離開宮室，回到獅子、稻草人和錫人那裡，他們都在等著聽奧茲怎麼跟她說。

　　「我沒希望了。」她悲傷地說：「奧茲要我除掉西方邪惡女巫，才肯送我回家，可是這我無能為力。」

　　她的朋友們聽了很遺憾，卻也幫不上忙。她逕自回到自己的房間，爬上床，哭著哭著就睡著了。

　　隔天早上，綠鬍子士兵去找稻草人，說道：「跟我來。奧茲傳見你。」

　　稻草人跟隨在後，進入了巍峨的宮室。進了宮室，他看到一位最美麗的女子正坐在翡翠寶座上。女子一身綠色絲質羅紗，一頭傾瀉而下的綠色捲髮上，戴著一頂寶石皇冠。她肩上還長了一對翅膀，翅膀色彩鮮麗，非常輕巧，彷彿一點點微風就能吹動它似的。

　　稻草人用他稻草紮成的身體，盡量擺出優雅姿態，向眼前這位美麗的女子鞠躬。女子友善地看著他，說道：「我是偉大而可怕的奧茲。你是誰，為什麼要來求見我？」

稻草人大吃一驚，他還以為會看到桃樂絲所說的大頭顱。他壯起膽子回答道：

「我是個稻草人，用稻草紮成的，所以沒有腦子。我來這裡，就是祈求您賜給我腦子，放在我的頭裡面，取代稻草。那樣，我就能變得和您的所有子民一樣了。」

「我為什麼要幫你做這件事？」女子問道。

「因為您充滿智慧，強大有力，而且沒有其他人可以幫我這個忙了。」稻草人回答。

「沒有報酬的請求，我是不會應允的。」奧茲說：「不過我可以答應你這件事，只要你替我除掉西方邪惡女巫，我就賜給你

又多又好的腦子。有了這麼好的腦子，你將會是奧茲王國中最聰明的人。」

「我以為您已經叫桃樂絲去除掉女巫了。」稻草人吃驚地說。

「是沒錯。誰除掉她，我都無所謂。不過除非她死了，不然我不會實現你的願望。現在你走吧，在你理應得到你所渴望的腦子之前，不要再來找我。」

稻草人傷心地回去找他的朋友，轉述了奧茲的話。當桃樂絲聽到偉大的巫師並非如她所見的是一顆頭顱，而是一位美麗的女子時，她很驚訝。

稻草人說：「她和錫人一樣，欠缺了一顆心。」

隔天早晨，綠鬍子士兵來找錫人說：

「奧茲傳見你。跟我來。」

錫人於是跟著他來到宮室。他不知道他看到的奧茲，會是一個美麗女子，還是一顆頭顱。不過，他希望見到的是美麗女子。他喃喃自語道：「因為如果是頭顱，我想他就不會給我心了，畢竟，頭顱自己也沒有心，是無法體會我的感受的。不過如果是美麗的女子，那我會懇求她給我一顆心，畢竟，常言道，女人比較有同情心。」

然而，當錫人走進巍峨的宮室後，他既沒看到頭顱，也沒看到女子，因為奧茲化身成了一隻最可怕的野獸。野獸身大如象，重得幾乎要把綠色的寶座給壓壞。這隻野獸的頭長得像犀牛，只不過臉上有五隻眼睛；身體長了五隻長長的手臂，和五條又長又細的腿，而且渾身濃毛密布，模樣超乎想像的可怕。在這種時候，還多虧了錫人沒有心，不然他的心會嚇得又急又快地砰砰跳。還好錫人是錫做的，他沒被嚇到，只是很失望。

「我是偉大又可怕的奧茲，」野獸咆哮說：「你是誰，為什麼要來求見我？」

「我是一位錫做的樵夫，我沒有心，無法愛人。我祈求您賜給我一顆心，好讓我和其他人一樣。」

「我為什麼要這麼做？」野獸問道。

「因為我要求了，而且只有您能做到我的請求。」錫人回答。

奧茲對此咆哮了一聲，粗暴地說：「如果你真的想要一顆心，你就自己去把它掙來。」

　　「怎麼掙？」錫人問。

　　「幫桃樂絲除掉西方邪惡女巫。」野獸回答：「等女巫死了，再來找我。我會賜給你一顆全奧茲王國中最大、最好、最深情的心。」

　　於是，錫人只好傷心地回到朋友那裡，告訴他們他看到的可怕野獸。奧茲能化身成那麼多樣子，他們都覺得驚奇。獅子說：

　　「我去見他時，如果他是野獸，我就要發出最大聲的咆哮，嚇死他，這樣他就會答應我的要求了。而如果他是美麗的女子，那我就假裝要撲向他，逼她答應我的請求。又如果他是顆大頭顱，那他就要向我求饒了，因為我會在房間裡把那顆頭顱滾來滾去，直到他答應我們的請求。所以朋友們，打起精神來吧，一切都會好轉的。」

　　隔天早上，綠鬍子士兵領獅子來到宮室，要牠去見奧茲。

　　獅子立刻走進宮門，環顧了一下四周。令牠吃驚的是，在寶座前的竟是一顆火球。火球燒得猛烈灼亮，讓牠幾乎無法直視。牠一開始以為，那是奧茲不小心著火，燒起來了。當牠想走近一點時，火球熱得燒焦了牠的鬍鬚，牠只好發著抖，爬回靠近門口的地方。

　　這時，一個低沉而平靜的聲音從火球裡傳了出來，如是說道：「我是偉大又可怕的奧茲，你是誰，為什麼來找我？」

獅子回答：「我是一隻膽小的獅子，我什麼都怕。我來這裡，是求您賜給我勇氣，讓我成為名副其實的萬獸之王。」

「我為什麼要給你勇氣？」奧茲詢問。

「因為您是最偉大的巫師，而且只有您有力量實現我的要求。」獅子回答。

火球猛烈地燒了一會兒。那聲音又說：「向我證明邪惡女巫被除掉了，我就賜給你勇氣。不過只要女巫還活著，你就繼續當個懦夫吧。」

獅子對這番話感到很生氣，卻也無話可說。牠靜靜地盯著火球看時，火球燒得更加熾熱了，牠只好轉身跑出王室。牠很高興看到朋友們還在等牠，並告訴他們牠和巫師見面的可怕經過。

「我們現在怎麼辦？」桃樂絲難過地問。

「我們能做的只有一件事，」獅子回答：「就是去維奇人住的地方，把壞女巫找出來，除掉她。」

「要是我們做不到呢？」女孩說。

「那我就永遠不會有勇氣了。」獅子說道。

「我就永遠不會有腦子了。」稻草人補充道。

「我就永遠不會有心了。」錫人說著。

「我就永遠見不到愛姆嬸嬸和亨利叔叔了。」桃樂絲說完，就開始哭了起來。

「小心！」綠色少女叫道：「眼淚掉到綠絲袍上，會留下斑點的。」

　　桃樂絲只好擦乾眼淚，說道：「我想我們總得試試看，不過我真的不想殺害任何人，即使是為了要再見到愛姆嬸嬸。」

　　「我跟你一起去，不過我太膽小了，不敢殺女巫。」獅子說。

　　「我也去。」稻草人說道：「不過我這麼笨，恐怕不能幫上什麼忙。」

　　「即使是個女巫，我也無心傷害她。」錫人說：「不過既然你們要去，那我當然也一起去了。」

　　於是他們決定隔天早上就啟程。錫人在綠色磨石上，把斧頭磨利，並把所有關節都好好地上了油。稻草人幫自己塞了新的稻草，桃樂絲還用新的顏料幫他畫眼睛，好讓他看得更清楚。那位親切的綠色少女，把桃樂絲的籃子裝滿各種美食，並在托托的脖子上，用綠色緞帶綁了一個小鈴鐺。

　　他們早早就上了床，一覺到天亮。直到破曉時分，宮殿後方傳來綠公雞的啼聲，和母雞下綠蛋的咕咕聲，才把他們給喚醒。

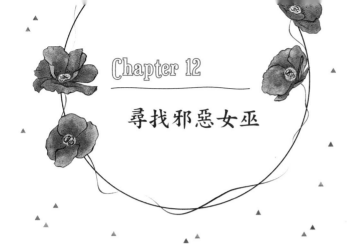

Chapter 12

尋找邪惡女巫

綠鬍子士兵帶他們穿過翡翠城的街道，回到大門守衛那裡。大門守衛幫他們解開眼鏡，把眼鏡放回大箱子裡，恭敬地為他們打開大門。

「通往西方邪惡女巫的路是哪一條？」桃樂絲問。

「無路可去。」大門守衛回答：「從來就沒有人想去那裡。」

「那我們要怎麼找到她？」女孩問。

「這簡單。」男人回答：「只要她知道你們在維奇人的國境裡，她就會來找你們，把你們變成她的奴隸。」

「那倒不見得。」稻草人說：「因為我們是要去打敗她的。」

「噢，那的確是不同了。」大門守衛說：「沒人打敗過她，所以我自然認為她會把你們變成奴隸，就像她對其他人一樣。你們要小心，她既邪惡又凶暴，不會讓你們打敗她的。往西方一直走，往太陽落下的地方去，就找得到她了。」

他們謝過守衛，向他道別後，便踏上綴滿雛菊和毛茛的柔軟草地，前往西方。桃樂絲仍穿著宮殿裡穿的美

The soldier with the green whiskers led them through the streets.

麗絲質洋裝，不過令她驚訝的是，衣服竟然變成了純白色，而不再是綠色的。托托脖子上的絲帶也由綠轉白，和桃樂絲的衣服一樣白。

不久，翡翠城就被遠遠留在身後了。他們一路前進，路面越來越崎嶇而多山丘。在這個西方之地，沒有農田，沒有房子，土地也無人耕種。

這裡沒有可以遮蔭的樹木，到了下午，太陽曬得他們的臉發燙。還沒到晚上，桃樂絲、托托和獅子就已經累了。他們在草地上躺下，睡覺休息，由錫人和稻草人在一旁看守。

那西方邪惡女巫只有一隻眼睛，但眼睛卻銳利如望遠鏡，哪兒都看得見。當她坐在城堡門口四處眺望時，恰好看到了正躺著睡覺的桃樂絲，還有她身邊的那些朋友。雖然他們遠在一方，但邪惡女巫看到有人進入她的王國，非常生氣，就吹響掛在脖子上的銀哨。

立刻，一群大狼從四面八方向她跑來。牠們的腿很長，眼神凶惡，尖牙利齒。

「去找那些人。」女巫說：「把他們撕成碎片。」

「您不把他們收為奴隸嗎？」帶頭的狼問道。

「不！」她回答：「他們一個是錫做的，一個是稻草紮的，一個是小女孩，一隻是獅子，沒有一個能工作。所以，去把他們撕成碎片吧！」

「遵命。」帶頭的狼說完，就和狼群迅速離去。

幸虧稻草人和錫人很清醒，他們聽到了狼群前來的聲音。

「這一仗我來打！」錫人說：「到我後面去吧，我來迎戰他們。」

他握住鋒利的斧頭，等帶頭的狼一來，他手臂一揮，狼頭便落了地，嗚呼哀哉。他斧頭又一舉，又來一隻狼，同樣斃命於錫人的利斧下。狼總共有四十隻，一次砍一隻，最後，狼屍在錫人面前堆積如山。

他放下斧頭，坐在稻草人旁邊。稻草人說：「朋友，這一仗真漂亮！」

隔天早上桃樂絲醒來時，看到一大堆毛茸茸的狼，嚇了一大跳。錫人一五一十告訴她事情的經過。她謝謝錫人救了大家，然後坐下來吃早餐。之後，大夥就再度踏上旅途。

這天早上，邪惡女巫來到城堡門口，用她的千里獨眼往外望，看到狼群全倒地斷氣，而那些陌生人仍在境內遊走。她大發雷霆，吹了兩聲銀哨。

立刻，飛來了一大群野烏鴉，天空一時暗了下來。

邪惡女巫對烏鴉王說：「立刻飛去那群陌生人那裡，把他們的眼睛啄出來，把他們撕成碎片！」

野烏鴉便成群飛向桃樂絲一行人。看到烏鴉飛來，小女孩很害怕。

稻草人說道：「這一仗換我來打了。在我旁邊躺下，就不會受傷了。」

除了稻草人，大家全都躺下。稻草人挺立著，伸出手臂。烏鴉一看到他，便被嚇住。這些鳥被稻草人嚇慣了，寸步也不敢靠近。然而，帶頭的烏鴉卻說道：「他只是稻草紮的人，看我把他的眼睛啄出來！」

牠往稻草人飛過去，卻被稻草人抓住頭，扭住脖子，直到牠斷氣。接著又飛來一隻，稻草人照樣扭斷

牠的脖子。烏鴉總共有四十隻，稻草人扭了四十個脖子，最後，牠們都陳屍在他的腳下。稻草人接著叫起夥伴，再度上路。

邪惡女巫又往外一看，當她看到烏鴉死成一堆時，簡直氣瘋了，就又吹了三聲銀哨。

立刻，空中傳來一陣蜂鳴，飛來了一群黑蜂。

「去那群陌生人那裡，把他們螫死！」女巫下令道。蜜蜂一轉，便往桃樂絲一行人那裡急急飛去。錫人已瞧見牠們飛來，而稻草人也有了對付的辦法。

「把我的稻草取出來，蓋在小女孩、小狗和獅子的身上。」他對錫人說：「這樣蜜蜂就叮不到他們了。」錫人照辦，桃樂絲則抱著托托，挨近獅子躺下，讓稻草把他們完全覆蓋住。

蜂群飛來之後，只找到一個錫人可以螫，便蜂擁而上。牠們對著錫人螫下去，蜂針全斷，錫人卻不痛不癢。蜂

針一旦折斷，蜜蜂就會死亡，所以牠們的下場就是如此了。牠們落在錫人腳邊，厚厚的一堆，宛如一堆黑煤。

桃樂絲和獅子隨後爬起來，女孩幫錫人把稻草放回稻草人的身體裡，回復原來的模樣，然後他們再度啟程上路。

看到黑蜂堆屍如煤，邪惡女巫怒不可遏。她跺腳扯髮，咬牙切齒，隨後又叫來十幾個維奇人奴隸，遞給他們鋒利的長矛，要他們去找那些闖入者，把他們殺掉。

維奇人並不是個善戰的民族，但他們不得不奉命行事，只好一路前進。當他們迎上桃樂絲時，獅子大吼一聲，往他們撲了過去，可憐的維奇人嚇得轉身拔腿就跑。

他們溜回城堡，被邪惡女巫抽了一頓鞭，然後被趕回去工作。女巫坐下來，思索對策。她搞不懂滅敵計畫怎麼會全都失敗，不過她畢竟是個法力高強又邪門的女巫，所以她很快又想到了辦法。

在她的櫃子裡，有一頂鑲著鑽石和紅寶石的金冠。這頂金冠具有魔力，誰擁有它，誰就可以使喚飛猴三

次，飛猴會完全遵照指示行事。可是
一旦喚過三次，飛猴便不再受命。
女巫之前已經使用過兩次金冠的
魔力，第一次是要飛猴幫忙她奴
役維奇人，統治他們的國家；
第二次是要飛猴幫忙對抗奧
茲國王本人，把奧茲趕
出西方國土。飛猴也幫
她完成了，因為只剩最
後一次使用的機會，所
以除非其他法寶都已用
罄，不然她是不會輕易動用
金冠的。如今，她那些惡狼、
野烏鴉和螫蜂都已經死了，而奴隸又被膽小的獅子嚇得
潰逃，所以她只剩一個方法，可以用來消滅桃樂絲一行
人。

　　邪惡女巫從櫃子裡拿出金冠，把它戴在頭上，然後
用左腳站立，慢慢唸道：

　　「耶——皮，佩——皮，喀——咳！」

　　接著她換右腳站立，唸道：

　　「西——囉，猴——囉，哈——囉！」

　　最後，她用雙腳站立，大聲喊道：

　　「瑞——西，蘇——西，立刻！」

　　咒語立刻開始生效，天空霎時暗了下來，空中傳來

一陣隆隆聲響。許多翅膀急速飛來，發出刺耳的喋喋聲
和嘻笑聲。當太陽從黑暗的天空中露臉時，照見了邪惡
女巫身旁正圍繞著猴群，每一隻猴子的肩膀上都有一對
巨大有力的翅膀。

　　其中，有一隻猴子的體型比其他猴子大上很多，似
乎是帶頭的領袖。牠飛近女巫，說道：「這是您第三次
叫喚我們，也是最後一次。您有什麼吩咐？」

　　「去找在我國土裡的那些陌生人，除了獅子以外，
把他們通通給我消滅掉。」邪惡女巫說：「把獅子帶來
給我，我要把牠當成馬來使役，叫牠作牛作馬。」

　　「我們會遵從您的命令。」領袖說罷，飛猴們便發
出一陣刺耳的嘈雜聲，飛向桃樂絲一行人。

　　幾隻猴子抓住錫人，飛到空中，把他帶到尖石林立
的地方，然後把可憐的錫人高高丟下。錫人從高空中落

到岩石上，摔得又塌又扁，躺在那兒，無法動彈，也發不出任何聲音。

又有猴子抓住稻草人，用長長的手指把他衣服和腦袋裡的稻草扯出來，然後把他的帽子、鞋子和衣服綁成一小捆，拋到大樹的樹頂上。

還有猴子用粗繩把獅子的身體、頭和腿纏繞住，使牠無法抓咬或是掙扎。然後牠們提起獅子，飛回女巫的城堡，把牠放在鐵籬高聳的小院子裡，讓牠無法逃脫。

不過，牠們完全沒有對桃樂絲下手。桃樂絲抱著托托站著，看著夥伴遭遇不幸，心想很快就會輪到她了。飛猴王飛向她，伸出長滿毛的長手臂，醜陋的臉上露出可怕的笑容。然而，當牠看到桃樂絲的額頭上有善良女巫親吻的印記時，牠便打住，並提醒別的猴子，不要去觸犯她。

「我們不敢傷害這個小女孩，她受到善良力量的保護，那比邪惡的力量還要強大。」牠對猴群說：「我們只能把她帶到邪惡女巫的城堡，把她留在那裡。」

牠們小心翼翼地用手臂抬起桃樂絲，很快飛到城堡，把她放在前台階上。然後領袖對女巫說：

「我們已經盡力遵從了您的指示。我們消滅了錫人和稻草人，把獅子綁在您的院子裡，不過我們不敢傷害這小女孩和她懷裡的狗。您對我們的使喚到此為止，您不會再見到我們了。」

說罷，所有飛猴在一陣嘻笑聲和嘈雜聲中，飛入空

The monkeys wound many coils
about his body.

中，一下子就不見蹤影。

　　當邪惡女巫看到桃樂絲前額上的印記時，她很吃驚，也很擔心。她知道，不管是飛猴還是她自己，都沒膽子傷害這小女孩。她低頭看桃樂絲的腳，看到了那雙銀鞋。她開始因為恐懼而戰慄起來，因為她知道那雙鞋具有強大的魔力。一開始，女巫打算逃走，但她恰好看到了桃樂絲單純無邪的眼睛，顯示出小女孩不知道銀鞋能帶來的神奇力量。邪惡女巫笑了起來，心想：「她不知道怎麼運用魔力，我還是可以讓她做我的奴隸。」

　　於是她粗聲粗氣地對桃樂絲說：「跟我來，記住我所吩咐的每一件事。如果你沒做到，我就要讓你死，就像錫人和稻草人一樣！」

　　桃樂絲便跟隨著她，穿過城堡中的許多華麗房間，最後來到廚房。女巫命令她清洗鍋子水壺、拖地板，並添柴看火。

　　桃樂絲順從地按照吩咐開始做活，她決定努力工作，因為邪惡女巫決定不殺她，讓她很高興。

　　桃樂絲忙著幹活，女巫心想該去院子馴服膽小的獅子，把牠當成馬一樣使役。她想，只要她隨時想駕車，就能叫獅子幫她拉車，那一定會很有趣。不過，當她一打開門，獅子就大聲咆哮，並且向她猛撲過去。女巫很害怕，就溜了出來，把門關上。

　　「我不能馴服你，那我可以讓你餓肚子吧。」女巫透過門柱對獅子說道：「除非你依令行事，不然就沒有東西可以吃。」

此後，她就不給被囚的獅子食物吃，不過她每天中午都會去門口問：「你準備好要像馬一樣受駕馭了嗎？」

而獅子會回答：「不。如果你進來院子裡，我就咬你。」

獅子之所以不必依女巫的命令行事，是因為每天晚上，等女巫入睡後，桃樂絲就會拿壁櫥裡的食物來給牠吃；吃飽後，牠就躺在乾草堆上，桃樂絲也會躺在一旁，把頭枕在牠柔軟又毛茸茸的鬃毛上，討論他們遇到的困境，並計畫逃脫的方法。不過他們苦無對策，因為城堡一直有黃色的維奇人在看守著。這些維奇人是邪惡女巫的奴隸，他們很害怕女巫，不敢抗令。

白天裡，女孩得拚命工作，女巫還常常威脅要用隨身攜帶的雨傘打她。但事實上，因為桃樂絲的額頭有印記，女巫根本不敢動她。但桃樂絲對此一無所知，所以總為自己和托托擔驚受怕。有一次，女巫用雨傘打了托托一下，這隻勇敢的小狗就衝過去咬她的腿。但女巫被咬的地方並沒有流血，因為她邪惡至極，她的血早在好幾年前就已經乾涸了。

桃樂絲的生活變得很悲慘，她慢慢了解到，要回到堪薩斯和愛姆嬸嬸身邊，是愈來愈困難了。有時，她會難過地哭上好幾個小時，這時托托就會坐在她腳邊，盯著她的臉，傷心地嗚嗚叫，為小主人感到難過。不管是要待在堪薩斯還是奧茲王國，只要能和桃樂絲在一起，托托都無所謂。但牠知道小女孩不快樂，這讓托托自己也難過了起來。

邪惡女巫現在很想把小女孩穿著的銀鞋占為己有。她的蜂群、烏鴉和狼已經枯屍成堆，金冠的魔力也已經用完，不過如果她能得到銀鞋，鞋子將會賜予她更大的力量。她仔細觀察桃樂絲，看她會不會脫下鞋子，心想或許可以偷走鞋子。但這雙漂亮的銀鞋讓桃樂絲深以為榮，所以除了晚上和洗澡時，她都不會脫下鞋子。女巫因為害怕黑暗，所以她不敢半夜跑進桃樂絲的房間拿走鞋子；而女巫不只怕黑暗，更怕水，所以在桃樂絲洗澡時，她也不敢走近。事實上，老女巫從沒碰過水，也沒讓水碰過她。

不過邪惡女巫老奸巨猾，她終於想到一個可以讓她如願的詭計。她在廚房地板中央放了一隻鐵棒，然後對鐵棒施加魔法，讓人的肉眼看不見它。因為人眼看不到鐵棒，所以桃樂絲走過地板時，便給絆得整個人都跌倒在地。她人是沒受什麼傷，但有一隻銀鞋在她跌倒時掉了下來。她還來不及撿回鞋子，鞋子就被女巫搶走，穿在她自己皮包骨的腳上。

邪惡女巫計謀得逞，不禁大喜，因為只要拿到一隻鞋子，就擁有一半魔力，而就算桃樂絲知道怎麼使用魔力，也對抗不了她了。

看到美麗的鞋子被搶去一隻，小女孩非常生氣，她對女巫說：「把我的鞋子還來！」

「不還！」女巫回答：「現在這是我的了，不是你的。」

「你真是可惡！」桃樂絲大叫：「你憑什麼拿走我的鞋子？」

「我就是要。」女巫嘲笑她說：「改天，我會拿走你另一隻鞋子。」

這把桃樂絲給惹火了，她拿起旁邊的一桶水，往女巫潑去，潑得她一身落湯雞。

女巫立刻恐懼得大叫一聲，桃樂絲驚訝地看著她。女巫的身體開始萎縮，然後倒了下去。

「看看你做的好事！」女巫尖叫：「我很快就要溶化了。」

「我真的很抱歉。」桃樂絲說道。看到眼前的女巫像黑糖一樣地化掉，她真是嚇壞了。

「你不知道水會殺了我嗎？」女巫用絕望的聲音哭叫著問道。

「我不知道！」桃樂絲回答：「我怎麼會知道呢？」

「我就快要完全溶化了，這座城堡是你的了。我一生作惡多端，只是我沒料到，像你這樣的一個小女孩，竟能把我溶化，終結我的惡行。看著──我走了！」

　　說完這些話，女巫就倒在地上，化成一堆棕色的液狀物，在廚房乾淨的地板上流成一片。看著女巫幾乎化於無形之後，桃樂絲拿起另一桶水，潑向那一堆東西，往門外清掃出去。她撿起老女人僅留下來的銀鞋，清理了一下，用布擦乾，再重新穿上。現在，她終於可以自由行事了。她跑到院子，告訴獅子說西方邪惡女巫已經死亡，他們不再是這個陌生地方的囚犯了。

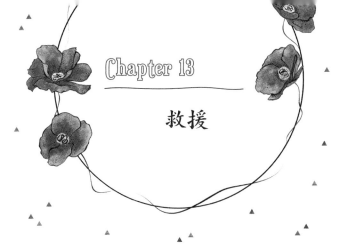

Chapter 13

救援

聽到邪惡女巫被一桶水給溶化掉了，膽小的獅子非常高興。桃樂絲立刻打開牢籠的大門，放牠出來。他們一起走進城堡，桃樂絲第一個舉動是把維奇人集合起來，告知他們現在已不再是奴隸了。

黃色維奇人欣喜若狂。他們已經被迫為邪惡女巫作牛作馬好幾年了，而且邪惡女巫待他們非常殘忍。此後，他們就把這一天訂為假日，設宴歡舞來慶祝。

「我們的朋友稻草人和錫人要是能跟我們一起，我一定會很高興的。」獅子說。

「你不覺得我們可以去救他們嗎？」女孩急切地問。

「我們可以試試看。」獅子回答。

於是，他們找來黃色維奇人，問他們是否願意幫忙營救他們的朋友。他們表示，非常樂意傾力相助，因為桃樂絲解放了他們。桃樂絲於是選了幾個看起來最有見識的維奇人，一起出發。他們走了一天半，來到錫人橫陳的石原上。錫人摔得整個都毀壞凹損，他的斧頭落在一旁，斧刃已經生鏽，斧柄也斷了一截。

　　維奇人把錫人輕輕捧起，帶回黃色城堡。路上，桃樂絲為老朋友的不幸遭遇掉下眼淚，而獅子也一副沉重又難過的樣子。

　　到了城堡，桃樂絲對維奇人說：「你們有人是錫匠嗎？」

　　「有呀，我們有很優秀的錫匠。」他們告訴她。

　　「那請他們來找我。」她說。隨後，錫匠便帶著工具籃來找她。她問：「你們能把錫人身上彎掉的地方弄直，讓他恢復原狀，再把他斷掉的地方焊接好嗎？」

　　錫匠們仔細檢查過錫人之後，表示他們可以把他修得完好如初。就這樣，他們在城堡中最大的一個黃色房間裡工作了三天四夜，把錫人的腿、身體和頭，又錘又扭，打彎焊接，磨亮敲打，直到錫人筆挺如昔，關節的運作靈活依舊。錫人身上是多了些補釘，但錫匠已經把他修補得很好了。況且錫人也不是一個愛慕虛榮的人，

The tinsmiths worked for three days and four nights.

他一點也不在意補釘。

　　最後，他走進桃樂絲的房間，向她感謝救命之恩時，不禁喜極而泣。桃樂絲只得用圍裙小心地幫他擦去臉上的每一滴眼淚，以免關節生鏽。另一方面，桃樂絲也因為與老友重逢，高興得眼淚撲簌簌地掉，只是她的眼淚是不需要拭去的。至於獅子，牠因為頻頻用尾巴末端來擦拭眼淚，尾巴都濕掉了，只好去院子裡把它曬乾。

　　桃樂絲告訴錫人發生的所有事情之後，錫人說：「要是稻草人能與我們重聚，我一定會很高興。」

　　「我們要去找他。」女孩說。

　　她找維奇人來幫忙。他們走了一天半之後，找到了那棵大樹。飛猴就是把稻草人的衣服，扔到這棵樹的樹枝上的。

　　這棵樹很高，樹幹又滑，沒人爬得上去。錫人立刻說：「我來把它砍下，這樣就可以拿到稻草人的衣服了。」

　　當錫匠們在修補錫人時，有一位做金匠的維奇人，打造了一把實心的金斧柄，把它牢牢地裝在斧頭上，以取代舊的壞斧柄。另有人把斧頭上所有鏽蝕都磨掉，所以斧頭現在就像剛磨過的銀器一樣，閃閃發亮。

　　錫人一說完，馬上開始砍樹。很快地，樹就砰地一聲倒下，稻草人的衣服也從樹上掉下，滾落地上。

　　桃樂絲把衣服撿起來，讓維奇人帶回城堡，然後塞

進又好又乾淨的稻草。看呀！稻草人又回來了，和以前沒有兩樣。稻草人向他們再三道謝救命之恩。

　　如今，他們團聚了。桃樂絲一行人在黃城堡裡度過了幾天歡樂時光，城堡裡應有盡有，好不舒適。但這一天，女孩想到了愛姆嬸嬸。她說：「我們必須回去找奧茲，要他實踐諾言。」

　　錫人說：「對，我終於要得到心了。」

　　「我要得到我的腦子了。」稻草人快樂地補充道。

　　「我要得到我的勇氣了。」獅子深思地說。

　　「我要回去堪薩斯了。」桃樂絲大叫，一面拍手。「噢，我們明天就往翡翠城出發！」

　　他們就這樣決定了。隔天早上，他們集合維奇人，向他們道別。維奇人很難過他們要離開，而他們已經很喜歡錫人，還求他留下來統治他們和西方的黃色國度。後來看他們決意要走，維奇人就贈送托托和獅子各一條金項圈，饋贈桃樂絲一個鑲鑽的美麗手鐲，致贈稻草人一根金頭手杖，好讓他不會絆倒，至於錫人，他們送的是一個鑲有珍貴寶石和金子的銀製油罐。

他們每一個人都說了好一段謝辭，當作答謝，並握手致意，還握得手都痠痛了。

桃樂絲去女巫的櫥櫃裡，把籃子裝滿旅途所需的食物時，看到了那頂金冠。她把金冠戴在頭上，大小正適合她。她不知道金冠具有魔力，只是覺得它很漂亮，便決定要戴著它，而把自己的遮陽帽放進籃子裡。

一切就緒之後，他們就啟程往翡翠城邁進。維奇人向他們歡呼了三次，道了許多祝福，送他們上路。

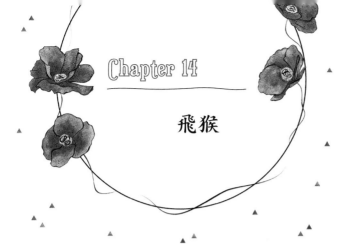

Chapter 14

飛猴

你們應該還記得，邪惡女巫的城堡和翡翠城之間是沒有路的，連一條小徑都沒有。這四個人去找女巫時，是女巫先看到他們，然後派飛猴去把他們抓來的。現在，要穿越這一大片毛茛和黃雛菊，找尋歸路，要比上次被抓去來得困難多了。當然，他們知道要往太陽升起的東方直直走去，所以他們也就朝那裡出發了。然而，到了正午，因為日正當中，無法辨別東西，他們就在遼闊的田野中迷了路。但他們依然繼續前進，到了夜裡，月亮升起，皎潔的月光遍照大地。他們躺在芬芳的黃色花朵之間，酣睡到天亮——除了稻草人和錫人。

隔天早上，太陽躲在雲的後面，但他們仍出發了，彷彿他們很確定該走哪個方向似的。

桃樂絲說：「如果我們走得夠遠，終會走到某個地方的。」

但是，一天一天地過去，眼前仍只見一片深紅色的田野。稻草人開始咕噥了。

「我們一定是迷路了。」他說：「除非趕快找到回翡翠城的路，不然我就永遠得不到我的腦子了。」

「還有我的心。」錫人說：「我等不及去見奧茲了，但這真是一條漫漫長路呀。」

　　膽小的獅子低聲說：「你看，這樣走下去要是都毫無結果，那我就沒有勇氣走下去了。」

　　桃樂絲也垂頭喪氣了起來。她坐在草地上，看著夥伴們，他們也坐下來看她。托托發現，這是牠有生以來，第一次累到連去追逐頭上的蝴蝶的力氣都沒有。牠伸出舌頭，喘著氣，看著桃樂絲，好像在問下一步應該要怎麼走。

　　「如果我們叫田鼠來，」她建議：「牠們也許可以告訴我們去翡翠城的路。」

　　稻草人叫道：「一定可以的，我們之前怎麼都沒想到？」

　　桃樂絲吹響脖子上的小哨子。田鼠皇后給她那個哨子之後，她就一直戴著。沒多久，他們聽到小腳步趴噠趴噠的聲音，有一群小灰鼠跑過來。皇后自己也在其中，她用小小的吱吱聲問：「我能為我的朋友做什麼？」

「我們迷路了。」桃樂絲說：「您能告訴我們翡翠城在哪裡嗎？」

皇后回答：「當然，不過去那裡還很遠，因為你們走反方向了。」她注意到桃樂絲的金冠，就說道：「你為什麼不使用金冠魔法，把飛猴給叫來呢？不用一個小時的時間，飛猴就能帶你們到奧茲的城裡去了。」

桃樂絲驚訝地回答：「我不知道金冠有魔力，它的咒語是什麼？」

「咒語就寫在金冠的裡層。」田鼠皇后回答：「不過如果要叫飛猴來，那我們就得告退了。牠們很會惡作劇，而且以捉弄我們為樂。」

「牠們不會傷害我嗎？」女孩擔憂地問。

「噢，不會的，牠們必須服從戴這頂金冠的人。再見了！」說罷，她就跑得不見身影，所有老鼠飛快地跟在後面。

桃樂絲往金冠裡瞧，看到內裡上寫了一些字。她想，這一定是咒語，就小心地看了說明，然後把金冠戴在頭上。

「耶——皮，佩——皮，喀——咳！」她用左腳站著唸道。

「你說什麼？」不明究理的稻草人問道。

「西——囉，猴——囉，哈——囉！」桃樂絲換用右腳站著，繼續唸。

「哈囉！」錫人冷靜地回答。

「瑞——西，蘇——西，立刻！」換用雙腳站立的桃樂絲唸道。咒語一唸完，他們就聽到刺耳的喋喋聲和振翅的啪噠聲，有一群飛猴朝他們飛來。

飛猴王在桃樂絲面前躬著腰，問道：「您有什麼吩咐？」

孩子回答：「我們想去翡翠城，可是我們迷路了。」

「我們會帶你們去。」飛猴王回答。話一說完，兩隻猴子立刻抱起桃樂絲飛去。其他猴子隨後帶著稻草人、錫人和獅子，一隻小猴子抓著托托，飛在後面，托托還竭力想咬牠。

稻草人和錫人一開始很害怕，他們還記得飛猴曾經凶暴地對待過他們。不過在發現牠們並無惡意之後，便愉快地翱翔空中，欣賞底下美麗的樹林和花園。

桃樂絲被兩隻最大的猴子帶著，其中一隻是飛猴王。牠們用手圈成椅子，小心地不弄痛她，而她坐在上面，也不用費力。

「你們為什麼必須服從金冠的咒語呢？」她問。

「這說來話長。」飛猴王笑著回答：「不過，既然我們還要飛很久，如果您想聽，我就講來給您打發時間。」

「我洗耳恭聽。」她回答。

領袖開始說：「我們曾經是一個自由的民族，居

The Monkeys caught
Dorothy in their arms
and flew away with her.

住在大森林裡，生活安樂。我們在樹木之間飛翔，以堅果和水果為食，隨心所欲，不必向任何人稱臣。我們有些猴子有時是過於調皮，會飛到地面拉扯無翅動物的尾巴，或是追逐鳥兒，或是向穿越樹林的行人丟堅果。不過我們無憂無慮，十分快樂，充滿歡笑，每天都過得很盡興。這是很久很久以前的事了，那時奧茲還尚未從雲端下來統治這塊土地。

當時，在遙遠的北方，住著一位美麗的公主，她是一位法力高強的魔法師。她的法力只用於助人，未曾用來傷害任何好人。她的名字叫做歌雅蕾，住在一座用大顆紅寶石所蓋成的華麗宮殿裡。她深受每一個人的愛戴，但她最大的憂愁，就是找不到一個足以匹配的人來愛。所有的男人都太蠢太醜，配不上這麼美麗又聰明的女孩。不過最後，她終於找到了一個既具有男子氣概，又聰明過人的俊美男孩。歌雅蕾打算等他長大之後，就要和他成親。她把男孩帶回紅寶石宮殿，使出所有的法寶，要讓他成為女人所夢寐以求的男人：強壯、善良又迷人。奎拉拉（大家都這麼叫他）長大成人之後，被公認是世上最優秀、最聰明的人，而且他又是那麼英姿煥發，歌雅蕾對他非常傾心，便急著張羅婚禮。

那時候，我的祖父是飛猴王，住在歌雅蕾宮殿附近的樹林裡。牠這個老傢伙，愛惡作劇甚於愛美食。就在婚禮前的某一天，我的祖父和一幫猴子出去，見到了奎拉拉正在河邊散步，身上穿著由桃色絲綢和紫色絲絨所做成的華麗衣裳。我祖父想看看他到底有什麼本事,就下令猴子們飛下去抓起奎拉拉,把他帶到河中央,然後扔下去。

『游上來吧,我的好友。』我祖父叫道:『看看河水會不會弄髒你的衣服。』奎拉拉很聰明,也會游泳,而且不自恃而驕。他浮出水面游到岸邊時,只是笑一笑。歌雅蕾趕來時,發現他的絲綢和絨子都被河水弄壞了。

公主大為光火。她知道惡作劇的是誰,便叫來所有的飛猴。起初她說要把牠們的翅膀綁起來,然後就像牠們對待奎拉拉那樣,把牠們丟入河中。猴子一旦被綁住翅膀丟進河裡,勢必滅頂,故我的祖父苦苦哀求,再加以奎拉拉也替牠們說好話,歌雅蕾才饒了牠們一命。只不過,交換的條件是:飛猴要聽從金冠擁有人的命令三次。這頂金冠是特地做給奎拉拉的結婚禮物,據說耗費了王國一半的財富。想當然耳,我的祖父和其他猴子立刻就答應了這個條件。就這樣,不管是誰擁有金冠,我

們都得聽命於他三次。」

「那飛猴後來怎麼樣了？」桃樂絲問。她對這個故事很感興趣。

猴子答道：「奎拉拉是第一個擁有金冠的人，也是第一個向我們施令的人。由於他的新娘子不想再看到我們，所以在他們結婚之後，他就把我們叫到樹林裡集合，然後命令我們待在永遠不會讓歌雅蕾看見的地方。這我們非常樂意從命，因為我們很怕她。

這就是金冠落入西方邪惡女巫手裡之前，我們所遵從的任務。西方邪惡女巫叫我們把維奇人變成奴隸，後來又把奧茲本人逐出西方國。現在金冠是您的了，您有權使喚我們三次。」

猴子王講完故事時，桃樂絲往下望去，看到了翡翠城閃耀的綠色城牆已經近在眼前。她很訝異猴子怎麼飛得這麼快，也很高興飛行結束了。這群古怪的動物小心地把他們安放在城門前。飛猴王對桃樂絲鞠過躬，就帶著猴群飛快離去。

「真是一次不錯的飛行。」小女孩說。

「沒錯，而且一下子就解決了我們的問題。」獅子說：「多虧你帶上了神奇的金冠！」

Chapter 15

露出馬腳

四個旅人走向翡翠城的大門，按了門鈴。按了幾次後，上次見過的那位大門守衛開了門。

「什麼！你們又回來了？」他驚訝地問。

「你沒看到正是我們嗎？」稻草人回答。

「我想說你們去找西方邪惡女巫了。」

「我們是去找過她了。」稻草人說。

「那她又讓你們離開了？」男人好奇地問。

「因為她無能為力呀，她溶化掉了。」稻草人解釋。

「溶化掉了！哇，這實在是個好消息！」男人說：「誰把她溶化掉的？」

「桃樂絲。」獅子正經地說道。

「天啊！」男人叫道，對桃樂絲深深行了一鞠躬。

守衛帶他們到自己的小房間，像上次那樣給他們戴上從大箱子裡拿出來的眼鏡，像之前那樣把眼鏡鎖上，然後穿過城門，進入翡翠城。人們聽大門守衛說，桃樂絲把西方邪惡女巫給溶化掉了，就簇擁而上，大批民眾一路跟隨她到了奧茲的宮殿。

守宮殿門的仍是那位綠鬍子士兵，只不過這一次，他立刻就讓他們進去了。接待他們的，也仍是那位美麗的綠色少女。少女隨即帶他們前往上次住過的房間，讓他們在奧茲準備好接見他們之前，可以先休憩一番。

士兵立刻向奧茲稟報消息，說桃樂絲一行人已經除掉邪惡女巫，回到城裡來了。奧茲聽了，只是默不作聲。他們以為偉大的巫師會立刻召見他們，但事實上並沒有。隔天、後天、大後天，他們仍然沒有接到奧茲的命令。等待是既無聊，又令人疲倦，他們最後對奧茲生氣了起來。奧茲送他們去歷經險難，受人奴役，現在又這樣對待他們。稻草人請綠色少女再去通報奧茲說，如果他不立刻召見他們，他們就要叫飛猴來幫忙，看他到底要不要遵守諾言。巫師聽到稟報後，非常害怕，就下令要他們明天早上九點四分到宮室裡來。奧茲曾在西方國和飛猴交手過，他並不想再看到牠們。

四位旅人整夜無眠，他們無不想著奧茲答應要賜給自己的禮物。桃樂絲只睡了一會兒，她夢到她人在堪薩斯，而愛姆嬸嬸正告訴她，說她多麼高興看到小女孩又回到家裡來了。

隔天早上九點整，綠鬍子士兵來傳他們。四分鐘後，他們就一起走進奧茲國王的宮室。

當然，他們每個人都以為，巫師的樣子應該和他們之前所見的一樣。他們環顧四周，卻驚訝地發現，房間裡空無一人。他們靠近門口，緊緊挨在一起。空蕩屋內的死寂，比奧茲之前的化身還更可怕。

不久，他們聽見一個嚴肅的聲音，似乎是從大圓頂那裡傳出來的。它說道：「我是偉大而可怕的奧茲，你們為什麼要找我？」

他們再仔細打量過房間的每個角落，仍不見任何身影。桃樂絲問：「您在哪裡？」

「我無所不在，但凡人的肉眼看不到我。」聲音回答：「我現在要坐上王位，讓你們可以面奏。」

果然，聲音聽起來就是從王位那裡發出來的。於是他們走向前，站成一列。桃樂絲說：「喔，奧茲，我們是來請您履行承諾的。」

「什麼承諾？」奧茲問。

「您答應過，只要一除掉邪惡女巫，您就要送我回堪薩斯。」女孩說。

「而您就要送給我腦子。」稻草人說。

「而您就要送給我一顆心。」錫人說。

「而您就要送給我勇氣。」膽小的獅子說。

「邪惡女巫真的被除掉了嗎？」聲音說。桃樂絲覺得他聲音有點發抖。

她回答：「是的，我用一桶水把她給溶化掉了。」

「我的天呀！」聲音說：「太突然了！好吧，明天來見我，我需要時間想一想。」

「您有的時間已經夠多了。」錫人生氣地說。

「我們一天也等不下去了。」稻草人說。

「您必須遵守對我們的承諾！」桃樂絲喊道。

獅子心想，嚇一嚇巫師也好，就大吼了一聲。牠的吼聲兇猛可怕，嚇得托托竄到一旁，撞翻了立在牆角的屏風。屏風應聲而倒，大家轉過身去，頓時一陣詫異。眼前，躲在屏風後面的，是一個矮小的老人。老人童山濯濯，一臉皺紋，看起來和他們一樣地驚訝。

錫人舉起斧頭，衝到矮小老人的跟前，大聲叫道：「你是誰？」

「我是偉大而可怕的奧茲。」老人聲音顫抖地說道：「別砍我，求求你，你要我做什麼我都答應。」

我們的朋友們又驚訝又失望地看著他。

「我還以為奧茲是一顆大頭顱。」桃樂絲說。

「我以為奧茲是一個美麗的女子。」稻草人說。

「我以為奧茲是一隻可怕的野獸。」錫人說。

「我以為奧茲是一團火球。」獅子喊。

「不，你們都錯了。」老人溫馴地說道：「那是假裝出來的。」

「假裝出來的！」桃樂絲喊道：「難道你不是偉大的巫師嗎？」

他說：「噓，親愛的，別大聲嚷嚷，如果被聽到，我就完了。大家都以為我是個偉大的巫師。」

「你不是嗎？」她問。

「才不是呢，親愛的，我只是個普通人。」

「你不只是個普通人，」稻草人悲傷地說：「你是個騙子。」

「你說對了！」老人一邊說，一邊搓著雙手，好像這話讓他很滿意似的。「我是個騙子。」

錫人說：「這太慘了，我要怎樣得到我的心呢？」

「我要怎樣得到我的勇氣呢？」獅子問。

「我要怎樣得到我的腦子呢？」稻草人邊哭，邊用外套的袖子拭淚。

奧茲說：「親愛的朋友們，我求你們別再說這些芝麻小事了，想想我吧，我被你們拆穿了，這是最可怕的事了。」

「沒有別人知道你是個騙子嗎？」桃樂絲問。

「除了你們四個和我自己，沒有人知道。」奧茲回

"Exactly so! I am a humbug."

答：「我騙了大家那麼久，還以為永遠不會被拆穿呢。我讓你們進來宮室，就是個天大的錯誤。我一向連我的臣子都不見，所以他們都相信我是個可怕的人。」

桃樂絲疑惑地說：「可是，我不懂，我上次見你的時候，你怎麼會是一個大頭顱？」

「那是我的一個把戲。」奧茲回答：「請來這邊，我來告訴你們細節。」

他們跟著他，被領到宮室後面的小房間裡。他指著一個角落，那裡放著一顆用很多厚紙做成的大頭顱，上面仔細地畫了臉譜。

「我用線把它從天花板上吊下來。」奧茲說：「我站在屏風後面拉線，讓它的眼睛會移動，嘴巴也會張開。」

「那聲音呢？」她問。

「噢，我會腹語。」老人說：「我可以讓聲音從我想要的地方發出來，所以你會以為聲音是從那顆頭顱發出來的。這邊是其他我用來騙你們的東西。」他給稻草人看他偽裝成美麗女子時所穿戴的裙子和面具，而錫人所看到的可怕野獸，原來不過是把一堆皮縫在一起，再用板子把它撐住罷了。至於火球，也是假巫師從天花板上吊下來的，火球原是一團棉花，淋上了油之後，就會猛烈地燃燒起來。

稻草人說：「真的，你這樣一個騙子，應該為自己感到可恥。」

「我是啊，我是覺得自己很可恥。」老人抱歉地回答：「但我別無他法。請坐下吧，這裡有很多椅子，讓我告訴你們我的故事。」

他們便坐下來，聽他說了如下的故事：

「我在歐馬哈出生……」

「什麼，那離堪薩斯不遠啊！」桃樂絲大喊。

「是不遠，不過離這裡很遠。」他一邊悲傷地對她搖搖頭，一邊說道：「我曾拜名師學藝，等我長大之後，我就成了腹語家。我可以模仿任何鳥類或動物的聲音。」說到這裡，他發出喵喵聲，聲音果然很傳神，讓托托豎起耳朵，到處找貓。「後來，」奧茲繼續說道：「我當膩了腹語家，就跑去當熱氣球人了。」

「那是什麼？」桃樂絲問。

「就是在馬戲團表演日坐著熱氣球上升的人，好吸引群眾，讓人們買票看馬戲團。」他解釋。

她說：「噢，我知道。」

「有一天，我坐著熱氣球上升，結果繩子纏住，熱氣球無法下降，就一直升到雲層上方，然後被空中的氣流，帶到好幾哩外的地方。我在空中飄了一天一夜，第二天早上我醒來時，發現熱氣球飛到一塊奇異又美麗的土地上面。

後來，熱氣球慢慢下降，我人沒有受傷，但我發現我旁邊有一群古怪的人，他們看我從天而降，就以為我是偉大的巫師。當然，我就恭敬不如從命了。他們很怕我，保證只要是我吩咐的事，無不照辦。

　　為了我自己的樂趣，也為了讓這些善良的人有事情可以忙，我就命令他們建造了這座城市和宮殿。他們樂於聽命，也做得很好。我想，這座城市一派碧綠，異常美麗，就把它取名為翡翠城。為了讓這座城更名副其實，我又叫所有人戴上綠色眼鏡，這樣，他們眼裡所見的，就莫不都是綠色的了。」

　　「難道在這裡，不是每樣東西都是綠色的嗎？」桃樂絲問。

　　「並不比別的城市來得綠。」奧茲回答：「不過，當然，戴上綠色眼鏡之後，就所見皆綠了。熱氣球把我帶來這裡時，我還很年輕，但現在我已經很老了，翡翠城也很有歷史了。長久以來，人民都戴著綠色眼鏡，把這裡真當成翡翠城了。這裡的確很美麗，寶石金銀，珍品奇物，隨處可見。我一向善待人民，他們也很愛戴我，不過建好了宮殿以後，我就把自己關起來，不見任何人。

　　我一個最大的恐懼，就是那些女巫了。雖然，我毫

無法力，但我很快就發現女巫們真的擁有神奇的魔法。這個國家共有四個女巫，分別統治北方、南方、東方和西方的人民。幸好，北方和南方的女巫很善良，不會危害到我，但是東方和西方的女巫邪惡透頂，要不是她們以為我的法力高過她們，她們一定已經毀掉我了。我很怕她們，也因此，我長年生活於極度的恐懼之中。所以你們可想而知，當我聽到你的房子壓死東方邪惡女巫時，我有多麼高興了。你們來找我時，我想只要你們能除掉另一個女巫，任何事情我都願意答應你們。但如今你已經把她溶化了，我卻只能很慚愧地告訴你們，我無法履行諾言。」

「我想你是個很惡劣的人。」桃樂絲說。

「噢，不是的，親愛的，我真的是個好人，但我必須承認，我是很彆腳的巫師。」

「你不能給我腦子嗎？」稻草人說。

「你並不需要呀，你每一天都學到新事物。小嬰兒有腦子，但所知不多。唯有經驗才能帶來知識，你生活在這個世上愈久，經驗就愈多。」

稻草人說：「你說

的也許沒錯,但是除非你給我腦子,不然我還是很不快樂。」

這位冒名巫師端詳著他。

他嘆口氣說:「好吧,如我所言,我並不算是個魔法師。但如果你明天早上來找我,我就幫你塞一些腦子到腦袋裡頭去。只不過,我無法告訴你腦子要如何使用,你要自己去發現。」

「噢,謝謝你,謝謝你!」稻草人叫道:「別擔心,我會自己找出使用方法的!」

「那我的勇氣呢?」獅子焦急地問。

「我確信你是很有勇氣的,你需要的只是自信。」奧茲回答:「沒有任何生物是臨危不懼的。真正的勇氣,是在恐懼時還能面對危險。你已經很有這種勇氣了。」

「也許有,但我還是一樣害怕。」獅子說:「除非你能給我可以忘卻恐懼的勇氣,不然我還是很不快樂。」

「好吧,我明天就給你這種勇氣。」奧茲回答。

「那我的心呢?」錫人問。

奧茲回答:「嗯,這個嘛,我想你不該渴望得到一顆心,心讓很多人快快不樂。如果你明瞭這一點,你就會很慶幸自己沒有心。」

「這只是你的意見罷了。」錫人說：「對我來說，只要能給我心，所有的不快樂我都甘心領受，毫無怨言。」

奧茲溫和地回答：「那好，明天來找我，你會得到一顆心的。我假扮巫師已經這麼久了，再多玩幾下也無妨。」

桃樂絲說：「那現在，我要怎麼回堪薩斯？」

「這我們必須想一想。」矮小男人回答：「給我兩三天思索，我會想辦法帶你穿越沙漠。在這期間，你們都是我的貴客，你們住在宮殿時，我的人會服侍你們，隨你們使喚。但我只想要求一件事，以做為我協助你們的回報，那就是：你們必須幫我保密，不可告訴任何人說我是個騙子。」

他們同意守口如瓶。之後，他們歡天喜歡地各自回房。桃樂絲這下子也指望那位被她稱為「偉大而可怕的騙子」的人，能找出方法送她回堪薩斯。如果他做得到，那她就什麼都不跟他計較了。

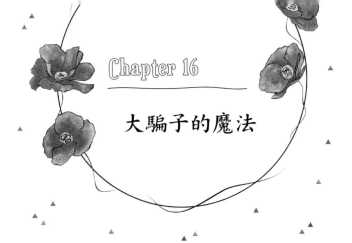

Chapter 16

大騙子的魔法

隔天早上，稻草人對他的朋友說：「恭喜我吧！我終於要去找奧茲拿我的腦子了。當我回來時，我就跟其他人沒有兩樣了。」

「我一直很喜歡你原來的樣子。」桃樂絲率直地說道。

「你很善良，會喜歡一個稻草人。」他回答：「不過，當你聽到我新腦子裡迸出來的絕妙想法時，一定會更看重我。」

他興奮地向大家道過再見，前往宮室，輕輕敲了門。

「進來。」奧茲說。

稻草人走進去，看見那矮小的男人正坐在窗邊沉思。

「我是來要我的腦子的。」稻草人有點不安地說。

「噢，對，請坐在那張椅子上。」奧茲回答：「為了找到放腦子的正確位置，請原諒我必須把你的頭拿下來。」

稻草人說：「這沒關係，只要頭放回去時會變聰明，

就儘管把我的頭拿下來吧。」

於是巫師把他的頭取下，清光裡面的稻草。接著，他走到後面的房間裡，拿了一團麥麩，混入許多別針和針狀物，把它搖一搖，讓針混得更勻，然後放進稻草人的頭頂，再用稻草把空隙塞滿，以固定位置。他重新把稻草人的頭接回身體時，說道：「從現在起，你就是一個完美的人類了，因為我給了你很多全新的腦子。」

稻草人最大的願望終於實現，他既高興又驕傲。他誠摯地向奧茲道謝，然後走回到朋友那裡。

桃樂絲好奇地打量著他。因為有了腦子，他的頭頂變得鼓鼓的。

「你覺得怎樣？」她問。

「我覺得真的變聰明了。」他認真地回答：「等我習慣我的腦子之後，我就無所不知了。」

「為什麼會有針和別針從你的頭頂上冒出來？」錫人問。

「那證明了他頭腦很敏銳呀。」獅子說。

「好，我要去找奧茲拿我的心了。」錫人說罷，便走向宮室敲了門。

「進來。」奧茲說道。錫人進去之後，說：「我是來要我的心的。」

矮小的男人回答：「好，但我要在你的胸口上割一個洞，才能把心放到適當的位置上。希望不會弄痛你。」

錫人回答：「噢，不會的，我根本不會有感覺。」

奧茲於是用錫匠的剪子，在錫人的左胸膛割了一個方型小洞。接著，他從五斗櫃拿了一顆外型很美觀的心。那顆心是用絲綢做成的，裡面塞了木屑。

「這顆心不是很美嗎？」他問。

「真的很美！」錫人雀躍不已地答道：「但這顆心善良嗎？」

「噢，非常善良！」奧茲回答。他把心放進錫人的胸口，然後重新放上那塊方形錫塊，把它齊整地焊接回割下來的地方。

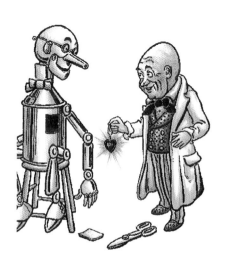

他說：「現在，你有一顆令人驕傲的心了。但很抱歉的是，你的胸膛上多了個補釘，

這也是萬不得已的。」

「那補釘無所謂啦。」快樂的錫人說道：「你的大恩大德，我沒齒難忘！」

「這不足掛齒。」奧茲回答。

錫人回到朋友那裡，大家都祝賀他的好運。

現在換獅子走向宮室，敲了門。

「進來。」奧茲說。

「我來要我的勇氣。」獅子走進房間後說道。

矮小的男人回答：「好，我去幫你拿勇氣來。」

他走去櫃子那裡，伸手取下最上層架子上的方形綠瓶子，把裡面的東西倒在一個雕刻精美的金綠色碟子上。他把碟子拿到獅子面前，獅子用鼻子嗅了嗅，似乎不喜歡它的味道。巫師說：「喝吧。」

「這是什麼？」獅子問。

奧茲回答：「這個啊，把它喝進你的身體裡，它就是勇氣了。你知道的，勇氣當然都是在身體裡面

的，所以除非把它喝了，不然它就稱不上是勇氣。所以我建議你，盡快喝下它。」

獅子不再遲疑，就把碟子裡的東西喝個精光。

「現在感覺怎樣？」奧茲問。

「勇氣十足。」獅子回答。牠高興地回到朋友那裡，告訴他們牠的好運道。

現在剩奧茲獨處一室，他笑了笑，心想，他成功地給了稻草人、錫人和獅子那些他們自認為缺乏的東西，他喃喃道：「我怎能不當個騙子呢？所有人都要我做那種明知道不可能的事。要讓稻草人、獅子和錫人稱心如意，還算容易，因為他們以為我無所不能。但是要送桃樂絲回堪薩斯，需要的可就不只是想像力了，而我很確定，我一籌莫展。」

Chapter 17

熱氣球怎麼
起飛的

接下來的三天，奧茲都沒有傳喚桃樂絲。雖然她的朋友個個心滿意足，但這幾天對小女孩來說是很鬱悶的。稻草人告訴大家，他腦子裡有偉大的想法，但他不肯透露是什麼想法，因為他知道，除了他自己，沒有人能夠了解那些想法。當錫人走路時，他可以感覺到自己胸膛裡的心正在跳動。他還告訴桃樂絲，他發現，他現在的心，比以前他還是血肉之軀時的心，還要來得更善良、更溫柔。獅子則宣布，牠現在一無所懼，就算來了一支軍隊或是一群兇猛的喀力軍，牠也會樂於迎戰。

除了桃樂絲，這一群夥伴個個都感到很滿足。此時，桃樂絲的歸鄉之心更是殷切了。

到了第四天，奧茲終於傳喚她，讓她欣喜不已。當她走進宮室時，奧茲和藹地對她說：「坐下，親愛的，我想我有辦法送你離開這個地方了。」

「然後回堪薩斯？」她急切地問。

「是不是回堪薩斯，我就不確定了。」奧茲說：「堪薩斯在哪裡，我毫無概念。不過，只要能夠越過沙漠，想找到回家的路就容易了。」

「我要怎麼穿越沙漠呢？」她問道。

「我來跟你說我的想法。」矮小的男人說：「你看，我是坐熱氣球來到這裡的，而你也是被龍捲風從空中帶來的。所以我想，穿越沙漠的最佳辦法，就是用飛的。如果要製造龍捲風，我無能為力，但是我一直在仔細思考整件事，我相信，我可以做一個熱氣球。」

「怎麼做？」桃樂絲問。

奧茲說：「用絲布來做熱氣球，然後把它塗上一層膠，再灌進瓦斯。我的宮殿內有很多絲布，要做熱氣球不成問題。只不過，在這整個國家裡，都找不到瓦斯可以用來灌熱氣球，讓它飄起來。」

桃樂絲說：「它要是飄不起來，那就沒有用了。」

「沒錯。」奧茲回答：「但是有其他方法可以讓它飄起來，我們可以改用熱空氣。熱空氣沒有瓦斯那麼好用，只要空氣一變冷，熱氣球就會降落在沙漠中，那我們就會迷路了。」

「我們！」桃樂絲喊：「你要跟我一起去嗎？」

「是的，當然。」奧茲回答：「我實在厭倦再當騙子了。只要我一出這個宮殿，人民很快就會識破我根本不是個巫師，他們會很生氣我騙了他們。所以，我只好整天關在房間裡，但這樣實在悶壞了。我寧願跟你回堪薩斯，回到馬戲團去。」

「我很高興有你作伴。」桃樂絲說。

「謝謝你。」他回答：「如果你願意幫我把絲布縫起來，我們就可以開始做熱氣球了。」

桃樂絲於是拿起針線，奧茲盡快地把絲布剪成適當的形狀，小女孩也盡快把布整齊地縫在一起。第一塊布是淡綠色的，第二塊布是深綠色的，第三塊布是翡翠綠的，因為奧茲想做一個有不同深淺綠色的熱氣球。他們花了三天的時間才把所有的布縫成一塊，最後，他們完成了一個二十餘英呎長的大型綠色絲綢布袋。

接著，奧茲在袋子的裡層塗上一層薄膠，好讓它不透氣，然後便宣布熱氣球已經大功告成了。

「不過，我們還需要一個用來乘坐的籃子。」他說。於是，他叫綠鬍子士兵去找一個大洗衣籃，並用許多繩子把洗衣籃固定在熱氣球的下方。

等一切就緒後，奧茲下諭令給人民，表示他即將去拜訪一位住在雲端的偉大巫師兄弟。這個消息很快傳遍全

城，人人都前來一睹這番奇景。

奧茲叫人把熱氣球抬到宮殿前面，引來人們好奇地圍觀。錫人用他砍好的那一大堆木柴升了火，奧茲在火的上方抓住熱氣球的底部，讓上升的熱空氣進入絲綢布袋裡。漸漸地，熱氣球膨脹了起來，並慢慢上升，最後只剩籃子立在地面上。

奧茲爬進籃子，大聲對所有人說：「現在，我要出訪去了。在我出門期間，由稻草人代理統治。我下令，你們得服從他，就像你們服從我那樣。」

這時熱氣球栓在地面上的繩子被拉得很緊，因為熱氣球裡的空氣很熱，重量比空氣輕很多，熱氣球直要往上飛入空中。

「桃樂絲，來吧！」巫師大喊：「快，熱氣球要飛走了。」

「我到處都找不到托托！」桃樂絲回答。她不想把她的小狗留在這裡，但托托跑進人群裡去對一隻小貓吠叫。最後，桃樂絲終於找到牠。她抓起牠之後，便向熱氣球跑去。

她還差幾步就到了，奧茲伸出手，要幫她爬進籃子裡，但就在這時，喀的一聲，繩子斷了，熱氣球升上天空，留下了她。

　　「回來！」她尖叫：「我也要去！」

　　「我回不來了，親愛的。」奧茲從籃子裡喊：「再見！」

　　「再見！」每個人都叫道。他們盯著奧茲乘坐的籃子，看著它慢慢地越飛越遠，直至天際。

　　這是他們最後一次看到奧茲這位偉大的巫師。我們只知道，也許他安全地抵達了歐馬哈，現在還住在那兒。

　　但是，人民十分緬懷他，他們口耳相傳道：「奧茲，我們永遠的朋友。他在這裡時，為我們建立了美麗的翡翠城，現在他離開了，留下睿智的稻草人來治理我們。」

　　然而，痛失偉大的巫師，讓人民悲傷了好些日子，無以慰藉。

回堪薩斯的希望再度破滅，桃樂絲痛哭不已。不過她又想了想，也很慶幸自己沒有坐上熱氣球。況且，她和夥伴們也都因失去奧茲而感到不捨。

錫人來找她，說：「如果我沒有為賜給我善心的人感到哀傷，那我就太不知感恩了。我要為奧茲的離去哭泣一下，能否請你好心地幫我擦眼淚，這樣我才不會生鏽。」

「我很樂意。」她話一說完，就去拿來一條毛巾。錫人哭了幾分鐘，桃樂絲緊盯著他的眼淚，然後用毛巾把眼淚擦掉。哭完之後，錫人親切地向她道謝，然後拿鑲有珠寶的油罐，來為自己全身上油，以防萬一。

稻草人現在是翡翠城的統治者了。雖然

他不是巫師，但人們都以他為傲，他們說：「在這世界上，再也找不到由稻草人所統治的城市了。」而就他們所知，確實是如此。

熱氣球帶奧茲飛走的隔天早上，四位旅人在宮室裡聚會，商議事情。稻草人坐在王位上，其他人恭敬地站在他跟前。

「我們也不算厄運連連。」新統治者說：「這座宮殿和翡翠城現在歸我們所管，由我們作主。記得不久前，我還被綁在一個農夫的玉米田裡的竿子上，而如今，我成了這座美麗城市的統治者。我對自己的命運甚感滿意。」

「我也是。」錫人說：「我很高興有了新的心，而且這確實是我在世上唯一想要的東西。」

「至於我，就算我不比其他野獸勇敢，但我很清楚自己也是很有膽量的，所以，我也就很滿足了。」獅子謙虛地說。

「桃樂絲要是能滿意於住在這翡翠城裡，」稻草人繼續說：「那我們就能一起過著幸福的日子了。」

「可是我不想住在這裡。」桃樂絲喊道：「我想回堪薩斯，和愛姆嬸嬸和亨利叔叔住在一起。」

「好吧，那麼，要怎麼做？」錫人問。

The Scarecrow sat in the
big throne.

　　稻草人決定好好想一想。但由於他想得太用力，腦袋裡的針和別針都迸了出來。最後，他說：

　　「何不把飛猴叫來，讓牠們帶你飛過沙漠？」

　　「我怎麼沒想到呀！」桃樂絲高興地說：「就是這樣了。我立刻去把金冠拿來。」

　　她把金冠拿到宮室裡，唸著咒語，一群飛猴很快從敞開的窗戶飛進來，站在她旁邊。

　　「這是您第二次召喚我們。」飛猴王向小女孩鞠躬說：「您要我們做什麼？」

　　「我要你們帶我飛到堪薩斯。」桃樂絲說。

　　但飛猴王搖了搖頭。

　　「恕難照辦。」牠說：「我們只屬於這個國度，無法離開。還不曾有飛猴去過堪薩斯，我想未來也不會有，因為飛猴不屬於那裡。我們很樂意在能力範圍之內為您效命，但是我們無法穿越沙漠，再會。」

　　飛猴王再次行過禮後，就展開雙翅，帶著飛猴群從窗戶飛走了。

　　桃樂絲失望得都快哭了。「我白白浪費了一次金冠的魔力。」她說：「那些飛猴幫不上忙。」

　　「太悽慘了！」軟心腸的錫人說。

　　稻草人又尋思起來。他的頭顱鼓脹得很厲害，桃樂絲很擔心他的頭會爆炸。

　　他說：「我們叫綠鬍子士兵進來，看他有什麼建議。」

被傳喚的士兵戰戰兢兢地走進宮室。奧茲還在的時候，都不准他進到門內。

稻草人對士兵說：「這個小女孩想穿越沙漠，有什麼辦法可行？」

士兵回答：「我不知道，至今尚無人能穿越沙漠，除了奧茲本人。」

「沒有人能幫助我們嗎？」桃樂絲真切地問。

「葛琳達或許可以。」他建議。

「葛琳達是誰？」稻草人問。

「葛琳達是南方女巫，統治垮德林人。在所有女巫中，她的法力最高強。此外，她的城堡就座落在沙漠邊緣，所以她或許有穿越沙漠的辦法。」

「葛琳達是個好女巫，是吧？」孩子問。

「垮德林人視她為好女巫，她對每一個人都很仁慈。」士兵說：「據說，她是一位很美麗的女子。她已經活了很久了，可是她知道青春永駐的秘訣。」

「我要怎麼去她的城堡？」桃樂絲問。

「往南方直走。」他回答：「不過，聽說路途上險惡重重。樹林裡有野獸，途中還有一個古怪的民族，不喜歡讓陌生人過境他們的領地。也因此，還未曾有垮德林人來過翡翠城。」

士兵說完便退下了。稻草人說：「看來，不

管沿途如何危險，桃樂絲最好還是前往南方國度，向葛琳達求助。桃樂絲要是一直留在這裡，怎麼說也回不了堪薩斯。」

「你要三思啊。」錫人說。

「我已經反覆想過了。」稻草人說。

「我跟桃樂絲一起去。」獅子說：「你的城市讓我覺得膩了，我渴望回到林間田野——我是隻不折不扣的野獸，你也知道的。況且，桃樂絲也需要有人保護她。」

「沒錯。」錫人同意。「我的斧頭也可能派得上用場，所以我也要跟她一道去南方國。」

「那我們什麼時候出發？」稻草人問。

「你也去嗎？」他們驚訝地問。

「當然。如果不是桃樂絲，我永遠也得不到腦子。桃樂絲把我從玉米田的竿子上放下來，帶我來翡翠城，我這一切好運都是因為她。所以，除非她動身返回堪薩斯居住，不然我永遠不會離開她。」

「謝謝你們。」桃樂絲感激地說：「你們對我真好。我想我們盡早出發吧。」

「我們明天早上就走。」稻草人回答：「那我們現在就準備吧，這將是一趟漫長的旅程。」

Chapter 19

樹林警察

第二天早上，桃樂絲向美麗的綠色少女吻別，然後一夥人和綠鬍子士兵握手道別，他一路送他們到大門口。大門守衛看到他們時，很納悶他們為什麼要離開這美麗的城市，再去經歷險難。但他很快解開他們的眼鏡，把眼鏡放回綠箱子中，並致上許多祝福。

他對稻草人說：「您現在是我們的君王，請務必早日歸來。」

稻草人回答：「我會盡可能早點回來，但我得先幫桃樂絲回家。」

桃樂絲向和藹的守衛最後一次道別時，她說：「我在你們這個美麗的城市裡，受到了親切的款待。每個人都對我很好，我的感激之情難以表達。」

「親愛的，那就別表達了。」他回答：「我們很想留你下來，但如果回堪薩斯是

你的心願，那我也祝你能找到方法回家。」他隨後打開外牆的大門，他們往前邁步，展開了他們的旅程。

我們的朋友們朝南方國土前進，一路上太陽高掛。他們精神奕奕，有說有笑。桃樂絲再度充滿了歸鄉的希望，而稻草人和錫人也很高興能幫上忙。獅子心情愉快地嗅著新鮮的空氣，尾巴搖來搖去，很高興能重返大自然。托托在一旁跑來跑去，到處追逐蛾和蝴蝶，一路上快活地吠著。

當他們踏著輕快的步伐往前走時，獅子說道：「城市生活一點也不適合我。住在城裡，我的肌肉都快不見了。現在，我可巴望著機會，能向別的野獸展現我是多麼的勇敢。」

他們轉身望了翡翠城最後一眼。他們現在只能看到綠色城牆後面的一片樓塔和尖頂，其中最高聳的是奧茲宮殿的尖塔和圓頂。

「怎麼說，奧茲也不算是個太差勁的巫師。」錫人說。他感到心臟正在他的胸膛裡跳動。

「他知道怎麼給我腦子，而且還是個很棒的腦子。」稻草人說。

「奧茲給我的那帖勇氣，如果他自己也服用，那他就會是個勇士了。」獅子補充道。

桃樂絲閉口不言。奧茲沒有對她實現承諾，但也算是盡力了，所以她原諒了他。如奧茲所言，他自己雖然是個蹩腳的巫師，但還算是個好人。

第一天的行程，是穿過翡翠城四周的綠地和美麗花田。當晚，他們以草地為枕，以星空為被，好好的休憩了一番。

　　到了早上，他們繼續前進，遇到了一座濃密的森林。看起來，森林往左右兩旁一直延伸下去，似乎沒有路可以繞過去，再加上他們怕會迷路，也不敢改變前進方向。所以，他們就開始找，看從哪裡進入森林會比較容易。

　　最後，帶頭的稻草人找到一棵樹枝廣布的大樹，樹下有空隙讓他們一群人通過。稻草人朝著大樹走過去，未料他一來到樹枝下，樹枝竟往下伸，纏繞住稻草人，然後把他從地面上舉起，頭朝前地往夥伴那裡拋過去。

　　稻草人是沒有受傷，但嚇了一大跳。桃樂絲把他扶起來的時候，他一副頭昏眼花的樣子。

　　「這裡還有一個空隙可以進去。」獅子叫道。

　　「我先走走看。」稻草人說：「反正我被丟出來，也是沒事。」他往另外一棵樹走過去，一邊說道。結果那棵樹的樹枝也立刻揪住他，又把他丟了出來。

　　桃樂絲說：「太奇怪了。我們該怎麼辦？」

　　「這些樹好像存心要跟我們作對，要阻撓我們。」獅子說。

　　「我想換我的方法來試試看。」錫人說罷，就舉起斧頭，往粗魯對待稻草人的第一棵樹走過去。這時一根粗樹枝彎下來，要攫住錫人，但錫人用力一砍，把它砍

The branches bent down and twined around him.

成了兩半。霎時，那棵樹的所有樹枝都顫動了起來，一副很痛的樣子，錫人也就得以從樹下安全地通過。

「來吧！」他向夥伴們叫道：「快！」

他們一齊往前跑，毫髮無傷地從樹下通過，只有托托，牠被一根小樹枝抓起來搖晃，因而叫了起來。錫人立刻把小樹枝砍斷，救出了小狗。

森林裡的其他樹並沒有阻攔他們前進，所以他們想，一定是只有第一排樹能夠彎下枝幹。它們大概是這片森林的警察吧，所以有這番本領，以使陌生人卻步。

他們輕鬆地通過森林，來到了森林另一端的邊緣。這時，他們很驚訝地發現，眼前竟有一座比他們還要高的高牆。高牆看起來是用白瓷做成的，牆的表面和盤子一樣光滑。

「我們現在怎麼辦？」桃樂絲問。

「我來做個梯子。」錫人說：「我們必定得爬過牆了。」

Chapter 20

精緻的瓷器國

錫人用樹林裡找到的木材做梯子時，桃樂絲因為長途跋涉太累了，就躺下來睡覺。獅子也蹭起身子休憩，一旁還躺著托托。

稻草人看著錫人工作，對他說道：「真想不通，這裡怎麼會有一道牆，也不知道牆是用什麼做成的。」

「讓你的腦子休息一下吧，別管牆的事了。等我們爬過牆，就知道牆那一頭是什麼樣子了。」錫人回答。

沒多久，梯子就做好了。這個梯子看起來雖然很簡陋，不過錫人有把握，用來爬牆是夠堅固的了。稻草人把桃樂絲、獅子和托托叫醒，告訴他們梯子已經備好了。稻草人率先爬上梯子，只不過他太笨手笨腳，桃樂絲只得緊跟在後，以免他摔下來。就在稻草人探出牆頭時，他叫道：「噢，天呀！」

「繼續爬啊。」桃樂絲喊道。

於是，稻草人就繼續往上爬，然後坐在牆頭上。接著，換桃樂絲探出牆頭張望，結果她也和稻草人一樣叫道：「噢，天呀！」

隨後上去的是托托。托托看到了之後，也立刻吠了起來。不過，桃樂絲讓牠安靜下來。

接著爬上梯子的是獅子和錫人。當他們一看到牆後面的樣子，也都叫道：「噢，天呀！」最後，他們在牆頭上坐成一排，往下望著這一片奇異的景象。

呈現在他們眼前的地面，就像大瓷盤的盤底一樣，又滑、又亮、又白。地面上，散布著瓷做的房子，顏色鮮艷耀眼。這些房子非常的迷你，最高的也只到桃樂絲的腰部。此外，還有蓋得很漂亮的小穀倉，穀倉周圍圍著瓷做的籬笆，而到處成群的牛馬豬羊和雞，也是瓷做的。

然而，最奇特的，還是住在這塊奇異地方的人。擠牛奶的女孩和牧羊女，穿著顏色亮麗的上衣，袍子上綴滿金色的斑點；皇室的女性成員，一身或銀色，或金色，或紫色的華服；牧羊人穿著及膝的短褲，短褲下擺綴著或粉紅、或黃、或藍的條紋，鞋子上還有金色的鈕子；而皇室的男性成員，戴著鑲滿珠寶的皇冠，穿著貂皮袍子和綢緞上衣；滑稽的小丑穿著褶邊袍子，兩頰上畫著紅色的圓點，戴著尖頂高帽。最奇怪的是，這些人都是瓷做的，連衣服也是，而且他們的個子很小，最高的還

These people were all made of china.

不及桃樂絲的膝蓋。

　　一開始，沒有人注意到這些旅人，只有一隻頭很大的紫色小瓷狗走到牆邊，用細小的聲音對他們吠叫，然後又跑走。

　　「我們要怎麼下去？」桃樂絲問。

　　他們發現梯子很重，拉不上來，所以稻草人就先跳下牆，讓其他人可以跳到他身上，以免因為地面太硬而傷了腳。當然，他們盡量不落在他的頭上，免得被大頭針扎到腳。等大家都安全跳下牆之後，他們扶起已經被踏扁的稻草人，幫他把稻草拍一拍，讓他恢復原狀。

　　「要走到另一頭去，必得路過這個奇怪的地方。」桃樂絲說：「如果不一直往南走，是十分不智的。」

　　他們便開始穿越瓷人國。他們最先遇到的，是一位正在為瓷牛擠牛奶的瓷姑娘。當他們走近時，瓷牛忽然把腿一踢，結果凳子、桶子，甚至擠奶姑娘都被踢到，嘩啦一聲，全倒在瓷地上。

　　桃樂絲看到牛竟把自己的腿給踢斷，十分震驚。桶子也碎成好幾片，而可憐的擠牛奶姑娘，她的左手肘也裂開了。

　　「喂！看看你們做的好事！」擠牛奶姑娘生氣地叫：「我的牛斷了腿，我得帶牠去修補匠那裡把腿黏上。你們來這裡嚇我的牛，到底是什麼意思？」

　　「我真的很抱歉。」桃樂絲回答：「請原諒我們。」

　　但美麗的擠牛奶姑娘正在氣頭上，沒理睬他們。她

悶悶不樂地撿起斷掉的腿，牽著
牛走掉。那隻可憐的牛，只好
用三隻腿一瘸一拐地走著。
她把自己受傷的手肘挨著
身體緊靠，然後一面走
開，一面還頻頻回頭，用
責怪的眼神瞄那些粗魯的
陌生人。

桃樂絲對這個意外感到
很難過。

「我們在這裡一定要非常小
心。」軟心腸的錫人說：「不然會弄
破這些美麗的小人兒，讓他們無法復原。」

走了一會兒，桃樂絲碰見了一位衣著異常華麗的年
輕皇家女孩。女孩看到這些陌生人時，先是停下腳步，
後來就開始跑了起來。

桃樂絲想看清楚那位女孩，就追在她後面。瓷女孩
叫道：「別追我！別追我！」

她小小的聲音，充滿恐懼。桃樂絲停下腳步，問道：
「為什麼？」

公主也停了下來，隔著安全的距離，回答說：「因
為如果我用跑的，可能會跌倒，而把自己摔碎。」

「可是，不是可以修補起來嗎？」女孩問。

「噢，是的，但你知道，修補以後就不會這麼漂亮

了。」公主回答。

「我想也是。」桃樂絲說。

「我們有一位叫做喬克先生的小丑，他老是想用頭站立。」瓷女孩繼續說：「所以他常常把自己摔破，他身上補過的地方就有上百個了，看起來實在不是很美觀。現在，他正往我們走過來，你可以自己看看。」

果然，有一位開心的小丑朝他們走過來。桃樂絲可以看到，儘管他的衣服又是紅，又是黃，又是綠的，煞是光鮮，可是他全身到處都有裂痕，東一條西一條的，一看就知道修補過很多地方了。

小丑把手插在口袋裡，鼓起兩頰，傲慢地向他們點個頭，說：

我的這位窈窕淑女呀，
怎對著可憐的老喬克
兩隻眼睛這樣愣怔怔？
你表情僵硬呆若木雞
好像是剛吞下了火鉗！

「先生！安靜！」女孩說：「你難道看不出來這些人是客人，我們應該以禮相待嗎？」

「噢，我相信，這就是尊敬。」小丑說，還立刻用頭倒立了起來。

「別理喬克先生。」女孩對桃樂絲說：「他的頭有很多裂縫，讓他變成了一個笨伯。」

「噢，我一點也不生他的氣。」桃樂絲繼續說：「只是你這麼美，我實在是愛不釋手。你要不要跟我回堪薩斯？我可以讓你站在愛姆嬸嬸的壁爐架上。我用籃子把你帶走就可以了。」

「那樣我會很不快樂的。」瓷公主回答：「你看，在我們這裡，我們知足安樂，可以隨心所欲地交談或行動。但只要一被帶離這裡，我們的關節就會立刻僵硬掉，變得只能直直地站立著，供人玩賞罷了。當然，人們就是希望我們這樣，好好地站在壁爐、櫃子或客廳的桌子上就好。但在我們自己的國度裡，我們的生活愜意多了。」

「我絕不想要讓你不快樂！」桃樂絲喊道：「那，我只好說聲再會了。」

「再會了。」公主回答。

他們小心地走過瓷器國。一路上，小動物和居民一看到他們，就逃到一旁去，生怕自己會被這些陌生人給碰傷了。大約一個小時之後，他們走到了瓷器國另一頭的邊界，又碰到了另一道瓷牆。

但這一道牆，沒有之前那道牆那麼高。他們站在獅子的背上，攀過了牆頭。最後，獅子靠緊腿，伏下身子，跳上牆。只不過，在牠跳躍時，牠的尾巴打到一座瓷教堂，把教堂打得粉碎。

「太慘了。」桃樂絲說：「不過我想我們還算幸運

的了，只弄斷了一隻
牛腿和一座教堂，沒
有弄碎這邊的小小居
民。他們真的是很容
易碎裂！」

　　「的確是。」稻
草人說：「還好我是
稻草做的，不太容易
毀損。在這個世間上，
還有比當稻草人更悲
哀的事啊。」

Chapter 21

獅子成為
萬獸之王

這些旅人爬下瓷牆之後，發現他們來到了一處不甚宜人的地方。這裡一片沼澤和溼地，草叢長得又高又茂密，看不到地面上的泥濘坑洞，很容易把人絆倒。還好他們很小心地踩著腳步，終於安全過關走到了硬泥地，不過這裡更是荒涼了。之後，他們走了一段又長又累人的路，穿越灌木叢，進入另一座森林，這裡的樹木比他們之前所見的都更高大、更古老。

「這座森林真是宜人啊。」獅子心情愉悅地看著四周，說道：「我從沒見過這麼美的地方。」

「看起來陰森森的。」稻草人說。

「才不呢。」獅子回答：「我會想終生在此落腳。看看你腳下的枯葉，多柔軟啊！還有老樹上的那些青苔，長得又肥又綠，這

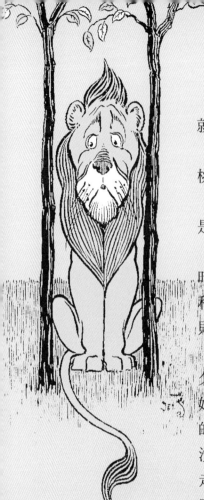

就是野獸們最想要的天堂樂園了。」

「也許森林裡現在就有野獸。」桃樂絲說。

「我想是有吧。」獅子回答：「只是我半隻也沒看到。」

他們在森林中行走，直到天色已暗，無法再繼續前進。桃樂絲、托托和稻草人躺下來睡覺，錫人和稻草人則照例在一旁守著。

到了早晨，他們再度啟程。沒多久，他們聽到了一陣低沉的隆隆聲，好像是很多不同的野生動物一齊吼叫的聲音。除了托托嗚咽了一下，他們沒有人被嚇到。他們繼續沿著許多人走過的小徑前進，最後，他們來到了森林中一處百獸聚集的空曠地方。獸群中，有老虎、大象、熊、狼、狐狸，和所有大自然裡頭的動物。桃樂絲一時之間被嚇到了，不過獅子解釋說，這些動物在舉行會議，而且從牠們的嗥叫和咆哮聲來判斷，牠們應該是遇到大麻煩了。

獅子說話時，有幾隻野獸看到了

牠，頓時，獸群像是著魔
般地安靜了下來。一
隻體型最大的老虎
走向獅子，鞠躬說
道：「歡迎您，
萬獸之王！
您來得正是
時候，請對抗
我們的敵人，讓森林中所有的動物重獲
和平。」

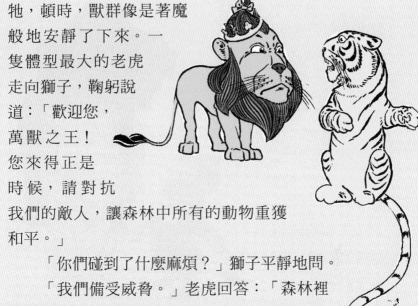

「你們碰到了什麼麻煩？」獅子平靜地問。

「我們備受威脅。」老虎回答：「森林裡
最近闖進了一隻凶殘的野獸。牠長得像一隻
巨型的蜘蛛，身體和大象一樣大，腳像一根樹
幹那樣的長，樣子極其可怕。牠有八隻腳，走過
森林時，會一隻腳抓一隻動物，然後把動物送入嘴巴
裡，就好像蜘蛛在吃蒼蠅那樣。只要牠還活著，我們
的生命就毫無保障。當你到來時，我們就是在開會，
看要怎樣做，才能自保。」

獅子想了一下。

「這座森林裡，還有其他的獅子嗎？」牠問。

「沒有。以前是有啦，但都被怪獸給吃掉了。況
且，那些獅子都不像您這樣高大威猛。」

「如果我解決了你們的敵人，你們會向我稱臣，尊我為森林之王嗎？」獅子問。

「我們欣然從命。」老虎回答。其他所有野獸也大聲吼：「欣然從命！」

「你們說的那隻大蜘蛛，現在在哪裡？」獅子問。

「就在橡樹林那裡。」老虎邊說，邊用前腳指著。

「好好照顧我的朋友們。」獅子說：「我立刻就去和那隻怪獸搏鬥。」

牠向夥伴們說再見後，就意氣風發地出征，去討伐敵人了。

獅子找到大蜘蛛時，大蜘蛛正在睡覺。牠的樣子非常醜惡，獅子看了不禁嗤之以鼻。大蜘蛛的腳，的確就像老虎所形容的那麼長，而且一身又粗又黑的毛，嘴巴很大，一排利牙長達一呎；牠的脖子，細如蜂腰，連接著頭和圓圓的身體。獅子靈機一動，想到了妙策，牠很清楚，趁敵人睡覺時進行攻擊比較容易。於是，獅子一躍，直接跳到怪獸的背上，然後巨掌一揮，閃出牠的利爪，打得蜘蛛頭顱落地。獅子跳回地面，等到蜘蛛的長腳停止了掙扎，確定牠已經斷氣才離開。

　　獅子回到空地，森林裡的動物都在等著牠。獅子很驕傲地說：「你們不需要再害怕你們的敵人了。」

　　野獸們隨之向獅子行禮，尊牠為王。獅子向牠們承諾，等桃樂絲平安返回堪薩斯，牠就會回來統治牠們。

Chapter 22

垮德林人的國度

四位旅人穿越森林，一路平安。當他們走出幽暗的林蔭時，橫在他們眼前的，是一座由大塊大塊的岩石所形成的陡峭岩山。

「這座山很不好爬。」稻草人說：「但我們還是得爬過去。」

稻草人當先鋒，其他人在後面跟著。當他們就要走到第一塊岩石前面時，傳來了一個粗啞的聲音，叫道：「退回去！」

「你是誰？」稻草人問。

一個頭從岩石後面探出來，用那粗啞的聲音說道：「此山歸我們所有，任何人都不准通行。」

「但我們得通過才行。」稻草人說：「我們要去垮德林人住的地方。」

「不准通行！」聲音回答。隨後，從岩石後面走出來一個長得再奇怪不過的人。

他又矮又壯，脖子很粗，皺紋一圈又一圈，撐著一個大頭顱，頭頂扁平。稻草人看到他沒有手，不信這樣一個無用的人，會有能耐阻隢他們爬過這座山。

The Head shot forward and struck the Scarecrow.

「很抱歉，難以從命。不管閣下意見如何，你們這座山，我們是爬定了。」稻草人說完，就逕自往前走。

突然，那個人的脖子一伸，頭顱快如閃電地一彈，扁平的頭頂就正中紅心，擊中了稻草人，讓稻草人一路翻滾下山。接著那個人同樣快如閃電地把頭收回，然後粗聲地笑道：「你想得美喔！」

其他岩石後面隨之傳出一陣陣狂笑聲。桃樂絲看到山坡上有數百個無臂扁頭人，一塊岩石後面站一個。

這一陣譏笑稻草人滾下山的笑聲，讓獅子很惱怒。獅子大吼一聲，回聲如雷響，然後直往山上衝去。

一顆頭又快速彈出，大獅子立刻滾下山，簡直像被大砲給打到一樣。

桃樂絲跑向稻草人，扶他站起來。獅子渾身疼痛地走過來，說道：「要跟這些彈頭人打硬仗是沒有用的，沒有人可以擋得過他們的攻擊。」

「那我們怎麼辦？」她問。

「叫飛猴來。」錫人建議：「你還有一次使喚權。」

「好。」她說罷，就戴上金冠，唸著咒語。飛猴還是一樣迅速，整批猴群很快就來到她面前。

「您有什麼吩咐？」飛猴王鞠躬問道。

「帶我們越過這座山，到垮德林人的國家去。」女孩回答。

「照辦。」猴王說。飛猴群立刻用手臂拉起四位旅人和托托飛走了。他們飛越山丘時，扁頭人氣得大叫，

把頭對著
空中彈射，只不
過，他們的頭搆不到飛
猴。飛猴帶著桃樂絲一行
人，平安飛過山丘，然後把他
們放在埼德林人的美麗領土上。

「這是您最後一次召喚我們了。」猴王對桃樂絲
說：「所以，再會了，祝你們好運。」

「再會了，非常謝謝你們。」女孩回答。猴子隨即
飛向空中，一轉眼就不見了。

埼德林人的國家，看來國富民樂。一畦畦的田地，
作物即將收成；縱橫的道路，鋪得很平坦；美麗的溪流
上，橫跨著堅固的橋樑；圍籬、房子和橋，都被漆成亮
紅色，一如維奇人的成片黃色，和芒奇金人的成片藍
色。體型矮矮胖胖的埼德林人，看起來圓滾滾的，脾氣
好像很好。人們都穿得一身紅，在綠草和黃澄澄穀物的
襯托下，顯得很鮮亮。

飛猴把他們放在一個農家附近，於是一行人就向農
家走去，敲了門。前來應門的，是農夫的妻子。桃樂絲
向婦人要點東西吃，婦人為他們準備了大餐，包括三種

不同口味的蛋糕、四種不一樣的餅乾，還有一碗要給托托的牛奶。

「葛琳達的城堡離這裡有多遠呢？」孩子問。

「不遠了。」農婦回答：「走往南的路，很快就到了。」

他們謝過好心的婦人，重新上路。他們沿著農田行走，穿越美麗的小橋，來到一座美麗的城堡下。城門前，有三位少女，她們都穿著英挺的鑲金穗紅色制服。桃樂絲走近時，其中一位少女問道：「你們來南方國，有何貴事？」

「我們是要來找統治這裡的那位善良女巫。」她回答：「你能帶我去見她嗎？」

「請報上名來，我去稟報葛琳達，看她是否要接見。」他們報上名字後，女士兵便走進城堡。不一會兒，女士兵回來報告說，立即召見桃樂絲一行人。

Chapter 23

善良女巫葛琳達
實現女孩的願望

在謁見葛琳達之前,他們先被帶到城堡內的一個房間裡。在那裡,桃樂絲洗了臉,梳了頭;獅子抖了抖鬃毛上的塵土;稻草人把自己整一整,弄出最好的形狀;錫人擦亮他的錫皮,也把關節上了油。

把自己整理得體之後,他們跟著女士兵走進一個大房間。房間裡,葛琳達女巫就坐在紅寶石的寶座上。

葛琳達女巫看來又漂亮又年輕。她的頭髮是暗紅色的,捲髮流瀉而下,垂在肩上。她一身純白的洋裝,而眼睛是藍色的,慈祥地望著小女孩。

「我的孩子,我能幫你什麼?」她問。

桃樂絲詳細地報告了自己的經歷,包括龍捲風是怎麼把她帶到奧茲王國、她這些夥伴是怎麼來的,還有他們的奇妙歷險。

「現在我最大的願望,就是回堪薩斯。」她說:「愛姆嬸嬸一定會以為

389

我遭遇了不幸，那會讓她為我服喪。還有，除非今年的收成比去年好，不然亨利叔叔會負擔不了的。」

葛琳達俯身向前，親吻了這位可愛小女孩微仰的可愛臉龐。

「祝福你那顆珍貴的心。我可以告訴你要怎麼回堪薩斯。」她說：「不過，如果我告訴你，你就要把金冠給我。」

「我願意！」桃樂絲喊：「金冠現在對我也沒有用了，但您有了它，就能命令飛猴三次。」

「我想，我也只需要牠們幫我三次忙。」葛琳達微笑著回答。

桃樂絲便把金冠給女巫。女巫對稻草人說：「桃樂絲離開我們以後，你要做什麼？」

「我要回翡翠城。」他回答：「奧茲派我統治，人民也擁戴我。我唯一擔心的，就是該怎麼穿越扁頭人的山丘。」

「我可以使用金冠，命令飛猴把你帶到翡翠城的大門口。」葛琳達說：「人民要是失去了這麼好的一位君王，那就太可惜了。」

「我真的有那麼好嗎？」稻草人問。

「你出類拔萃。」葛琳達回答。

接著，她轉向錫人，問道：「桃樂絲離開這裡之後，你有什麼打算？」

錫人靠在斧頭上想了一下。他說：「維奇人對我很

You must give me
the Golden Cap.

好，而且邪惡女巫死了以後，他們想要我去統治他們，而我自己也喜歡他們。如果能再回到西方國土，我最想做的，就是永遠在那裡統治他們。」

「我會下第二個命令給飛猴，要他們把你平安地帶到維奇人的國家裡。」葛琳達說：「雖然你的腦子看起來沒有稻草人那麼大，不過你把頭擦亮了以後，是比稻草人的頭亮多了。我相信，你一定可以英明地領導維奇人，把他們治理得很好的。」

接著，女巫看著體型龐大又毛茸茸的獅子，問道：「桃樂絲回到自己的家以後，你有什麼打算？」

「在扁頭人的山丘那一頭，有一片高大而古老的森林，在那裡，萬獸已經尊我為王了。」牠回答：「如果我能回到那片森林，我會非常快樂地在那裡度過我的一生。」

「我會下給飛猴第三個命令，把你帶到你的森林去。」葛琳達說：「用完金冠的三次魔力之後，我要把金冠交予飛猴王，讓牠和牠的子民從此得到自由。」

稻草人、錫人和獅子由衷謝過善良女巫的恩德。桃樂絲說：「您的人，就如您的外貌一樣地美麗！只是，您還沒告訴我怎麼回堪薩斯。」

「你的銀鞋子就能帶你穿越沙漠了。」葛琳達回答：「如果你知道銀鞋的魔力，在你來到這個國家的第一天，就能回去愛姆嬸嬸的身邊了。」

「但是那樣的話，我就不會有這個聰明的腦子了！」稻草人喊道：「那我就要在農夫的玉米田裡度過一生了。」

「而我就不會有一顆美麗的心了。」錫人說：「那我就會站在林子裡，一直生鏽下去，直到世界末日。」

「而我就永遠會是個懦夫了。」獅子說：「那樣，所有森林中的任何動物，都不會好聲好氣地對我說一句話了。」

「他們說的都是真的。」桃樂絲說：「我很高興能幫助這些好朋友。現在，他們都得到了他們最想要的東西，也都成了一方之主，而且心滿意足。所以，我想，我還是希望能回堪薩斯。」

「那雙銀鞋具有神奇的力量。」善良女巫說：「其中，最奇妙的力量是，它能在三步之內，帶你到世界上任何的

角落去，而且每一步只要一眨眼的工夫就到了。你只要
把鞋跟互相敲三下，就可以命令銀鞋帶你到任何你想去
的地方。」

「如果是這樣，那我要銀鞋立刻就帶我回堪薩
斯。」孩子高興地說。

她抱住獅子的脖子，親了牠一下，溫柔地拍拍牠大
大的頭。接著，她親了錫人；錫人正在哭泣，這對他的
關節來說實在危險。最後，她抱住稻草人塞著稻草的柔
軟身體，而沒有親吻他那一張用畫的臉。要與這些親愛
的夥伴分離，她自己也傷心地哭了。

善良女巫葛琳達從紅寶石寶座上走了下來，給小女
孩一個吻別。桃樂絲謝謝她對他們一行人所做的一切。

桃樂絲莊重地將托托抱在懷裡，道過最後一次再見
之後，就將鞋跟併攏，互敲三次，說：「帶我回家，到
愛姆嬸嬸身邊去！」

　　立刻，她被捲入空中，速度如此之快，她能感覺到
的，只有耳邊呼呼的風聲。

　　銀鞋走了三步後，她忽然停住，落在草地上滾了好
幾圈，還沒弄清楚自己在哪裡。

　　最後，她坐起來，看了看四周。

　　「天啊！」她喊道。

　　現在，她就坐在堪薩斯廣闊的大草原上。眼前，是
亨利叔叔新蓋的農舍，那是在舊農舍被龍捲風捲走之後
重建的，而亨利叔叔正在穀倉裡擠牛奶。托托掙開桃樂
絲，往穀倉跑去，高興地吠叫著。

　　桃樂絲站起來，發現自己只穿了襪子。她的那一雙
銀鞋，在飛行時掉了，永遠地消失在沙漠之中了。

Chapter 24

重返家園

愛姆嬸嬸正從房子裡走出來,準備去幫甘藍菜澆水。她一抬頭,卻看到桃樂絲正朝著她跑過來。

「我的寶貝孩子!」愛姆嬸嬸大喊道,對她又是抱又是親的。「你到底是從哪裡跑回來的呀?」

「從奧茲王國呀,托托也是喔。」桃樂絲認真地說:「噢!愛姆嬸嬸,能回到家,我真是太高興了!」

國家圖書館出版品預行編目資料

綠野仙蹤（原著雙語彩圖本）/ 李曼‧法蘭克‧
鮑姆（Lyman Frank Baum）著；朱文宜 譯. —
初版. —[臺北市]：寂天文化, 2018.3 面；公分.
中英對照; 譯自：The Wizard of Oz

ISBN　　978-986-318-661-8 (25K平裝)

874.59　　　　　　　　　　　　107001073

The Wizard of Oz

作者 _ 李曼・法蘭克・鮑姆（Lyman Frank Baum）

譯者 _ 朱文宜

編輯 _ 安卡斯

中譯校對 _ 蔡裴驊

英文校對 _ 于姍秀

製程管理 _ 洪巧玲

發行人 _ 周均亮

出版者 _ 寂天文化事業股份有限公司

電話 _ +886-2-2365-9739

傳真 _ +886-2-2365-9835

網址 _ www.icosmos.com.tw

讀者服務 _ onlineservice@icosmos.com.tw

出版日期 _ 2018年3月 初版一刷（250101）

郵撥帳號 _ 1998620-0 寂天文化事業股份有限公司